THE MOON DANCERS

The MOON DANCERS

JOHN PITMAN

FOR LINDA

She made me do it.

DRAMATIS PERSONAE

His Britannic Majesty's Navy

Lieutenant Roger Alexander Ellis - A young officer of His Britannic Majesty's Navy, a serious fellow much given to the study of modern philosophy.

Captain Gardiner - Captain of HMS *Demetra* and one time close friend of Roger's mother.

Lieutenant Charlie Edwardes - An erudite and serious minded Scotchman and friend of Roger.

Lieutenant Harry Felgate - Harry and Roger's less serious companion, much given to making bad jokes.

Mr Evan Napean - Secretary to the Board of Admiralty.

Mr Richard Prowse - Master Attendant of Woolwich Royal Naval Dockyard.

Captain William Radford - Captain of HMS Eros.

Lieutenant Pertwee - First Lieutenant of the *Eros*.

Mr Midshipman Jenkins - a 'young gentleman' serving

1

aboard the *Eros.*

The village of Canewdon, Essex

Mr Arthur Ellis - Roger's father, a gunsmith.

Mrs Sally Dowsett - A lusty widow woman and keeper of the Anchor Inn at Canewdon.

Master Thomas Dowsett (Young Tom) - Mrs Dowsett's son and general factotum.

Billy - A young, ferret-faced friend of Tom Dowsett.

Hercules - A gentle old horse kept at the Anchor for the use of patrons.

Cuddy Smith and *Ned Symonds* - Two old codgers who drink regularly in the Anchor.

Reverend Thomas Gildersleeve - Vicar of St Nicholas' Church, Canewdon, a most curious clergyman indeed.

Perkins - The reverend's manservant.

Mrs Biddy Baker - An old woman of Butts Hill, Canewdon.

Sir Henry Spurgeon - Squire and magistrate, owner of Canewdon Hall.

Lady Mary Spurgeon - Sir Henry's wife.

James - Sir Henry's coachman, not in fact this worthy fellow's name but rather a name of convenience oft used by those from wealthy or noble families when addressing their coachman.

Miss Elizabeth Saunders - A free spirited young woman of Canewdon, once Roger's childhood friend.

THE MOON DANCERS

Mr Nathaniel Saunders - Elizabeth's father and Sir Henry's Reeve.

Mrs Annie Saunders - Elizabeth's mother.

Susannah - The Saunders' maidservant.

'Sourface' (Jemmy Webb) - A low, mean footpad.

'Ratty' (John Kettle) - Sourface's even more low and mean confederate, and would be political agitator.

Willie Fisher - Canewdon's village constable.

Mr Aaron Rolfe - The blacksmith, accomplished cricketer and handy with his fists.

Mr Edward Sawkins - The butcher and notable singlestick player.

Mr Hugh Nichols - The miller.

Mr John Salmon - The apothecary.

Dr Joseph Lipscomb - A Scotch physician, and great believer in the restorative powers of the poppy.

George, *Dick* and *Little Ben* – Honest labourers at Canewdon Hall Farm.

Mr Will Cook - A very worried gentleman from the neighbouring parish of Paglesham.

Mr John Hanson - High Sheriff of Essex.

Port Royal, Jamaica

Mr Wilkins - A rather dissolute officer of the Royal Regiment of Artillery.

'Juno' - A sultry Jamaican tavern dancer much given to

debauchery and vice.

Susie - A friend to Juno, also a tavern dancer and a willing partner in all of that lady's amorous adventures.

LEXICON

A

A wry mouth and a pissen pair of breeches: The results of a hanging.

Adamite: A member of any religious sect that is wont to practice ritual nakedness in imitation of the denizens of the Garden of Eden.

All my eye and Betty Martin: A tall tale or untruth.

Arsy varsey: Head over heels.

As melancholy as a gib cat: As out of spirits as a tomcat who has been out on the tiles. *Omne animal post coitum est triste* (every animal is depressed after coitus) - Aristotle.

B

Ballocks: Testicles; or an uncouth sobriquet for a parson.

Balum rancum: An organised ball whereat the whole company would dance completely naked.

Bana-bhuidseach dhubh: A black witch (Scotch Gaelic).

1

Barking-iron, or Barker: A pistol.

Barky: A ship, from the Old French *barque.*

Baubles: Testicles.

Bedlamite: A lunatic, in reference to those poor unfortunate residents of Bedlam, the Hospital of Saint Mary of Bethlehem, a London institution for the insane.

Beggars' bullets: Stones.

Beldam: A malicious or hateful old woman.

Betwattled: Greatly surprised or nonplussed.

Black Creole: A person of pure African heritage (Jamaican parlance).

Black fly: A parson who insists upon collecting his tithe of the harvest.

Blackbirders: Persons engaged in the slave trade.

Blue ruin: Gin.

Bone-rattler: An old and worn out coach.

Boot catcher: A tavern servant charged with cleaning the boots of the guests.

Bring your arse to anchor: To sit.

Brothers of the bung: Brewers.

Buck fitch: An old lecher.

Buck of the first head: A young man who is considered a leader in the field of debauchery.

Buggans: Evil spirits.

Buss: Kiss.

C

Calfskin fiddle: A rustic drum.

Cast up one's accounts: To vomit.

Cat-heads: Wooden beams used to support a ship's anchor, otherwise used to denote a woman's breasts.

Chalk: To punch someone in the face.

Chick-a-biddy: A young woman.

Chive: A knife.

Cinder garbler: A maidservant whose job it is to tend the fires and sift the ashes from the cinders.

Claret: A red wine, or sometimes blood.

Clod hopper: A country farm boy.

Cock Alley: A woman's vagina.

Conveyancer: A thief.

Cove: A man.

Criss: Good (Jamaican patois).

Cuff: A shortened form of 'cuffin', meaning a man.

Cully: A fop or a fool.

Cunny: The vagina.

Cup shot: Drunk.

Cupid's arbour: The vagina.

Cupid's kettle drums: A lady's bosoms.

Cure: In ecclesiastical terms, the exercise of his office by a clergyman.

Cushion thumper: A parson who, when in full cry, furiously pummels the cushions.

Cyprian: A high-class courtesan.

D

Dairy: A lady's chest.

Daisy kickers: Ostlers stationed at an inn or tavern.

Dance the blanket hornpipe: To fornicate.

Dance the hempen jig: To be hanged.

Dasher: A showy harlot.

Davy: A corruption of the term 'affidavit'.

Dell: A young lady.

Demi-rep: A respectable woman of doubtful chastity.

Devil walloper: A parson.

Dhoti: A cloth tied around the waist and extending to cover most of the legs (Hindi).

Dinnae fash: Don't worry (Scotch dialect).

Down at heels and out of elbows: Impoverished.

Doxy: A low wench or whore.

Drury Lane vestal: A prostitute who plies her trade in that area of London.

Duck fucker: Keeper of the poultry brought aboard a ship.

Duds: Clothes.

Duddering rake: An extremely lewd person.

E

Expended: Killed.

F

Facer: A violent blow to the face.

Feague: To insert ginger into a horse's rectum to make it lively and hold its tail up.

Feather bed jig: Sexual intercourse.

Fiddle-faddle: Nonsense.

Fizgig: A promiscuous woman.

Flag of distress: The cockade worn on the hat of a half-pay naval officer.

Foxed: Drunk.

Fundament: The buttocks or anus.

G

Game pullet: A young woman who is up for anything of an amorous nature.

Gammon: Nonsense.

Glim: A lanthorn, or sometimes a candle.

God's acre: A churchyard.

Goosecap: A silly man or woman.

Groggified: Drunk.

Gulled: Deceived or cheated.

Gumba: A West Indian drum.

H

Half seas over, or half cut: Partially drunk.

Haud yer wheesht: Be quiet (Scotch dialect).

Humpty-dumpty: Clumsy.

Hush the cull: Kill the fellow.

Huzzlecap: A childhood game of pitch and toss in which coins are thrown into a hat.

J

Jarvis: A coachman.

Johnny Crapaud: A name used by British sailors to designate a Frenchman. The Flemish people originally called the French *Crapaud Franchos*, in reference to the toads that once appeared on the arms of France.

L

Lay out quiet: Kill.

Light-heeled wench: A willing young woman who is more often than not like to be found flat on her back with her heels in the air. Some wags are wont to unjustly contend that this sort of girl is more to be found in Essex than in most other counties of England.

M

Merry arse Christian: A lady of easy virtue.

Milling: Boxing.

Miserable rip: A sad, worn out old horse.

Miss Molly: An effeminate fellow; a sodomite.

Mopsqueezer: A housemaid.

Mount of Venus: The *mons pubis*, the cushion of flesh situated over the pubic bone.

Muckworm: A miser.

Mulatto: The offspring of a white European and an African person (Jamaican parlance).

Mustee: a person of one-eighth African ancestry (Jamaican parlance).

Mustifino: The child of a *mustee* and a white European person; considered to be legally white and having the rights of a British citizen (Jamaican parlance).

Muzzler: A blow to the face.

N

Narthex: An antechamber at the entrance to a church, separated off by a railing.

Nazy: Drunken.

Negro: A person of African origin.

Nutmegs: Testicles.

O

Oaten pipe: A simple reedpipe made from the dried stalk of the oat.

One and a kick: One shilling and sixpence.

P

Palaver: Excessive talk or fuss, from the Portuguese *palavra* meaning a discussion between tribespeople and traders.

Pani-wallah: A water carrier, informal Indian word combining the Urdu *pani* with the Hindi suffix *vālā*.

Paps: A woman's breasts.

Parry-garrick: Corrupted form of 'Panegyric', a published text in praise of something.

Peg trantrums: Gone to peg trantrums, dead.

Pelf: Money.

Phyz: Face.

Pike off: Run away.

Pintle: Penis.

Play old gooseberry: Play the Devil.

Polt in the nutmegs: A kick in the testicles.

Popper: A pistol.

Prad: A horse.

Prancer: A horse.

Prattling box: A pulpit.

Pree: To watch (Jamaican patois).

Puff-guts: An overweight man.

Pumping ship: Being heartily sick.

Put to bed with a mattock and tucked up with a spade: Dead and buried.

Q

Queen of Elphame: The elfin queen of Faerieland (Scotch

dialect).

Queer as Dick's hatband: Very ill.

Quim: A woman's private parts.

R

Rum crowd: A good crowd.

Rum prancer: A mettlesome steed.

Rummelieguts: Windbag (Scotch dialect).

S

Sandy: A general term used to indicate a Scotchman, in the same way that Welchmen are oft called Taffy.

Scouts: In cricket, fieldsmen upon the field of play.

Scrag: To carry out an assault, typically by hitting, kicking, or punching a person repeatedly.

Scrub: A mean, dishonest looking fellow.

Shift your bob: Go away.

Snaffle: To steal.

Sniltch: Look upon something very closely.

Snub Devil: A parson.

Soul doctor: A parson.

Spiritual flesh broker: A parson.

Spreets and bousiemen: Sprites and bogeymen (Scotch dialect).

Squelch: A fall.

Stand Moses: When a man has another man's bastard

child foisted upon him.

Swive: To engage in sexual intercourse.

T

Tantwivy: At full speed, from the sound made by the hunting horn or post horn.

Three to one: Three to one though bound to lose: the amorous congress.

Tiffing: Eating or drinking.

Tit: A girl.

Toby lay: The practice of robbery upon the King's highway.

Top-hamper: A seaman's term for a ship's masts, spars, and rigging; or a woman's breasts.

Topper: A blow to the head.

Trumpery: Rubbish.

Trusty trout: A true friend.

Tup: To mate; said of a ram mating with a ewe.

Turned off: Hanged.

Turn-off guns: Pocket pistols.

U

Under the weather bow: Unwell.

W

Water scriger: A doctor who bases his diagnosis on the state of his patients' urine.

Water souchy: Fish, usually perch, stewed with herbs, especially parsley, and onion, served in the stewing water.

Wrapped up in the tail of his mother's smock: A description sometimes applied to a man lucky enough to experience some degree of success with the opposite sex.

Y

Yahoos: Noisy, violent persons; from the name of a race of brutish human-like creatures appearing in *Gulliver's Travels*, a novel by Jonathan Swift.

Yellow boy: A guinea.

CHAPTER 1

The winter of 1794-5 was bloody cold. Damme but it was! 'Tis true that I spent it all wrapped up snug in London, largely thanks to their Lordships of the Admiralty expecting to me to wait upon their good graces day after day, but still the snow was thick in the streets, and even old Father Thames froze solid. And the fog - damp as a freshly swabbed deck and cold as ice almost every night! Why, even allowing for the new oil lamps, anyone brave, or foolhardy, enough to venture abroad after sunset was obliged to carry a glim just to see their way clear. It was a long winter too. The cold and frost continued through to spring, with the thermometer rarely above twenty below zero of Fahrenheit, causing extreme distress to all, and especially to the poor and labouring classes who had already been hit by the catastrophic effect of the previous year's devilish bad harvest. Coal, when it could be obtained, fetched more than three guineas a chaldron and water-pipes were all frozen, so that many perished that year through a fearful lack of fuel and water.

For sure, Billy Pitt and his cronies did little to help. The unshakeable belief of a Tory Government wildly out of touch with the common people was that a strong economy was ever the key to victory in the war old England was waging, in concert with the Austrians, Prussians, Sardinians, Dutch, and even the despicable Dons, against the newly emergent French Republic. Consequently, the Treasury had committed to a punitive fiscal policy that was set to ruin all but the rich through the imposition of unconscionable taxes on essential goods and services. Westminster steadfastly ignored the plight of the poor and any form of relief was fobbed off on to the Justices, or else left to common charity. Collections were regularly made by the clergy and others and public kitchens had begun to spring up all around town. I remember *The Times* carried a long parry-garrick extolling the virtues of forgoing any sort of food that was deemed essential to the poor and confining one's diet solely to the consumption of fish. And so, in order to make sure that I could not be accused of failing in my duty, I oft found myself alone in my modest rooms at the Bell Tavern in King Street sitting down to a meagre and depressing meal of boiled trout or water souchy.

Mark you, I was no stranger to such privation, having served the last twelve years of my life on several of His Britannic Majesty's ships, ofttimes sailing some most inhospitable waters. But I will confess that I was glad to see winter turn to spring and with it the return

13

of some, albeit feeble, sunshine in April, when I joined a small and slightly disinterested crowd outside St. James' Palace to try to catch a glimpse of Prince George and his bride to be, prior to their wedding. Like most royal weddings this one was a private affair to be held in the Chapel Royal, and especially so, some said, because the Prince considered his future queen to be a somewhat unsavoury creature. But, all things considered, I thought that it might be worth a shot and sure enough, after some degree of idle loitering, I was rewarded with a brief sighting of the couple in the Palace grounds. Sadly, however, the spectacle was somewhat less than edifying.

The Prince, dressed in a brown coat covered all over with overblown embroidery and other such fripperies, was clearly as drunk as Davy's sow, and Princess Caroline looked for all the world like a lewd Dutch doll in her gauzy, almost bare bosomed, silver dress and velvet robe. A pretty pair they made indeed - neither of them no better than they should be, and especially so our noble Prince of Wales. It was common knowledge that the Prince had only agreed to the marriage in order that the King might pay off his debts and that, before consenting to marry Caroline, Prinny had been carrying on a liaison with that arch tart Maria Fitzherbert for over ten years past. Why, it was even said that at one time they went through a distasteful, clandestine, and ultimately illegal form of marriage, with the supposedly sacred rites actually taking place in as unhallowed a setting as Mrs Fitzherbert's own drawing room!

I declare though that I was not at all surprised by all this, for it was in no way out of the ordinary. During my time in our fair Capital I had become all too aware of the inherently self-centred, sinful nature of the city and it's proliferation of such moral vices as duelling, suicide, gambling, and debauchery. Indeed, the Londoner's wanton desire to engage in three to one permeated all levels of society and could be seen everywhere, from the ubiquitous presence of draggle tail harlots in the streets at night and the regular staging of common balum rancums attended by various rakehells, libertines, whores, and painted Cyprians, to the execrable excesses of *roués* like Old Q, the Duke of Queensbury. Ever present in society, Old Q was the epitome of London licentiousness and had seemingly dedicated his life to seduction and swiving. It was even rumoured that he once re-enacted *The Judgement of Paris* with three of the most beautiful and respected women of the town exhibiting themselves before him, as bare as nature intended; simply in order to compete for the spurious prize of a golden apple!

I will confess that it can be said that my own experience of these matters at the age of twenty-four was by no means great. My mother died when I was but a babe and I could only boast one female childhood friend. Her name was Elizabeth Saunders and she was a pretty little thing, with auburn hair falling in loose ringlets around her face, a radiant and ready smile, and an insatiable propensity for all kinds of mischief. But, although we resided in close proximity, I did not really see very much of her, save at church, and any contact was completely lost after I entered the Navy. Even when at sea I was seldom part of the atmosphere of wine, women, and song that permeated the wardroom, and most certainly never party to any of the hugger-mugger Miss Molly antics sometimes practiced by members of the more undisciplined of ship's companies!

I had joined my first ship at the age of twelve as a gentleman volunteer - servant to Captain Gardiner of the old *Demetra*, 74. My family has always been of the middling sort and when I was a boy my father, God rest his soul, worked as a gunsmith in our home village of Canewdon, an isolated place set deep within the Essex marshes. The old man was an ambitious fellow, both on his own part and on behalf of his family, and, after I had plainly failed to show any aptitude whatsoever for the gun maker's art, he conceived that the Navy should be the place for me. He knew right well that high rank within the Sea Service was not solely the prerogative of the titled and the wealthy and that, given a good measure of talent and wit, and no small amount of luck, success, fame, and fortune was open to a much wider class of 'gentlemen', wherein he was happy to categorise his only son. Obviously, with such humble origins and lack of influence in high places I was unable to enter the Service at the rate of midshipman, but Captain Gardiner, a local man, had apparently been an old friend of my mother's before I was even born, and so was kind enough to take me aboard as part of his following.

So it was that under the assiduous tutelage of the Captain, and by dint of my own hard work and exceptional diligence, I was rated midshipman at the age of sixteen, consequently serving as such on a number of ships for another four years before I entered and passed the examination for lieutenant. It was at this point that my sad lack of connections fully hit home. Notwithstanding that I had passed the exam at my first attempt, it proved singularly difficult for me to secure my promotion and I found myself continually passed over in favour of the milksop sons of the aristocracy or the snotty relatives of high ranking officers. Then, at the outbreak of the current hostilities, I had a stroke of uncommon good fortune. I was at that time serving in the *Dione*, 32, under Captain Thomas Horne when we took the French frigate *Amazone* off Cape Finisterre, following a long chase and a sharp action which culminated in my having the honour to lead a party on to the very decks of the Frenchie and, by and by, to personally haul down her flag. It was on account of this singular feat that I finally gained my commission, and very proud I was too. Lieutenant Roger Alexander Ellis, Royal Navy - how grand it sounded - and I were sure that this was but my first step on the road to glory.

The following year, however, *Dione* suffered a mort of damage in the great fleet action of the First of June and, subsequently being paid off, was brought into Chatham for an extensive refit. I therefore found myself dumped somewhat unceremoniously on shore with a small amount of prize money from the sale of the *Amazone* and showing the flag of distress with a modicum of half pay. Thereafter, in common with scores of my fellow officers, I was obliged to petition the Admiralty Board for a new berth.

At first I was ever hopeful. Having good qualifications and a record of gallantry, I was sure of finding a new ship right speedily. But, notwithstanding this, as the months wore on the spectre of my bourgeois upbringing once more raised its ugly head and my lack of access to the high and mighty began to tell against me. In those days the supply of sea officers was rapidly outstripping demand and it seemed to me that, without interest, I might remain in my sorry situation some thirty or forty years without once having any notice taken of me! At times, I even began to envy the Frenchman, against whom we were currently pitted. Johnny Crapaud appeared to fully espouse the enlightened ideas of egalitarian and meritocratic advancement in his military establishment, and indeed, since the revolution, the country seemed to have totally adopted the true philosophies of enlightenment - particularly the excellent concept of reason as the primary source of authority, the sweet ideals of liberty, freedom, and equality, and the laudable acknowledgement of the importance of religious toleration.

But, just as one had come to expect, the damned Jacobins once more went too far and, having bravely elevated the concept of reason itself to the status of religion, proceeded to tarnish the whole idea by holding a series of obscene Rabelaisian festivals dedicated solely to anarchy and the wanton pursuit of free will and pleasure. It was reported that in Paris, for example, that damn fool Hébert, who famously decried the actions of the bishop of Rome in excommunicating all the French by declaiming 'fuck the court of Rome, its cardinals and its bishops', presided over an indecent, so called 'Festival of Reason' at Notre Dame. By all accounts, after that venerable church had been thoroughly plundered by the *sans culottes*, it became the stage for a blasphemous and orgiastic public affair in which a seductively dressed young strumpet wearing a Phrygian bonnet and holding a pike so as to signify that she was the 'Goddess of Reason', was fairly worshiped at the high altar; and all whilst a gaggle of other half naked doxies danced around her singing ribald songs in celebration of the revolution.

But I digress; suffice to say that by mid-April 1795 I was kicking my heels in St James', heartily sick of it, and feeling damned sorry for myself. Most mornings I would rise, pull on my old single breasted blue coat with its grubby white piping, don my white waistcoat and breeches, and my shiny black Hessians (they weren't regulation, but I did so love those boots), strap on my short, straight bladed fighting sword, clap on my tricorne, and walk the short distance from King Street across the Cockpit to the Admiralty Building in Whitehall. Once there I would wait upon the word of one of the pettifogging clerks to Mr Napean, the Secretary to the Board, as to whether there was any news for me - which, invariably, there wasn't. And to cap it all I had to drop the little conveyancer tuppence for the privilege.

One good thing though, there was always a chance to catch up with some of the other fellows who were in the same straits as me, and thus I could often be seen killing time around town in the company of Harry Felgate and young Charlie Edwardes. Felgate was a jolly fellow much given to jests and other low wit and I confess I did not much take to him, but unfortunately he and Edwardes came as a pair and so I found I could not really avoid his company. Charlie was a much more serious young man, whose erudite conversation pleased me greatly. Being a Scotchman, Charlie was considerably interested in the natural histories of religion that had been produced some years earlier by his fellow Hibernians, Messrs Hume and Robertson. These works, he oft contended, sought to apply the science of human nature to the study of the origins and development of religious beliefs.

One afternoon, the weather being rainy and most inclement, we three had repaired to Bedford's, a coffee house located under the Piazza in Covent Garden. Bedford's, a dark and dingy place with wainscoted walls and shaved wooden floors, smelled foul and was permanently hung with tobacco smoke. And it was one of our favourite haunts. Its patrons were almost invariably men of parts - scholars and wits mostly, so that within the grimy bulwarks of that establishment jokes and bon-mots would echo from box to box and every branch of literature and philosophy would be minutely and critically examined. At this hour, it being a little after four o' the clock, the place was not too overcrowded so that we were able to secure a box at the upper end without being troubled too much by cries of 'what news have you' and suchlike from other members of the assembled multitude. After shrugging off our wet and steamy outerwear and ordering three bowls of the house's bitter Mohammedan gruel, we fell into conversation.

Harry started in along his customary lines.

"I say, you fellows," he grinned, as Charlie and I exchanged rueful glances. "Did you hear that last year, when the Frogs were taking the Duchess of Gramont to the guillotine she continually complained about the miserable rainy weather - that is until one of her guards said loudly, 'I don't know what you've got to complain about Madam - we've got to walk all the way home in this!'"

Of course, Charlie fairly fell about, and, thus encouraged, Harry prepared to launch into another groaner from his latest jest book. But, as was my wont, I was quick to bring things around to more serious matters.

"Charlie," I said. "On the subject of the French, let us hear some more of your latest hypothesis concerning the origins of that troubled nation's radical philosophies."

"Why, but of course," said Charlie. "To begin, might I ask if you were aware that, in framing their accounts of the natural development of religious belief, both Hume and Robertson appealed to the evidence of the pagan past?"

"Really?" said I, recognising the course we were about to embark upon, for it was not the first time that we had sailed these particular waters and so caused those two celebrated Sandies to raise their heads in our discourse. "Please, do explain, old fellow, how so?"

"Well, all throughout their writings, both of those learned scholars have clear recourse to the study of ancient texts that show that pagan religions have always provided a crucial support for popular morality. And I have lately been minded that this has never been more evident than in the revolution's overriding clarion call for universal *égalité* which, to their credit, the Jacobins apply even as between the sexes, don't y'know?"

"It appears to me that the Frenchies are certainly very keen on equality between the sexes," Harry put in, as a cherubic young lad appeared at the table with our drinks. "They don't rightly care whose head they chop off - man or woman!"

"Hush, Harry, let the man finish," I admonished, realising that it wouldn't take much for the conversation to shift once more from the intellectual to the farcical. "Carry on Charlie, let's hear your point".

Charlie carried on.

"You see," he said. "In ancient times nearly all pagan religions regarded men and women as true equals, subject to the biological realities of gender of course. They also had a clear understanding that these natural differences did not in any way privilege one sex over the other. And this, it seems to me, is something of what the Frenchies are getting at. Your Frenchman, in common with his pagan ancestors, believes that man and woman are equal in the eyes of God, or as Robespierre would have had it, the Supreme Being, and as such should, for example, be allowed to enjoy the equal right to petition for divorce, or the equal right to inherit. But, and here's the rub, unlike their ancestors the Frogs still maintain that, because women inhabit bodies with different physical attributes, they must necessarily possess fundamentally different qualities and virtues which, though not impacting upon their right to equal treatment as human beings, will, as Rousseau himself has argued, inevitably render them unsuitable to vote, say, or hold any kind of public office."

"I take your meaning," said Harry, leaning back in his seat and taking a pull from a long clay pipe. "Men are undeniably the stronger sex, and therefore more intelligent, courageous, and determined. Women, on the other hand, God love 'em, though undoubtedly sweet and nurturing, are far more governed by their emotions, and indeed their lusts."

"That's most likely why we are now seeing French women in another kind of role," replied Charlie. "I don't know if you have become aware of this, but it is a reported fact that most of the French revolutionary values - liberty, equality, reason, and so on - are now being represented in the arts through the depiction of female figures from antiquity, and, should you chance upon such images, as I have, you'll plainly see that those figures are more often than not shown dressed in skimpy togas or else are displayed half, or even fully, naked."

At which point, I weighed in with what was, well, almost, my own opinion. "Are either of you gentlemen perhaps familiar with Mary Wollstonecraft's work, *A Vindication of the Rights of Woman*?" I asked.

Both my companions shook their heads, and so, taking a tentative sip of the noxious brew before me, I went on.

"It is a very thought provoking work, to be sure - although it is damned wordy! By my reading of it, the author's central tenet is that women are not naturally inferior to men and that it is only because women are subject to what she calls a 'false system of education' - that is, a system that is based only on what men consider women should be - that women inevitably become frivolous, silly, and ultimately unable to make a meaningful contribution to society."

"In that respect, then," said Charlie. "Could not this lady's work be compared to the ideas put forward a few years ago by that French playwright, Olympe de Gouges? Although I believe de Gouges dared to venture even further by declaring women to be not only man's equal but his partner?"

"Quite so," I replied. "Women are as naturally rational as men and therefore it follows that, if they were given access to the same educational opportunities as their opposite sex, they must surely have every chance of working alongside men in the furtherance of all manner of trades, professions, commerce, and even, it must be said, politics. Indeed, it occurs to me that our current assembly of ineffectual Jacks-in-Office would most certainly benefit from a more compassionate and empathetic, or dare I say feminine, representation amongst them."

At that point however, a perhaps not so random thought struck me, and I paused to take another draught from my cup before turning to Harry.

"Mark you, on the question of lust, Harry" I mused, "I think you may have hit upon some truth. Though whether such passions are innate or no is a matter for conjecture."

"Whether it be innate or learned, Roger, perhaps the counterbalance to the delimiting effects of a woman's high propensity to sensuality can be seen as simply a matter of needing to properly weigh up the effects of pleasure against any resulting pain, like that fellow Bentham says," suggested Harry."

"Perhaps so," says I. "Certainly Bentham's principle of utility allows that any kind of action is right if it tends to promote happiness or pleasure, and only wrong if it tends to produce unhappiness or pain. And you are in the right of it, Harry, Bentham does tell us that happiness is a balance of pleasure over pain, and so it may be that instances of overt sexuality in both women and men can always be overlooked or condoned in as far as no consequential harm emanates from them."

Charlie and Harry nodded their agreement, but as they did so I abruptly changed tack.

"But I don't know," I said, sadly. "I have a mind that Bentham's philosophies, though eloquently defined, might well merely be a veiled attempt to justify the unfortunate dedication to the blind pursuit of hedonistic pleasure that so blights our society these days."

"Come now, Roger, it's not as bad as all that," said Charlie. "Everyone needs to blow off a little steam every now and then, even you, I'm sure."

"Ah, but it is as bad as that, Charlie. And it's not only the common types either, barely a day passes without reports and letters being published in the press telling of the adulterous liaisons and amorous adventures of Lady So-and So and the Duchess of What-Not - people of high standing who must surely be conscious of a need to maintain a suitable level of decorum in these dangerous times? I myself will have no truck with it, damme if I will, and I'll go so far as to declare that it is the bawdy and perverse self-gratification that is so prevalent around town that is causing me to become so deadly tired of London life."

"But you do recall what the Good Doctor said, laddie?" Charlie asked with a smile. "When a man is tired of London, he is tired of life!"

"That's all very well and good," I replied. "But, if I

add the frustrations of needing to continually kow-tow to those damned Admiralty clerks to the complete lack of morals I have seen since I arrived, I despair of finding any pleasure in my current situation - beyond the chance of snatching a few moments of civilised conversation with you both, of course. London is a mean and ugly place that has sunk to the very depths of depravity in its veneration of Cytherea. Why, if evidence be needed of the extent of the moral degeneration in this city, one need only stray among the old 'dark walks' of Vauxhall, which, even though now dimly lit, are still exceedingly secluded. Any visitor spending his evening among those arbours is certain to see women of the utmost social respectability willingly and publicly entering the amatory lists alongside various so called demi-reps, dashers, and your common or garden Drury Lane vestals. I tell you gentlemen, this city is in truth beginning to repel me and I have a mind to take a break from London for a while."

CHAPTER 2

I do believe that my friends fully understood my plight, for they took the utmost pains to encourage me in my desire for a brief vacation away from the fleshpots of London. Their Lordships would know where to find me should an opportunity arise, they argued, and I would most surely find a stay in the country to be an excellent fillip, so that I might return to the city in a few weeks, refreshed and once more ready for the fray. Eventually, I succumbed to their entreaties and in late May determined upon paying a short visit to Canewdon, that fond remembered hamlet that was once my childhood home.

Though places were scarce, I was fortunate enough to be able to catch a ride on a stage-coach from the Blue Boar Cellar in Aldgate to Brentwood (a bustling place, where I must say that, in company with divers other travellers, we dined rather well for a shilling: partaking of beef steaks, bread and beer at the Gardener's Arms) and then on to the old market town of Rayleigh. I had eschewed my uniform coat and travelled in civilian clothes: a plain brown jacket, mustard waistcoat trimmed with brass buttons, leather breeches and a pair of battered old brown topped boots that I had been meaning to send to the menders for some time. These boots were as nothing beside my Hessians but I steadfastly refused to pair those beauties with anything but my Navy rig. To provide some insurance against the ever present danger of highway robbery l carried a small, stubby pistol in the pocket of my grey broadcloth greatcoat. This little barking iron represented the remaining half of a pair of short barrelled twelve bore guns made by my father in the Irish style, which he presented to me on the day I left our home to join the *Demetra* - its twin having been lost when I chucked it at the head of an ugly great brute of a Frenchman who was trying to skewer me with a boarding pike on the deck of the *Amazone*. Notwithstanding its overall size, make no mistake, the pistol was a manstopper, and it must be said that feeling the weight of it dragging at my coat tail provided me with no small amount of comfort on the road.

The journey to Rayleigh, around thirty miles as the crow flies, set me back over just under fifteen shillings and meant spending almost six hours perched next to my sea chest atop a racketing old leather sprung bone-rattler, with the added bonus of being made to get down and walk all the way up Brentwood Hill because our four nags were considered unable to manage the steep incline when harnessed to a fully laden coach.

Therefore, though faced with the prospect of laying out an additional ten bob, I was more than willing to dip into my funds so as to change to a hired two horse post chaise for the remainder of the journey from Rayleigh through the villages of Hockley and Ashingdon, and on to my final destination, the Anchor Inn at Canewdon. And right glad I was to have done so, for by the time we rolled into the village a monstrous storm had set in and the little chaise was being lashed by heavy rain and wind, whilst thunder rolled and ragged bolts of lightning split the sky. Luckily the postboy was an experienced hand and, though the horses were uncommon spooked, he managed to keep them under control. God help sailors on a night like this, I thought, for this was one occasion when I was glad to be washed up on shore.

Now, with me being an orphan, I no longer had a home in the village to return to and so I had sent ahead to obtain simple lodgings at the Inn. As I alighted from the coach I was greeted by the widow Dowsett, the esteemed proprietor of this most welcome of ports in a storm, who ushered me quickly inside, out of the rain. The Anchor was an unpretentious establishment, more akin to an oversized alehouse than a coaching inn, but it did boast a large kitchen, several moderately appointed rooms, and a small stable block wherein horses were kept for the guests - and at three shillings and sixpence a week it suited me admirably.

Sally Dowsett was a woman approaching middle age, slim, shapely and still, to my mind, of quite handsome appearance. She wore an old fashioned sack dress and apron topped off with a white cap stretched over her own short brown curls. And she fussed over me like a mother hen as she led me into the kitchen.

"You come right in sir," she said, after I had announced myself. "Take off that heavy coat and sit yourself down at that table by the fire there while I send someone to get your chamber ready and fetch you a morsel to eat. Tom!" she called to a lad of about ten years old who was hovering behind her. "Tom, fetch the Cap'n here some bread, cheese and mutton. He must be famished after so long on the road. Then get yourself upstairs with his baggage and ready his room. The postboy will help you with that big chest, I'm sure."

"Thankee, Mrs Dowsett," I replied. "I have eaten on the road, but a little cold mutton and a drop of ale would go down right well."

The kitchen of the Anchor Inn was a Spartan affair with whitewashed walls and a large brick fireplace. The fireplace was hung with a large cookpot and festooned with a host of other gleaming cooking utensils. On the wall beside the fireplace was mounted the large wheel of the turnspit dog. The dog himself, a crooked, ugly old cur, sat below it, surveying the room with a suspicious, unhappy look on his face. Simple wooden tables, chairs and benches stood on the flagstone floor and were in part occupied by some of the inn's other patrons, rustic types nursing pots of ale or, in some cases, glasses of blue ruin.

"Have you ever seen anything like this weather of late, sir?" Mrs Dowsett asked as Tom arrived at the table carrying a plate heavy with victuals. "Cold as any stone all winter and not much better now with all this rain."

"It is indeed most unpleasant, Mrs Dowsett. Still, I would hope for better things to come as we enter the summer months."

"Please, Cap'n, call me Sal. Everybody else does, and I would be pleased if you would too. For sure, the weather in these parts tends to improve around midsummer, so I have every hope that you will have a pleasant stay in the village."

Quite so... er... Sal," I said. "I do recall some very long and temperate summers from my boyhood, which, to be sure, I was lucky enough to spend in these very environs."

"Why, I had no idea you were a local man, sir," smiled Sal. "May I then be the first to give you joy of your return. Pray tell, do you still have connections in Canewdon?"

Whilst finishing my supper I provided Sal with some brief particulars of my history. She in turn informed me that, as she and her late husband had only taken over the Anchor some five years past, she had not known of anyone by the name of Ellis living in the village, my father having died some while before. Indeed, it appeared that there had been a lot of newcomers arriving of late. There was a new squire, she told me. Sir Henry Spurgeon and his family had taken up residence at Canewdon Hall just two years ago, and not soon after, he had appointed the Reverend Thomas Gildersleeve to the parish living in place of old Reverend Cuthbertson, whom I had known as a child. There was one bright spot, however, Mr and Mrs Saunders and their daughter still lived in the High Street - Elizabeth had grown into a fine young woman, Sal said - and I instantly resolved to reacquaint myself with the family at my earliest convenience.

At length, I asked my host if I might repair to my room.

"But of course, sir," said Sal. "Young Tom will have finished now, so I'll get him to take you up. He's a good lad, sir, is Tom, and he's been a good son to me, helping me run this place ever since my husband passed last year."

Tom duly showed me up to the clean and spacious room on the first floor that was to be my home for the next few weeks. The room was well appointed with good mahogany furniture and, most surprisingly, boasted an immense four poster bed with a fine feather mattress and heavy curtains. There were curtains too at the window, and tallow dips on the mantle. There were even one or two, albeit rather dreary, pictures affixed to the walls.

"This is the best room in the house, Cap'n," Tom chirruped, as he pulled the door to. "Mother and I both hope that you will enjoy your stay with us."

I slept well that night, probably the best I had slept for some weeks, and woke up refreshed. The last night's rain had cleared up and the day dawned bright with promise. Having breakfasted on some hearty bacon and eggs, I took a turn round the village to see if it was truly as I remembered.

The Anchor stood on the corner of the High Street and my first thought was therefore to turn left out of the front door and walk down, past the small, neat village pond, and the old cage and stocks to view the nondescript single storey cottage wherein I had once lived with my father. Across the street I could see that since I was last there an imposing new brick built parish workhouse had sprung up on the site of what had once been Pond House.

My father's cottage was empty and beginning to fall into disrepair, and I soon found myself succumbing to a feeling of deep melancholy as I peered through its tiny windows at the scraps of furniture left behind. At the rear of the cottage was my father's old shop, still fitted out with forge and bellows at which he would often stand for hours heating, filing, and boring barrels to be fitted to firearms of every shape and size. I wondered, had I really sat there beside the old man, trying my best to help and to learn from him all those years ago, or was I just half remembering; conjuring up some kind of idyllic vision of the past, a vision that was leagues apart from the harsh, disciplined, and dangerous reality of the life I had since led in the service of the King? Whichever the case, there can be no doubt that the sight of those old buildings at once engendered within me a strong feeling of loneliness and a deep desire to have my father back with me, if only for one last time.

Wrenching myself away from the cottage and its associated memories, I walked back up the High Street in the direction of St Nicholas' Church, with Canewdon Hall away to my right, and the windmill and the Saunders' family home on my larboard beam. Given my melancholy state and, if I am honest, perhaps some measure of shyness too, I thought it best to wait awhile before presenting my compliments to Mr and Mrs Saunders. I therefore did not tarry at their large, stucco-fronted house with its tall sash windows but instead continued on up the hill in the direction of the church, passing the premises of the various local shopkeepers, who nodded and waved politely to me as I went by.

St Nicholas' Church was as I remembered it. Standing on a ridge overlooking the village to the east and the salt marshes of the River Crouch to the north, the grey ragstone church dominated the landscape. As I looked up at the high square tower and around me at the marble stones marking the final resting place of those who had gone before, I was reminded of winter evenings long ago, when Father would sit by the fire and tell chilling tales of the faceless grey lady floating out of the west gate down to the river, and Old Nick himself skulking in his lair under one of the broken tombstones. There were also the usual tales of fly by night witches, and cunning warlocks who roamed the churchyard by moonlight. The old man loved a ghost story, and he loved sending me off to bed all wide-eyed and quick to pull the blankets tight over my head. It was all my eye and Betty Martin, of course, but it was fine fare for frightening the children, so that they would be sure to toe the line. Indeed, back then, Father's stories were enough to keep me away from the churchyard in the evenings to be sure, but having now, as the scripture says, put away childish things, I knew for certain that such tales no longer had any place in this modern, rational world.

Emerging from the churchyard, I turned into Church Lane and continued my perambulation down to the crossroads, passing the parsonage on the way. Now presumably occupied by the Reverend Gildersleeve, the parsonage was another fairly modest single storey building, but unlike my father's cottage, the parsonage sported two fine dormer windows to allow the sunlight into what I supposed were attic bedrooms. I could also discern a formal garden and various outbuildings to the rear. As with my former acquaintances, the Saunders, I resolved to pay my respects to that no doubt august member of the clergy as soon as I felt it apposite to do so.

Turning left at the crossroads at the foot of Church Lane and, by and by, steering left again, took me through fields of tillering wheat and barley, back up to the door of the Anchor where I hove to once more, right ready for a bite of roast beef, pease soup and gooseberry pudding. This meal I was pleased to partake in the comfort of my room so as to allow for some more gentle reflection on my childhood days, and also no little sad consideration of those things that now seemed lost forever.

In the evening I took myself down to the kitchen, ordered wine, cheese and a little of the toasted bread soaked in ale, sugar and grated nutmeg that was known as sugar sops. I then fell to talking with my esteemed landlady and a couple of other fellows there present.

"Did you enjoy your walk this morning, sir?" asked Sal.

"I did, Sal," I replied. "It brought back many sweet boyhood memories, I declare."

"'Ave you visited Canewdon afore then, Master?" enquired one old clod hopper who was lounging at the end of the table clad in a short mud stained brown jacket and heavily patched breeches.

"Oh, Ned Symonds, do you not know, you having lived here all your life?" Sal scolded. "The Cap'n here is Arthur Ellis' son, y'know the gun maker who used to have the shop across the lane."

"Bless me! Young Roger, is it?" said the old codger. "I wouldn't 'ave recognised you, you 'aving filled out so well. I remember your da, though. 'E were a good and trusty trout t'me, f'sure."

"I remember you too, Mr Symonds" said I, with a smile. "Especially the clout round the ear you gave me the day you caught me snaffling fruit from Squire

Devereaux's orchards."

"Heh, heh. You always was a young scamp, Master Roger," Ned chuckled, looking down at his ale in an effort to feign some embarrassment. "Though not as bad as some around these parts, I'll warrant..."

"Squire Devereaux..." mused another old goat in the corner. "Now, 'e were a kind and fair man."

"That 'e was, Cuddy," agreed Ned.

"Why, you're Cuddy Smith!" I said warmly, addressing the second man. "I remember you too, now I come to take a good sniltch."

"Thankee kindly, Master Roger," said Cuddy, tugging at the place where his forelock must once have been. "D'you mind Squire Devereaux, up at the 'All? 'E died a few year ago and the 'All got shut up for ages until Sir 'Enry bought it. But this Sir 'Enry's not a patch on the old squire, damn me if 'e is. 'E wouldn't 'ave treated Mrs Baker so bad, an' you can have my word on that."

"Mind what you say, Cuddy," said Sal, in a low whisper. "Sir Henry has only done what the law prescribes."

"What's this?" I said, intrigued. "Is there a whiff of scandal about the village?"

"No scandal," replied Sal. "It's just that last night Biddy Baker, who lived up by Butts Hill, poor old soul that she was, took her own life. She must have been driven to it by some hidden heartache that no-one around her knew anything about. And it's a sad and terrible thing to tell, sir, but she was found this morning by her neighbours, and, upon them bringing the news to Sir Henry, who y'know is our magistrate, and to the new vicar up at the church, they were told in no uncertain terms that according to the law she could not be admitted to the churchyard and must needs be buried at the crossroads without benefit of clergy."

"That is a sorry tale indeed," I opined. "But alas, suicide is becoming so prevalent lately and the law does clearly state that to take one's own life must be counted a *felo de se*, by which I mean a crime against oneself, and as such requires that its sad victims be punished in this way. Times are changing though, Sal," I continued, having recalled something Charlie Edwardes told me that his beloved Mr Hume had once said. "Modern rational thinking now suggests that to take one's life is actually no crime at all in that the commission causes no harm to any but the perpetrator. And it is in fact most often the case that the very act of suicide itself can be of considerable potential advantage to that individual."

As I spoke I found my companions nodding sagely in agreement, but I suspected that as far as Ned and Cuddy were concerned, my words had passed somewhat over their heads. There was something about Sal's demeanour, however, that seemed to hint at some knowledge and understanding.

"That is true to say, sir," she murmured. "In this, as in many other things in life…"

"Pray tell, when is this burial to take place?" I asked, for, having never seen such a thing, I had a mind to witness the proceedings, if only to satisfy my curiosity.

"Ah, it'll likely be of a morning, two days hence," said Cuddy, solemnly. "They'll want to make sure they wash poor old Biddy properly and then get 'er wrapped up in a nice flowery smellin' shroud. An' then o'course they'll need to get the grave digger to prepare the ground for 'er."

So it was then, that on a damp and misty morning two days later, I took a turn down across the fields to the crossroads at the end of Church Lane in time to see several stout yeomen dragging a crudely fashioned bier, upon which lay the unfortunate Biddy Baker's corpse covered with a heavy cloth pall, up to an open grave hastily dug by the side of the road. As I watched from a discrete distance, I saw the bier tipped and the woman's body slipped into the ground. And then a most shocking occurrence took place. One of the bearers brought a wooden mallet and a sharpened stake from the back of the cart, and so armed, jumped straight into the grave on top of the body. I saw the man's fist rise and fall as he fair drove the stake through the heart of his victim, spurting black blood up his outstretched arm and pinning her to the earth. For sure, I had seen my fair share of violence and gore in many a sea fight, but even so, this disgusting spectacle truly turned my stomach and I was moved to withdraw as the man was assisted out of the hole by his fellows in order that the gravedigger might begin the task of filling in with quicklime before closing the grave.

Mark you; I knew full well why this grisly deed had been done. It was all superstitious nonsense. In times past it had been the custom that suicides be buried with a stake driven through the body to prevent the spirit from 'walking' or leaving the grave in order to plague the living. The same treatment was meted out to those poor wretches condemned as witches in the last century, as I remember. Lately such beastly practices had begun to be dispensed with in London and the other larger cities at least - and rightly so, to my mind - and metropolitan juries had virtually stopped punishing suicide altogether twenty or thirty years previously. But I was not in London any more. I was in the heart of deepest rural Essex where no doubt the old religious ideas that linked suicide and immorality, and the even older belief that a stake through the heart would serve as protection against the escape of evil, still held sway amongst those lacking an adequate education.

I retired that night still with a feeling of some trepidation concerning the things I had seen and the true nature of the place I found myself in - a place that somehow was starting to feel so different to the warm, secure and comforting vision of home that I had so long held in my memory. Although perhaps it had ever been so, and the truth was simply that as a child I had always been well sheltered from the harsh realities of rural life and its less savoury lore and customs. After a while I drifted off into a sleep beset by dreams of being

41

pursued through the churchyard by old Cuddy Smith got up as the Devil himself and threatening to spit me on a long pole if I didn't give up the huge bag of stolen cherries I was dragging along behind me. In truth, I have always been prone to night terrors - and I blame the old man for that - but this particular dream was, as I remember, one of the most vivid I ever had.

Betimes I was suddenly awakened from my dreaming by the click of the Suffolk latch that fastened the door of my room. My eyes widened and I listened intently as soft footsteps padded towards the bed. To my shame, my first thought was of spirits and spectres and I was in a cursed funk as I saw a delicate, white hand grasp the edge of the curtain and begin to slowly pull it open. But, soft, it was no shade that approached that night. As the curtain parted I realised that it was Sal who had entered.

"Don't be alarmed. Master Roger," she whispered. "Tis only I, come to offer you some tender comfort this night. I can see you have been sore affected by some of the things that occurred this morning - things that, by rights, you ought not to have been given to see. So, if you'll allow me, I'll do my very best to sooth those troubles away."

Well, to say that I had been put in fear by the prospect of being confronted by the revenant of poor old Biddy Baker was as nothing when compared to the fear conjured up by the knowledge that I was becoming subject to the advances of the landlady of the Anchor Inn. It was, however, at the same time oddly stimulating. I could see by the light of the candle she carried that she was clad only in a thin chemise, the laces of which were undone to the waist so that the shape of her still pert breasts could be fully discerned beneath the diaphanous, semi-transparent fabric. As she moved closer to place her candlestick down upon the bedside table and perch on the side of the mattress, one smooth, milk-white, naked thigh was exposed to my astonished gaze.

"I am deeply sorry madam," I stammered, instinctively pulling the covers up to my chin. "But my moral philosophies, and indeed my own sensibilities, prelude me from taking advantage of you by engaging in such pleasures outside the bounds of wedlock."

"Ah, I see" breathed Sal. "It is of no consequence my darling, I understand. I'm no stranger to the tales they tell of sailormen so long at sea. Hush now then, and let us forget this ever passed between us."

Moral philosophies or no, I wasn't having this. And I told the brazen fizgig as much, too.

"Why, Sal... erm... Mrs Dowsett. Do not mistake me, I am no Molly. And indeed you are a most comely and beguiling woman, b'Gad!" and she was too I thought, especially with those pretty little pink nosed puppies poking out of her shift. "But I avow that I have far too much respect for you - as indeed I have for all others of your sex - to so trifle with your chastity in this way."

"Chastity is it? Well I wouldn't trouble yourself

too much with that now, sweetheart, for that horse has long since left the stable. And I see now that I was indeed mistaken," Sal said archly, as she slowly insinuated her hand under the covers to brush over that which was now growing apace between my legs.

I became aware that I had begun to tremble somewhat as she bent over to kiss me tenderly on the forehead, whilst at the same time affording me a most glorious full view of the dairy.

"But, in truth, I do understand," she said, taking one final squeeze as she straightened up. "So we'll say no more about it. And now I shall bid you goodnight. Sleep well, sir, and, just before I go, would there be anything special you might be wanting... For your breakfast, I mean?"

Damme, but I was bloody well fit to burst. "Er... Bacon and eggs will be fine again, Mrs Dowsett, thank you." I squeaked.

"If it please you sir, do call me Sal...," she said as she gently closed the door.

CHAPTER 3

The next day, it being Sunday, I thought it best if I were to attend church. The events of last night had affected me greatly and, it must be said, in a not entirely unpleasant manner, so as to cause me some confusion in my emotions. I therefore felt that a good sermon might be just the thing to set me back on the narrow way which leadeth unto life. So, directly after breakfast, served by my erstwhile nocturnal visitor with a beauteous smile and nary a word on what had passed in the wee hours, I repaired to St Nicholas' to forgather with the rest of the village to hear the wise words of the Reverend Gildersleeve.

The old church had been built in the time of Henry V and was accessed via two massive timber doors on the south side of the building. Inside, an enormous, carved three decker pulpit dominated the chancel, illuminated by a large stained glass window, beneath which was situated the altar and an ornately carved stone font. The nave was flanked by two rows of imposing, high partitioned pews that afforded complete privacy to those within. Only the vicar himself could see into them from his perch at the top level of his prattling box. I could tell from the lively buzz of conversation that most of the congregation were already ensconced in their pews by the time I entered to take my seat at the back, just in front of the narthex.

On the appearance of the Reverend Gildersleeve the conversation stopped. The reverend was of medium height, still a fairly young man, perhaps in his mid-thirties, with a mildly pockmarked face which was no doubt a legacy of the smallpox. He wore a black gown and a full length black cassock with bright white bands at his throat. On his head he wore a floured wig with rows of tight curls down each side and on his feet he sported a fine pair of silver buckled shoes that click-clacked up the wooden steps as he mounted his pulpit.

Once settled on his lofty perch, the little cushion thumper let fly with a most unusual and at first, well at least as far as I was concerned, curiously appropriate oration.

"Brothers and sisters," he intoned. "This day, I would like to talk to you about adultery and fornication."

I'faith, I thought, does this fellow know something? He couldn't surely, and anyway I had resisted temptation, hadn't I?

"Thou shalt not covet thy neighbour's wife, sayeth the tenth of God's commandments passed down to Moses on Mount Sinai," continued the vicar, as I let out a small sigh of relief. Sal was a widow, when all was said and done. "Nor shalt thou commit adultery, sayeth the seventh. And this, you will say, is both right and proper - for the act of adultery is a sin that can lead to scars and wounds that cut deeper than any that were ever made by a blade. But, I ask you now to consider, what of the act of fornication itself - the giving in to a simple animal instinct which... alas... man only too readily allows to arise wherever the opportunity presents itself. Is this too a sin?"

Get ready for a spot of good old fire and brimstone, I fancied, this'll shake 'em up. But no, this singular cleric evidently had different ideas.

"You will all, in no doubt, be familiar with *Corinthians* Chapter 6, which tells us not to be deceived, for 'neither fornicators, nor adulterers shall inherit the kingdom of God'. You must also know, however, that this is but a reference to what in those far off days was considered no more than a crime against property. At that time a woman's bride-price would be reduced should she no longer be seen to be a virgin and, by engaging in the act of fornication, a man was, in fact, considered to be a thief, stealing away a valuable commodity from the woman's father. I must tell you though that nowhere in the Bible does it say that amorous congress outside the bounds of matrimony is a sin!

On the contrary! The Old Testament *Song of Solomon* fully celebrates sexual love, with no reference to marriage at all, thus affirming to us, with the highest authority, that physical passion is in itself both good and beneficial. So then, what of a man and a woman drawn to satisfy their sexual appetites when both are free from vows? Are they sinners? I say not! I say God in his wisdom made us sexual beings and our sexuality is not something to be denied or made shameful. Yay, our sexuality should be celebrated as part of the very order of creation.

But, as in all things there must be discipline. In his sermon on the mount Jesus speaks of the Law of Love, and this law must be equally applied to the service of Venus as it is to all other things. The sexual act is a powerful thing and from it can come great pleasure and also great pain, both for others and for your own self. Even our late Brother Wesley urged that in everything we should abide by three rules: love God, do good, and do no harm. And, in another sphere altogether, the great physician Hippocrates himself declared that the fundamental rule of medicine must be *primum non nocere*, 'first do no harm'. And so I say also to you that, as with the physician, the first ethical principle of amorous congress must be to do no harm by it, nor indeed allow it to cause any harm to be done."

Lord, save us! I thought (perhaps appropriately given my surroundings) as the reverend ran on with gathering enthusiasm. He's a bloody Benthamite, and he's game enough to trot out all that 'morality of an action is decided by its consequences' fiddle-faddle straight from the pulpit of all places. I must say, I didn't approve of this at all, and it seemed to me to be naught but an encouragement to profligate behaviour, and ample evidence too that the tendency to moral degeneration that was rife in the city was beginning to spread its tentacles ever further.

For the nonce, however, despite my moral disapprobation, I did not wish to offend so early in my sojourn in the village and so I perceived it best to keep my views to myself, especially since on emerging from the church to engage in the customary gathering on the greensward, the rest of the congregation appeared completely unaffected by the vicar's rhetoric, almost as if they had heard it all before. When announcing my presence to Reverend Gildersleeve I therefore avoided any comment on his extraordinary sermon.

"Ah, if it isn't our sailor, home at last," said the reverend. "I had heard of your arrival in the village and I have been looking forward to meeting you."

"And I you, Reverend," I replied politely. "Pray forgive me for not making myself known to you far sooner, I have been a while settling myself into my new surroundings."

"And are your new surroundings to your liking, Lieutenant?"

"They are, sir, but I confess that Canewdon does not seem quite the place it was when I left all those years ago," I said, sadly. "But perhaps this is only to be expected. In truth, to the child all things seem everlasting, and as children we are rarely alert to change outside of our own introspection, and nor are we always fully aware of everything that is happening around us."

"Those are indeed wise words, young man," said the vicar, nodding. "Alas, there has been much change in the world in recent years, and unfortunately the village has not been immune to it."

"How so?" I asked, curiously.

"I am afraid to say that the folk here have suffered greatly of late. Last year's was a bad harvest and, as you know, it has been an uncommon harsh winter," the vicar went on. "And the price of bread is forever rising. D'you know, a quarten loaf now costs all but a shilling? Money is ever scarce, and if this situation continues for much longer I fear that many more of my flock must surely be driven on to the parish lest they starve."

"These are uncommon hard times, Reverend. For I have lately heard much made of the fact that, because of the very high price of all the other articles of life, many of the labouring poor are forced to live chiefly on bread alone. And if even that poor staple is denied them... Why, as indefensible as it may be, it would be small wonder were some of them to look at events lately occurring across the channel and begin to cry out for change."

"No, no, Lieutenant, you must never doubt that the people of this village remain good people all the same. As you must have seen, Canewdon folk will always greet you with a bow or curtsey and a cheery 'good morrow' - and, though they may occasionally speak ill of the King and Mr Pitt over a pot of ale in the Anchor, they are fiercely patriotic, sir. They'll have no truck with any Frenchified excesses or Jacobin blasphemies, indeed they will not."

Although a little shagging outside wedlock should always be encouraged, I presumed. But, nevertheless the Reverend Gildersleeve did seem prepared to emphasise with the plight of those of his spiritual charges less fortunate, and, moreover, he clearly held the people of the village in high regard.

Whilst we conversed, a number of other persons hove into view.

"Sir Henry!" called the vicar, hailing the leader of the group, a tall, vigorous looking figure decked out in the latest of country finery: a suit of matching green coat, waistcoat and breeches. He wore his own hair, clubbed and tied with a black ribbon, and topped it off with a tall, conical hat. "Might I introduce Lieutenant Ellis, newly arrived in the parish, though it must be said, no stranger to it. Mr Ellis, Sir Henry Spurgeon, of Canewdon Hall."

"Y'Servant, sir," said Sir Henry, nodding in my general direction.

"An honour to meet you, Sir Henry," I replied.

"May I present my wife, Lady Mary?" went on the squire, indicating a pleasingly plump and fairly unassuming woman in a burnt orange close fronted gown and a broad-brimmed shepherdess hat. "And may I also present our great friends Mr and Mrs Saunders and their daughter Elizabeth?"

Of the appearance of Mr and Mrs Saunders that day, I cannot rightly recall very much, for my eyes were all for Elizabeth. The pretty little girl I had once known had grown into a truly radiant beauty. Of middling height, Elizabeth still wore her own auburn hair, unpowdered and artfully curled around her face. Arched eyebrows, tapered at the ends, crowned large brown eyes set atop an elegantly straight nose and rosebud lips. Her simple cream coloured dress emphasised her slim waist and upright, virginal breasts.

"How delightful to see you all again," I gushed.

"My dear Mr Ellis, the pleasure is all ours," said Mrs Saunders sweetly. "We have such fond memories of you - chasing around this very churchyard playing Huzzlecap or London Bridge with our dear Lizzie and the other children. How splendid it is to see you grown into such a dashing young man!"

"Thankee, madam," I replied gallantly. "May I say how good it is too, to see Miss Saunders having blossomed into such a beautiful and charming young lady?"

"*La*, sir, you do me too much honour," said Elizabeth, blushing prettily and with downcast eyes.

"And if I may also say, Mrs Saunders," I oozed, thinking to pour on the charm. "You yourself remain as youthful as when I last saw you. Forsooth, did I not know better, I would have taken you both to be sisters."

"You are too kind, sir," said Mrs Saunders, smiling brightly. "And, even if your words have no basis in fact, your flattery does you much credit. Now, tell me, are you intending to stay awhile in Canewdon?"

"Somewhat, yes," I confirmed. "I have a mind to spend the summer here, for I confess that I find London to be a trifle hard to bear at this time of year, and I long to experience the pleasures of the countryside once again."

"Such excellent news," exclaimed Mrs Saunders, clapping her hands together excitedly. "I do hope that during that time we will be able to see much of you. We have oft called you to mind over the years and wondered what may have become of you."

"To be sure, Lieutenant, if you are able, you must call upon us tomorrow morning," Mr Saunders decided. "It would be most satisfying for us to properly renew our acquaintance with you, sir. What say you, Annie...? Elizabeth...? Shall we have this young blade over to us for coffee tomorrow?"

"That would be most agreeable, Mr Saunders," said Mrs Saunders.

"It most certainly would," said Elizabeth.

And so it was settled.

The next morning I presented myself at the door

to the Saunders' house, freshly scrubbed and in my best buff coat. The door was answered by the family's maidservant, who, after taking my hat and cane, showed me into the drawing room. The room was spacious and airy, benefitting from a good amount of natural light from the full length windows that looked out onto the neat little garden to the rear of the house. A large painting depicting some woebegone looking hounds was hung on one wall directly above a white Adam style fireplace. The fireplace was itself flanked by two matching chairs. Some other bits and pieces of furniture had been arranged formally around the edge of the room and four further chairs had been placed in the centre, around a small mahogany pedestal table. It was here that Mr and Mrs Saunders, and Elizabeth, waited to receive me.

The family welcomed me profusely and we made such small talk as propriety required, while the maidservant, Susannah, was dispatched to fetch coffee and chocolate. It transpired that Nathaniel Saunders, a stout, florid faced man most likely into his late forties, now acted as Reeve to Sir Henry, managing the not insignificant acreage that comprised Canewdon Hall Farm and had, in consequence, become quite a *Grand Panjandrum* about the village. Soon the conversation turned to the conduct of the war, with Mr Saunders becoming keen to know if I were in possession of any particular insight into the recent disastrous campaign in Holland.

"I am sad to say that I most likely know no more

of that than you, sir," I informed him. "Our Generals in the Low Countries have not exactly covered themselves in glory over the past year or so. The recent evacuation can only be described as shameful, and it is reported that upwards of 20,000 men have been lost by the Duke of York since the start of the campaign. The French and their allies now control the entire continental coastline with only the Navy and Dundas' few units of cavalry left behind at Bremen betwixt us and them."

"Well, I thank God for the Navy, Lieutenant," said Mr Saunders. "We are indeed fortunate that our wooden walls continue to stand firm against the Jacobin menace, eh Annie?"

"Amen to that, Nathaniel," replied his wife, a lady of gently rounded, womanly proportions, slightly younger than her husband. "Earl Howe is certain to put paid to any wicked French designs on our poor country. Why, did he not hand out such a drubbing to the French Fleet last summer as to take from them six line of battle ships and completely destroy another - sending the rest of them scurrying back home with their tails between their legs?"

"That he did, madam," I confirmed. "Though it is somewhat unfortunate that Black Dick's overall objective, that is to capture the Frog's vast grain convoy and so deprive the French people of their daily bread, was not properly achieved by his heroic deeds."

"May I ask you if you played any part in the battle, Mr Ellis," Elizabeth asked, smiling coyly. Gad, she was a looker.

Aye, I did, Miss," I replied as modestly as I could manage under that delightful scrutiny. "Our little barky, the *Dione*, though not by rights part of the line, was called into action to assist the *Billy Ruffian* when that worthy vessel found herself running into difficulty during the melee."

"The *Billy Ruffian?*" queried Mr Saunders. "I have not heard of a ship by that name. Is she newly built?"

"*Billy Ruffian* is the name by which we sailors know HMS *Bellerophon*, sir. But you are right in thinking her but lately built; she was launched in '86, a few years after the American war, and is a third-rate mounting 74 guns."

"Ah, the *Bellerophon*, yes, I have heard of her, certainly. Lord Cranston commands her, does he not?"

"He does. His Lordship took over from Captain Hope last November. Hope commanded the *Ruffian* during the battle and Commodore Pasley also flew his broad pennant aboard her. It was shortly after the Commodore lost his leg to an eighteen-pounder ball that passed through the quarter-deck that the *Ruffian* found herself beset by two, or maybe three, Frog ships simultaneously and had her masts and spars pretty much ripped apart by their gunnery. She was unable to manoeuvre and was thus in grave danger of becoming overwhelmed when, seeing this situation, our captain brought us between the *Ruffian* and the Frenchies. We opened a brisk fire on one of them, helping to drive them off, and afterwards we contrived to bend some lines onto the *Ruffian* so as to tow her out of the engagement to safety."

"How brave of you all!" exclaimed Elizabeth, clapping her hands in that same excited manner that I had observed in her mother outside the church - it must have been some kind of family trait I supposed. "And what glory must have been bestowed upon you for your actions!"

"Well, glory was bestowed on our captain at least," I said ruefully. "He was, in truth, one of the favoured few to receive a gold medal from King George after the battle. But no such honours were bestowed upon the rest of us and, by reason of our ship having been so badly knocked about as to be paid off; my own reward appears to have been naught but a goodly spell on dry land in search of a new berth."

"That is most regrettable," Mr Saunders said sympathetically. "But I have no doubt that you will soon be rewarded in your search. Pray tell, have you been able to enjoy your run ashore in the meantime?"

"I will allow that it has its frustrations, definitely, but I strive to keep myself as fully occupied as possible - I am a prodigious student of modern philosophy, don't y'know," I declared loftily, wishing to present myself to my hosts in the best light possible. "And I frequently find that I can become deeply immersed in the quest for the fundamental nature of reality and existence."

"Your father would have been very proud of you," said Mrs Saunders. "I remember him dearly and I know that he would have been pleased as Punch to see you become so distinguished an officer, and a scholar to boot."

"It pleases me greatly to hear you say that," said I, and you can be sure I meant it. "For my father's approval was something that I always have, and will ever, aspire to."

And to what conclusions have your studies led you thus far?" Elizabeth enquired.

"Ah, yes," this ought to raise my stock, I decided happily. "Well, I have most recently been applying some thought to the theories concerning the political, economic, and social equality of the sexes. My reading of Wollstonecraft, for example... do you know her...? No...? Oh, well, in this erudite lady's treatise, entitled *A Vindication of the Rights of Woman*, she endeavours to set out a vision of equality between men and women. Women are only considered inferior, she says, because they lack education. Women are after all human beings, and are therefore deserving of the same fundamental rights as men. This is why, in any social order that is founded on reason, they should be treated equally and allowed to contribute as much to society as men."

Bravo, Mr Ellis!" cried Elizabeth. "This equality between the sexes is something that is crystallised in my own beliefs. There must be balance in all things, and I agree wholeheartedly with any philosophy that affords an equal place to men and women in our society."

I saw Mr and Mrs Saunders exchange a surreptitious glance. Then, before Elizabeth and I could develop these arguments further, Mr Saunders cut in.

"Ah, now, I can see that you two have much to talk about, and I can see too that our young friend here is a gentleman of the utmost respectability and learning. I therefore propose that we older folk withdraw and leave you both alone to talk awhile. Y'servant, Mr Ellis. It has been a pleasure. Come, Annie, let us away and leave the young people in peace."

O'ho! Here's a piece of luck, I realised. All my cards had come up trumps here. It was dashed unusual for a young couple to be left alone so soon in their acquaintance. And so I set out to make the most of it.

"Shall we converse some more on the nature of Miss Wollstonecraft's propositions, Miss Saunders?" I said after our elders had left the room.

"Please, call me Lizzie," this enchanting young woman replied, growing somewhat more animated in her speech. "And, if it please you, I would much rather hear more about your time in London, and about the fashions and entertainments to be had in that great city, Do tell me of how the gentle folk of London disport themselves around town, Roger. Purely in the spirit of furthering my education in such matters, of course," she added mischievously.

I do not really know what came over me at that point, and mayhap I was emboldened by my earlier aphrodisiacal encounter with Sal, for, notwithstanding my normally puritanical view of the nature of London society, I somehow hit upon the rather *naïve* notion of trying to impress the girl with my 'worldliness'.

"I confess, I know little of fashion, Lizzie, but I understand that the French Directoire fashions are all *a la mode* this season, and that they are most singularly daring."

"Daring? Oh how intriguing, you must enlighten me further."

"I shall," I said, lowering my voice so that it should not carry beyond those four walls. "Let me tell you, when I left London the wearing of low cut bodices was very much the *vogue*, with ladies vying enthusiastically with one another as to how much *décolletage* they put on show. Those more modest will only allow their bodice to come just above the point of exposing their charms, but it must be said that some of the more emboldened ladies of the town are sporting necklines so low that, with but the slightest movement, their 'most delicate points' are wont to make a surprise appearance."

This last revelation elicited a little gasp from Lizzie which did nothing but encourage me to rattle on. "Of course, if that does occur, the lady in question will act only slightly shocked, as it is well known that, when wearing gowns of that cut, such accidents are bound to happen. Some even apply rouge to those particular parts to ensure that, when they do appear, they always appear in their best light! And, dare I say it, I know of a number of young bucks of the first head who will routinely wager on the precise moment when madam's nipples will surface during some or other ball or late night supper party."

"Oh, Roger, if this is the sort of thing that goes on, the city must be quite a dissolute and intemperate place." Lizzie breathed.

I then noticed what could only be described as an eager, excited expression beginning to cross my companion's lovely face and in recognition of this, to my shame, it seemed now that I could not stop.

I told her, in great detail, of the late Dr Graham's Temple of Health where, until very recently, young women were wont to pose in a supposed demonstration of perfect health and beauty with literally nothing at all to preserve their modesty. I spun lurid tales of 'posture girls' stripped bare and served up to young gentlemen diners on a silver platter, and I went on at length about certain aristocratic ladies daring to appear in public wearing veils of transparent muslin and nothing more. And she fairly lapped it all up, asking questions and generally encouraging me to embroider my already exaggerated stories even further. This is what comes of listening to that degenerate old soul doctor every Sunday, I reasoned. Finally, I regaled my eager audience with tales of respectable females rubbing shoulders with highwaymen, pimps, and whores at the Dog and Duck in St George's Fields, and recounted the awful goings on at a cock and hen club in Clerkenwell where both 'ladies' and gentlemen engaged in such excesses that it was often necessary for the neighbours to call in the constables. Not that I had actually seen any of this for myself, of course, but you may be sure that I made every effort to convey that I thoroughly disapproved of the very idea, nonetheless.

By the time I had finished, Lizzie and I both found ourselves worked up into a somewhat agitated state. So much so that it became necessary for Lizzie to call for more refreshment to cool us down, lest we be so discovered by her good parents re-entering the room. Therefore, by means of copious amounts of carrot beer, delivered by Susannah with a smile and an impudent, knowing wink in my direction, we were, at last, restored and thinking ourselves very fortunate that things had calmed down a little before Mr and Mrs Saunders did eventually make their reappearance.

Once more in a state of *comme il faut*, I was thus able to respectfully take my leave of the family, having first requested, and received, permission to call upon Lizzie again. On returning to the Anchor I spent the rest of the day re-reading my Voltaire, and in particular that great man's slightly scandalous poem *What Pleases the Ladies?*, before retiring early to my bed. I soon discovered that my mind could dwell on nothing other than thoughts of Lizzie and, as you may imagine, my dreams that night were as far distant from the stuff of my usual nightmares as they could have possibly been.

CHAPTER 4

As the days wore on I began to spend more and more time with Lizzie. Her parents seemingly equally pleased for us to either bide indoors playing chess or backgammon or to take long walks around the village and through the surrounding countryside. Our talk during these times together touched upon many things and, as ever, Lizzie was keen to hear more of London society. I did my best to steer clear of the seamier side of life (for the most part, at least) and told her instead of the theatres, the gaming houses and the circuses. I also expounded on the more civilised joys of Vauxhall, where for just two bob one could witness hot-air balloon ascents, firework displays, and tightrope walkers, and the exclusive pleasures of Ranelagh and its famed rotunda, within which anyone in possession of half a crown could enjoy genteel concerts, drinking and dining. Throughout all our meetings, however, there was always an underlying frisson of excitement, with our mutual attraction finding expression through gentle teasing, the fluttering of eyelashes, or fleeting mild caresses.

We also talked more seriously on many an occasion, and Lizzie began to impress me greatly with her radical ideas and her passionate belief in the need for complete social and political equality between the sexes. I remember one such conversation taking place on a most delightful early summer afternoon when we were alone together in the flower garden of her parents' house. Lizzie and I were seated on a rustic bench, taking tea on the small terrace that was situated outside the drawing room window. The garden was springing into life all around us. Roses and delphiniums were beginning to bloom in the herbaceous borders and bright orange oriental poppies were starting to unfold their silky bowl-shaped petals, adding an explosive and exotic burst of colour to the overall prospect.

"Why should men always be the dominant force in making any kind of political or cultural decisions, Roger?" Lizzie asked me. "Women comprise one one-half of the population, after all. Surely, true social progress can never be achieved without the full participation of women?"

"I agree entirely, my dear," I replied, sipping my tea, which had been served in the Chinese style, in a basin without a handle.

"I cannot believe that this has always been so," Lizzie continued. "And I think that, maybe at one time, women might even have been privileged to hold a much more prominent position in the world."

She paused and moved closer towards me in a conspiratorial manner.

"Did you know that some while ago in a field near the Hall, a dozen or so Roman urns were dug up, and that at the same time a curious stone statue of some heathen deity was also unearthed?"

I shook my head and confirmed that this was indeed news to me.

"'Tis true," said Lizzie. "And what is most remarkable is that this statue was of a female form, completely unclothed, and with her hands touching herself… down below…"

This last revelation, delivered as it was, in no more than a whisper directly into my ear, caused me to shiver slightly in anticipation of things perhaps to come.

"I believe this little figure to be compelling evidence that in prehistoric societies women were actually revered for their ability to create life," Lizzie said quietly, laying her hand upon my arm. "I have heard that effigies like these have been found all over England - which must mean that the ancient people were in the habit of worshipping some kind of mother goddess, or spirit of fertility, if you will. And, what is more, I think that a similar tradition might once have been a vital part of early Christian beliefs too. Why, if you look carefully, and although the vicar will be at pains to deny it, you can see a similar carving high up in the church roof!"

"Surely the presence of such a thing in the church

is merely a warning against the sins of the flesh?" I responded.

"I don't think so; for surely those who placed the carving would not have really wanted to remind people of those things the clergy would clearly rather they forgot?

"Perhaps not," I concurred. "But you must agree, it is a fact that Christianity has always undermined women, seeing them only as a physical distraction for men, incapable of any form of spirituality in their own right. This is why there have never been, and nor can there ever be, any women priests, is it not?"

"God forbid that women should be seen as a distraction to the men around them!" Lizzie retorted, angrily. "Pah! We must ever be quiet and subservient and must never take up too much space at the table! Nor, it seems, must we dress so as arouse men. And that notwithstanding the increasing trend towards the depiction of scantily clad women in art and literature, seen most especially in some of those supposedly aesthetic publications disseminated by the scurrilous members of the Dilettanti Society. Oh, how I envy those ladies of *le bon ton* of whom you spoke when first we met. They are not afraid to embrace their femininity, and to celebrate it by exposing their bodies howsoever, and to whomsoever, they wish."

In truth, to hear this last pronouncement from my dear sweet Lizzie was a little disquieting, but increasingly I was discovering that I was blind to even any small indication that my young friend was anything but perfect, and so I stowed her comments firmly in the back of my mind.

It was shortly after this that an invitation arrived from Canewdon Hall. Sir Henry and Lady Spurgeon had requested the company of both Lizzie and me at dinner a week on Friday. It was to be a rather grand affair, with ladies and gentlemen of quality present from most of the surrounding manors and Lizzie's parents were, in consequence, exceeding happy to allow me to act as her escort.

On the appointed day I got myself up in my full dress uniform of blue coat, with its blue standing collar, white lapels and cuffs, white single breasted waistcoat, breeches, stockings and pinchbeck buckled shoes (reluctantly worn in place of my favoured Hessians) and so attired repaired to the Saunders' house to await Sir Henry's coachman, James, who had been sent to convey us up to the Hall. Susannah showed me once again into the drawing room to wait whilst Lizzie finished dressing upstairs. It was not long 'til the squire's *calèche* drew up outside and Lizzie made her appearance, descending the stairs in a long velvet travelling cloak with the hood pulled up over a natural tousled hairpiece that she had woven into her own hair. After bidding farewell to Mr and Mrs Saunders, I handed Lizzie up into the *calèche* and the driver whipped up the two horses to get us under way. The *calèche* was a light carriage with small wheels, a body in the form of a boat, and a folding top that afforded some degree of privacy within, and Lizzie and I snuggled cosily into it as we rode up past the church and round to the Hall.

Canewdon Hall was a smart Palladian style villa, with a grand pedimented doorway opening onto a wide, panelled entrance hall that was painted in a rustic stone colour. A mahogany and iron staircase led to the upper rooms and two large doors on either side of the staircase led into the drawing room and dining room. Two small doors to the left of the entrance afforded access to the breakfast room and Sir Henry's study, and another small door on the far right opened onto a powder room. Also tucked away to the right was a much less imposing staircase leading down into the kitchen and servants' accommodation.

As we entered, a liveried Negro footman appeared to take Lizzie's cloak, which she duly unfastened and handed to him, revealing a sumptuous high-waisted, short sleeved gown of periwinkle blue satin complimented by a pair of long white gloves. My jaw dropped open in surprise, but it was not the dress that betwattled me. Lizzie's neck, shoulders and bosom were unveiled as far as delicacy could possibly allow and the uplifting effect of her short stays meant that just the slightest hint of pinkish areolae could be discerned above the shimmering material of her gown. Lizzie flashed me a dazzling smile, but I could only gape at the sight of this stunning display of *décolletage* as we moved into the drawing room, where, together with the squire's other dinner guests, we were first met by our hosts.

The drawing room of Canewdon Hall was a far

more impressive affair than its modest counterpart at the Saunders' house. This room, with its thick carpets, stylish furniture, and lavish paintings, had an air of richness and grandeur reminiscent of the finest of London mansions. A door at the far end of the room provided egress into a narrow gallery that ran along the whole side of the house, and enormous windows afforded a splendid view across rolling lawns to the South Fambridge Marsh and the river beyond. On entering, I found myself further taken aback to see that the largest painting in the room depicted a youthful Mary Spurgeon as Peitho, the Greek spirit of seduction, clad in an audacious *robe de gaulle*, the thin material of which was shown to be spilling provocatively from one delicate white shoulder. On closer inspection, I noted the signature of the illustrious George Romney at the foot of the canvas, indicating that Squire Spurgeon was indeed a man of means.

"Welcome to our home, Lieutenant Ellis… Miss Saunders…," cried Sir Henry as we made our entry. "I am so glad you could come. And might I say, Miss Saunders, you look ravishing."

"Thank you, Sir Henry," replied Lizzie. "I confess that I did wonder whether I might be slightly overdressed."

"Haw, haw! Not at all, not at all, my dear," laughed the squire, as my eyebrows shot up in amazement. "Do they not say that these days being fully dressed requires the breast and shoulders to be bare, while being under-dressed must necessitate that the neckline reach right up to the chin! What d'you say, Mary, does Miss Saunders not look splendid?"

"Most splendid, Henry," said his wife, looking Lizzie over with an appreciative eye. Lady Spurgeon was, in fact, similarly attired in a crimson satin dress, although she wore a much more modest neckline as befitted her years, and my sensibilities. Sir Henry himself cut a dandified figure in an elegant dark blue cutaway coat and breeches, and a high waisted striped waistcoat.

We lingered in the drawing room until the Reverend Gildersleeve, the last of Sir Henry's guests, arrived. We then filed into the dining room in order of precedence, with Sir Henry and Lady Spurgeon in the van and Lizzie and me bringing up the rear. The dining room was another fine room which was dominated by a large extended dining table. After the latest fashion, the seating was arranged 'promiscuously' (but, of course - why would it not be so arranged?) with ladies and gentlemen sitting alternately. Lizzie and I sat together, the reverend sat opposite Lizzie and I faced a shy looking young woman who had come over from one of the outlying farms. The first course, fried celery and oyster loaves, was already laid out and we set to helping ourselves to those dishes nearest to us. As Lizzie reached across to lay claim to some of the inviting looking crispy celery sticks I clearly saw that the vicar's attention was fully focused on her bulging top-hamper. Becoming aware that I had noted his impudence he looked across to me and, with a wolfish grin, nodded in the direction of the target to which his eyes had been drawn. Damn the fellow, has he no shame, I thought as I fairly glared back at him; and he a man of the cloth, too.

Polite conversation bubbled around the table and various toasts were called as Sir Henry's footmen cleared the remains of the first course and laid the next, which comprised chicken fricassee and a ragout of pigs' ears. As was to be expected in such company, the talk was mostly of farms and farming - and, understandably, given the grim trials that these husbandmen were lately experiencing, the emphasis was put firmly upon the most effective means to promote a bounteous harvest, which it seemed, involved such esoteric practices as the winter fallowing of the fields every second or third year and the rotation of hardy crops such as oats or barley, clover, trefoil and rye grass, and beans. Not that I had a mind to pay attention to any of it, for I was simmering away in a high dudgeon throughout the whole of the second course and well into the third: a groaning board of sirloin of beef (carved by our host in an elaborate and symbolic display of his munificence), veal escalope with lemons, and stewed venison. It was when someone mentioned the recent sad case of suicide in the village that my ears pricked up once again.

"I hear that old Mother Baker from up at Butts Hill did herself in the other week," said a porky looking fellow at the end of the table.

"Yes, indeed," Sir Henry replied, sawing at a substantial slice of beef with a wide bladed knife and then stabbing it with his two pronged fork. "It was a bad business. Her neighbours came to me desirous of a church burial y'know? But what could I do? The law is clear; there is no room in the churchyard for such sinners."

"Quite so," said the porky fellow. "The act of self-murder is a sin which violates the sixth commandment. Thou shalt not kill sayeth the Lord, even if you yourself are the only victim."

"That is truth indeed," added the Reverend Gildersleeve, piously. "Did not that great theologian and philosopher, St Thomas Aquinas, tell us that suicide is contrary to natural self-love, and that not only does it injure the community of which we are a part, it also flies in the face of our duty to the God who gave us life?"

"It seems I've heard quite a lot of the commandments of late," I piped up, staring directly at the vicar.

All throughout the meal, the reprehensible reverend had hardly once taken his eyes off Lizzie's paps and, though I could not in all propriety call him to account for it in public, I was angry enough by then to be determined to put a shot across his bows for any other cause I could think of.

"And I've also heard a great deal about what the bible does and doesn't say in certain circumstances…"

As I left this unspoken challenge to hang in the air I felt Lizzie grip my arm tightly.

"Please Roger, don't," she whispered in my ear.

But it was too late for any of that, my blood was up and, ignoring her entreaties, I turned again to Sir Henry.

"I agree, sir that, notwithstanding the moral arguments put forward by Hume and Bentham, of which I am sure the reverend gentleman is aware, and also notwithstanding the recent tendency for coroners to summarily reject charges of *felo de se*, the law is, as you say, clear on this matter. But, in this case of the poor woman from Butts Hill, I would take serious issue with the manner of punishment."

"How so, sir?" barked Sir Henry, clearly put out by my effrontery.

"I am sad to say that I was a witness to the burial of Mrs Baker, Sir Henry, and I own that such a loathsome act I never yet saw. Her sentence was carried out with both a repugnant desire to mutilate the corpse in punishment for her actions, and a ridiculous superstitious desire to pin-down her ghost to prevent it from returning to haunt the living."

At that point, I swear you could hear a pin drop. Then, up spoke the Reverend Gildersleeve once again.

"My dear Lieutenant," he said, smarmily. "You must realise that the folk in this village are simple people with simple beliefs. They expect things to be done in a certain way…"

"And, does that mean the continuance of brutal mediaeval practices that have no basis in rational thought?" I interrupted. "This whole episode reeks of the kind of delusion that surrounded the witch hunts instigated in this very county by Hopkins and Stearne during the late civil war!"

"Please, calm yourself, Lieutenant," said Sir Henry, evidently disconcerted by my vehemence and seeking to mollify me before matters got out of hand. "I understand your reasoning, and I do find sympathy with some of your arguments. 'Tis true that our small community is slow to throw off the yoke of unfounded beliefs and it is a known fact that magic and witchcraft has a long tradition in Canewdon - as the reverend here will testify."

"Indeed so," answered the vicar, while around the table the buzz of conversation sparked up again as people realised that daggers were now less likely to be drawn. "Canewdon's association with witchcraft goes back many years and I am afraid to say that this association is sadly and most unfortunately centred upon my church. It is said, for instance, that the village was once the home of six witches who were wont to conduct dark rituals involving incantations and necromancy in the grounds of the church, and there are several cases actually on record that tell of malicious old beldams bewitching young children to death. These witches, some said, could shimmer into the shape of mice or white rabbits and that on one occasion a poor man from Canewdon Wick who tried to catch one of these animals took sick and died soon after. Legend also has it that six witches will always remain in the village so long as the church tower stands, and that every time a stone falls from the tower, one of the witches will die, and another will take their place."

"These are simply folktales," I scoffed. "I oft heard such stories when I was but a child at my father's knee."

"Folktales or not, Lieutenant, these stories, and others, continue to be believed around these parts. There is another legend, for example, which tells that those who dare to walk round the church tower at midnight will be taken up and forced to dance with the witches until they drop to the ground with exhaustion. Heh! I'll allow though that some good has come of this, as it is largely thanks to this tradition, and its attendant tales of demons and goblins flitting around the stones at night, that trespassers rarely, if ever, venture into my churchyard after darkness falls."

I was now beginning to tire of the vicar's yarns and with a dessert of strawberry fritters and syllabub now being served, my attention turned once more to the table. But I could not resist one last broadside.

"Reverend," I said, sternly. "I do believe that you have a prodigious talent for the melodramatic, which I might suggest you strive to keep in check. The dinner table is no place for such frightful stories, especially when there are ladies present."

"Pray forgive me, Lieutenant," the vicar said with an irritatingly sardonic smile and a nod. "I mean no offence. I simply think that, now more than ever, it is good for us to face our fears; and perhaps even, for a while at least, to become children again, fearing no longer those dread horsemen of famine and war, but rather merely being affrighted by the thought of ethereal spirits and other such things which, even if they do exist, can surely do nothing to harm us."

"Hear, hear!" exclaimed Sir Henry, now in cheerful agreement. "It ain't the dead who will hurt you, but rather the living, eh Reverend. Haw, haw!"

"H'rumph!" I grunted, annoyed that the supercilious sermoniser had managed to have the last word.

After dessert the ladies retired to the drawing room while I stayed with the gentlemen, smoking moodily, drinking port and looking as melancholy as a gib cat. A footman then called us to tea and cake with the ladies. As soon as I entered Lizzie bore down upon me with an ominous expression clouding her face. She took me up and propelled me peremptorily through the door at the end of the room and into a quiet corner of the gallery.

"What on earth were you thinking, Roger?" she hissed. "To treat Sir Henry and the vicar so shamefully!"

"I am sorry, Lizzie," I replied. "And as respects Sir Henry I will allow that I regret my actions. But, as for that lecherous little ballocks, he deserves all he gets - and you ask me what *I* was thinking? Rather would I know what you were thinking, to turn up tipping

Cupid's kettle drums to all and sundry. By m'faith, girl, such provocative behaviour is… well… it's just not decent."

"How can you say that, Roger," demanded Lizzie, eyes flashing like diamonds. "I have only dressed *à la mode* in the style of the London fashions that you yourself described to me. In any case, as you would no doubt agree, it is only 'rational' that ladies should have the freedom to wear whatever they want to wear, and not be blamed for the consequential actions of such uncouth gentlemen who plainly cannot keep their thoughts to themselves, or themselves under proper control."

Once again, I could not bring myself to think any ill of this lovely creature, and she was right, the fault was all with that bloody vicar. How dare he ogle my Lizzie in such an overt manner?

"I am truly sorry, my dear, please forgive me," I entreated, taking her hands in mine. "It is but jealousy that drives me. I vow that I will not behave in such an uncivilised way again."

"Very well, you are forgiven," Lizzie allowed, albeit grudgingly. "Now come, there are cards at play and later there will be dancing. Let us try to enjoy the rest of the evening."

And I did enjoy the rest of the evening. I was lucky enough to come away from a hand or two of Faro with some small change jingling in my pocket and Lizzie and I danced a delightful *Cotillion* with another young couple, performing its sequence of choreographed steps with gay abandon. And then, at last, it was time to leave and, having bidden a stiff but polite farewell to our hosts, Lizzie and I once more climbed into the squire's *calèche* to make the short journey back to her parent's house. As the carriage turned into the High Street I requested that James halt a while and rest the horses.

"Why are we stopping?" murmured Lizzie, sleepily. "Is there something amiss?"

"No, my dear, there is nothing amiss," I reassured her as I leant in closer and took hold of her arm. I could feel the warmth of her body against me as we looked deeply into each other's eyes. "There is just something I must do before we reach home."

So saying, I inclined my head forward and brushed her lips with mine. I broke contact after that first tingling touch, but in one smooth movement Lizzie's hand came up behind my head and, with closed eyes, she pressed her lips to me in a long lingering kiss. I felt her tongue dart out to explore my mouth and I reciprocated with a will, finally sinking back into my seat after what seemed an eternity of pleasure. Gathering my wits, I made to take another pass but was stopped by a most beautiful smile and a small raised finger that was laid upon my eager lips.

"That's enough for now, my darling," Lizzie breathed. "Let us be off again. Mama and Papa will be wondering what has become of us."

THE MOON DANCERS

And with that, we settled back down into our seat and I signalled the, thankfully very discrete, coachman to proceed.

CHAPTER 5

As we entered the month of July, Lizzie and I took advantage of the long hours of daylight and rove further afield, mostly on foot, but occasionally also on horseback. Wheat and barley had begun to ripen in the fields, and the meadows around the village had now reached maturity so that, in common with the overgrown ancient hedgerows, they were crowded with wildflowers, the sight of which afforded Lizzie endless delight. Rich purple knapweed and betony complimented the golden yellow of lady's bedstraw and meadow vetchling, with the whole being home to myriads of butterflies, bees and other insects, thus contributing to an idyllic English pastoral scene that might well have inspired Mr Wordsworth himself to add some additional stanzas to his *Evening Walk*.

One afternoon we determined to ride out a couple of miles or so past an impressive thirteenth century manor house, which I gathered was the home of the porky fellow I had encountered at the squire's dinner, to Paglesham, in search of the many species of birds known to be present in that location. Lizzie was wont to travel far and wide for a brief sighting of an avocet, curlew, or oyster catcher, and as ever I was keen to help her in whatever quest she set her heart on. But, all the same, before we set off I made sure of the priming and general condition of my little short barrelled pistol for I had heard that Paglesham could be a somewhat lawless place with a long reputation for smuggling. The various creeks and inlets around Paglesham afforded a convenient landing for contraband spirits, silks and lace and it was said that nearly every family in the area was involved in the nefarious running of these goods across the county and even as far afield as the City of London.

My nag that day was a bit of a miserable rip that young Tom had brought round from the Anchor's stable block, whose name was, apparently, Hercules. The poor beast was fairly long in the tooth and promised a slow, plodding hack at best, but as I was but a poor horseman, having spent so long riding naught but the waves; I was, in truth, grateful for that. Lizzie's horse was by contrast a rum prancer, obtained for her by her father from the stables at Canewdon Hall. At around fifteen hands and jet black, the trim little animal served to set off Lizzie's excellent seat most charmingly as she perched sidesaddle, with her right leg hooked over the pommel and her left extended down with a dainty foot placed firmly in the slipper stirrup. She was dressed immaculately in a scarlet habit comprising a neat little feathered hat, a high necked jacket with a false waistcoat front, and a long skirt that had clearly been designed to show off her shapely ankle and calf to their best advantage.

"Good afternoon, Roger," she called, as I put my foot into my stirrup and clumsily swung myself aboard Hercules' broad but sagging back.

"Afternoon, Lizzie," I said. "Fine afternoon for a ride, is it not?"

"It is, but mind you don't go tiring poor old Hercules out, now," Lizzie admonished, smiling playfully. "He's a dear old thing and not accustomed to being an officer's charger."

"I fear he is in no danger from me, Lizzie," I replied sheepishly. "He and I are of a mind, I'll wager. Neither of us will be going at our fences or galloping pell-mell across country right soon."

Once I was settled in the saddle, we set off along the road, Lizzie at a stylish jog-trot and me clop-clopping along behind. As we rode past the pond and under the looming shadow of the workhouse, we drew level, and began to converse. At first I thought to comment on how well the fields around us were looking.

"Does it not do your heart good to see the brightness of the corn, Lizzie?" I ventured. "A good harvest will be welcome indeed, I think, and should provide much needed relief for many who have found themselves tightening their belts following last year's poor returns."

"I hope that we will see an improvement this year," replied Lizzie. "But I worry that we may yet find ourselves again experiencing a shortfall come harvest time."

"Oh, really? Do you then foresee some problem arising that may yet blight the crops?"

"I do. Papa has told us that that black stem rust has been found in some of the squire's fields and that, if this takes proper hold, the crops could be ruined. He says that it has been seen mostly on plants growing near barberry bushes and so he has been at pains to order all those bushes to be destroyed in the hopes of interrupting the spread of the disease."

"Then I pray that his efforts are rewarded," I said. "The people have lately suffered enough from the combined effects of enclosure, high prices and shortages of food, and I fear that further privations might well result in unrest such as that which is just now being reported from Saffron Walden."

"That is a frightening prospect; to be sure. Is it true that in that unfortunate town it has been necessary to call in the soldiery to quell rioting in the streets?"

"Aye," I confirmed. "It seems that the mob there was being whipped up by one or two politically motivated firebrands who were plying them with strong drink. Lord Cornwallis over at Warley Camp was unable to send any men to restore order given that he only had raw, untrained fencibles at his command and the whole was close to getting out of hand. In the event, the Surrey Light Dragoons had to be sent over from Lexden instead."

"May it please God that such miseries do not extend to our little community," Lizzie said. "And, by my troth, I for one will endeavour to do all in my power to prevent it."

"I'm afraid that there may be little you or I can do in that respect, Lizzie," I opined, shaking my head sadly.

"Well, we shall see…," my companion responded, a trifle enigmatically. Well, to my mind at least.

We rode on through the lanes and at length came to a small wood just outside Paglesham. The sky had clouded over slightly by this time and a brisk south-westerly was starting to get up, promising rain. The bird population had been playing hide and seek with us and so I proposed that we think about turning back.

"You are probably right, Roger," Lizzie agreed. "It is becoming a little bleak and I would rather not be caught in the rain."

"Indeed not, for in truth neither of us has taken pains to dress for bad weather," I said, taking the chance to look Lizzie over once again and avidly drinking in the trim manner in which she sat her horse: her straight back causing her to thrust out her chest most alluringly, and her skirt stretched tight over one shapely thigh which rested on the saddle directly in front of her.

As we turned our horses I noticed something odd

out of the corner of my eye. There was a movement among the trees that now lay on our starboard bow. At first I thought it to be a roebuck disturbed by our passage, but as I looked more closely I could see it was the figure of a man picking his way gingerly through the spiny gorse and out onto the road but a few yards before us. Instantly I was put upon my guard and my right hand went to my pocket to feel the reassuring bulk of my pistol within. Seeing this, the man stood square before us and presented two heavy horse pistols. One he pointed directly at me and the other he discharged into the air, causing both our nags to shy so that we were hard put to keep them under control.

"Hold, cully!" shouted our assailant, an unkempt and ill-dressed scrub in a coat the colour of the Devil's nutting bag and with a sour looking visage that had been marked heavily by the pox. "I would advise against anything rash, you are covered from both sides and neither I nor my pal here will hesitate to lay you both out quiet if you seek to have a brush with us."

Lizzie let out a small yelp of fear and I saw that another man had approached her from the side, grabbing at her bridle and brandishing a long bladed chive in her face. In appearance he was younger, smaller and, if it were possible, scruffier than his confederate.

"Now, get down from those prads and let 'em run loose!" demanded Sourface. "Ratty! Help the lady down from her horse."

Knowing that it was most prudent to comply with

the fellow's request, given the brutality such footpads regularly displayed to their victims, I cocked my right leg over the front of my saddle and slid to the ground, loosing Hercules' reins as I did so. Lizzie similarly unhooked her right leg from the pommel of her saddle and slipped off, straight into the arms of the grinning Ratty. Her skirt and petticoats riding up indecorously, first catching on the pommel, and then on Ratty's coat as he pressed hard against her, revealing pretty coral pink silk stockings tied above the knee with red ribbon. On their release, both horses trotted away towards the wood and bent to crop the grass.

"Come away from the lady now, Ratty, she doesn't need you pawing at her like a cur on heat," said Sourface, smiling. "Now get over to keep this fine gentleman quiet whilst we have a talk."

"What are you after, you thieving blackguard?" I spat. "Money? The horses? What?"

"Now, now, sir, I'll thank you to keep a civil tongue in your head, lest Ratty here be tempted to cut it out for you."

Ratty giggled at this and shook his dagger at me as Sourface continued.

"And as for what it is I want, I'm afraid to admit that I am a devilishly greedy cove and I want everything you have, even down to the very clothes you and your pretty little tit stand up in. But, pray do not think too ill of me. I would ask you to believe that I deeply regret that circumstances should have reduced me to the necessity of relieving you two handsome young people of your property. These are desperate times and hunger can make a thief of any man for, in truth, it is only fit for boys to starve, not men."

"So, its hunger that drives you, is it? Well, there's plenty in that same boat with you that don't feel themselves obliged to have recourse to highway robbery, you bastard!"

Curiously, the man seemed to reflect upon this for a while before he answered.

"Ah, well that's as maybe, but, when all's said and done, by m'faith the toby lay makes for a fine life and it takes but a small contribution from generous provenders like you to keep us toby men in flash company and willing doxies. Now, stand aside, cully, for I've a mind that the first thing I shall take is a kiss from your fair lady, and mayhap later, once she is stripped, I might even venture further to lay claim to that most valuable thing she can offer besides."

Lizzie let out a gasp as the villain cast down his empty pistol and moved toward her, pulling her to him and roughly forcing his mouth over hers. I saw that Ratty's eyes were bright with excitement and that he was gawping open mouthed as Sourface tried to lift Lizzie's skirt and shove his free hand into the folds of material in an attempt to force his fingers up between her legs. Squealing, Lizzie struggled vainly to push him away, her terror at this assault only serving to inflame both men's passions further. I knew then that this was my one chance. Ratty's distraction was enough to afford me the opportunity to lash out with as much force as I could muster and plant a heavy boot plumb into his groin, dropping him like a stone and setting him clutching in agony at his ruined baubles. At once I tore my pistol from my pocket, frantically clawing the hammer back to full cock as I ran at Sourface. The man had only time enough to half turn in my direction when I blundered into him, knocking him to the ground. Being totally off balance, I could not avoid falling on top of him and as we went down in a flurry of arms and legs the barrel of my pistol jammed square into the bastard's throat. The pan spurted a shower of sparks and the wonderful little gun went off with a deafening crack. Sourface's head jerked back and my own face was hit by a spray of deep red blood. The ball must have travelled clean through the man's neck, for when I regained my feet he remained prostrate upon the road, dead as a nit.

Lizzie was frozen to the spot, staring wide eyed at the dead thing before her. Her face and clothes were splashed with blood and I could see her mouth beginning to form into a piercing scream. After quickly scanning the situation with regard to friend Ratty and seeing him haring off into the distance as if the hounds of hell were after him, I ran to Lizzie and held her tightly in my arms. She clung to me like a limpet, sobbing uncontrollably as I tried my best to comfort her. I was bloody shaken myself, to be sure, but I was no stranger to killing and I calmed down quickly enough, feeling nothing but contempt for the damnable thief and would be rapist who now measured his length on the track. It took longer for Lizzie's distress to subside, however, and I found that I needs must hold her for some considerable time, feeling the warmth of her body, the dampness of her tears, and the rapid rise and fall of her breast against me. My head was spinning, and I confess that at that moment I felt an overwhelming rush of love for this splendid, irresistible young woman wash over me like a spring tide.

Once we had gathered our wits we began the long, weary walk back to Canewdon, dampened by the light rain that had started to fall. The horses had cantered off homewards of their own accord when the fracas erupted and when they arrived, riderless, outside the Anchor, alarums were raised and a party headed by Mr Saunders and Willie Fisher, the parish constable, set out to investigate what had befallen us. We were thus met halfway along the road and Lizzie was taken up into the strong, comforting arms of her father. After hurried explanations it was determined that the hour was too late for it to be safe to double back to where the unlucky footpad lay dead, and Lizzie and I were therefore hastened, with much attention and sympathy, back to the village.

Early the next morning, Willie Fisher and some other men took a cart to retrieve the body and bring it to the Anchor, so that it could be laid on a table in the kitchen and prepared for burial. Before this party arrived back, however, I was summoned to Canewdon Hall to appear before the squire. On arrival, one of Sir Henry's flunkeys ushered me into the study to stand before the squire's huge mahogany, black leather, and gilt writing table. Seated behind the table with his nose seemingly buried in a sheaf of papers, Sir Henry waited a few moments before raising his head to look at me. Then, grinning like the cat's uncle, he stood and reached across the table to grasp my hand, pumping it furiously.

"My boy, we are so proud of you," he declared. "Were it not for your courage and skill at arms Miss Saunders could well now be deflowered, injured, or worse!"

"My thanks to you, Sir Henry," I responded. "But, I only acted as any other gentleman would, had they found themselves in my place."

"Not so, m'lad, not so. Please do sit down. Will you take a drink with me?" said Sir Henry, pushing a glass across the table and sloshing a good measure of red wine into it. "Such valour in these dark days is becoming a rare commodity and we are all grateful to you, sir, indeed we are. These days, violent and unprovoked attacks on the road are becoming all too commonplace, and it is sad to say that the threat of the hangman's rope is proving less of a deterrent to crime than it once did."

"That is indeed a melancholy fact of life, Sir Henry. Hardly a day goes by but there is a report of some further outrage committed upon the King's highway, whether it be open robbery or bloody murder. And it seems that these dreadful doings are forever to be lionised in tawdry chapbooks and broadside ballads;

almost as a challenge to the law itself - and even to the point of implying that the poor of this country are alone in feeling the full weight of the judiciary whilst the vices of the rich go unpunished."

"Quite so, Lieutenant, quite so. And if we are to have any chance of stopping this villainy we need fewer folk to play the willing victim and must instead embolden more to have recourse to the gun and the sword, not only to protect themselves, but also to supplement the fear of Jack Ketch in these devils. It is the only way, sir, the only way. The law alone will not suffice. Now, with regard to proceedings against you…"

Despite being warmed by the wine, I blanched at this, for, although I knew that the right of armed self-defence had been firmly entrenched in common law since long years past, I knew also that I could face indictment for murder or manslaughter should the dead man's accomplice come forward to lay charges against me.

"I believe," Sir Henry continued. "That the snivelling little wretch who assisted in this act of wickedness is unlikely to come forward for fear of bringing a wry mouth and a pissen pair of breeches upon himself for his part in the cruel deed. And, my boy, I want to make it plain that, should the rogue have the temerity to so gainsay you, I'll readily take m'davy that you have no case to answer!"

To hear this came as some considerable relief and I own that I returned to the Anchor that afternoon in a better frame of mind to that in which I had left it earlier in the day. Nevertheless, I thought it prudent to avoid the kitchen that evening and also throughout the whole of the next day, taking my meals in my room to avoid further sight of my erstwhile assailant being dressed in his winding sheets. The day after, however, I did make it my business to repair to the church to witness his quiet burial. The Reverend Gildersleeve was officiating, as one might expect, but the only other persons present were a couple of fellows who had been recruited to manhandle the bier along the High Street and through the east gate of the churchyard. Being a felon, and unknown in the parish, Sourface was afforded no more than a simple pauper's grave at the far west end of God's acre, beyond the church tower. He also merited no sermon, although the reverend was moved to say a few words from the book of *Genesis* as the gravedigger plied his final shovelful of good Essex clay.

"And the Lord God commanded the man, saying, 'of every tree of the garden thou mayest freely eat: but of the tree of knowledge of good and evil, thou shalt not eat of it: for in the day that thou eatest thereof thou shalt surely die'."

When the gravedigger had finished his task of tamping down the earth, an eerie stillness descended on St Nicholas' churchyard, broken only by the caw and rattle of the crows nesting nearby. I stood awhile, watching the men making preparations to trundle the bier back along the path to the east gate, and otherwise generally taking stock of my surroundings. As I cast my eye up at the tower I noticed that some slight damage had occurred to the crenulations atop the south wall. Curious, I asked the reverend if he was aware that, as it appeared to me, some stones had somehow become dislodged and fallen from the tower.

"I am aware of the damage, Mr Ellis," the vicar replied, stiffly. Despite his obligation to turn the other cheek, I was obviously not yet fully forgiven for challenging him as I had. "But it is of no consequence. The collapse is merely the result of a minor lightning strike that occurred during the recent storm. I have asked the stonemason to attend to it as soon as he is able."

"And beneath the tower?" I said. "There appear to be the marks of a fire on the grass; would that also be attributable to the lightening, d'you think?"

The vicar gave me a strange look.

"No, Mr Ellis. The fire was set by the verger. He has recently been at work pollarding some of the trees and has been burning leaves and small branches. It is perhaps unfortunate that he has chosen so central a location for his pyre, but I am sure that when he has finished he will rake over the embers, break up the surface, and restore the turf."

Pollarding during the summer months struck me as somewhat unusual, given the likelihood of any new growth being impaired by heat or drought, but I supposed that the verger knew his business and so thought no more of it.

CHAPTER 6

U nderstandably, Lizzie's behaviour and perspective after the attack was somewhat altered. At first she expressed feelings of guilt, seemingly blaming herself for the assault but somehow rationalising it as a natural consequence of women's propensity towards temptation.

"It must surely be as everyone says, Roger," she said to me on one occasion, when we were, once more, ensconced in her parents' drawing room. "All women have a tendency to be ruled by their bodies and their emotions, most especially lust, and excessive passion. Had I not taken such pains to make my appearance pleasing to you when we rode out - and that I did, you should make no mistake on it - that loathsome man might not have been so inflamed in his passion as to attempt to satisfy his fancy so violently. My intention was to make the most of my charms, to titillate, if you will, so that you would be moved to like me more, nay even to desire me. And had I not acted in this stupid way our encounter on the road may have ended otherwise than in blood and death."

"No, Lizzie, I cannot accept or encourage your attitude in this," I declared. "These men, like many of their ilk who are wont to prey on travellers, were evil-minded, rapacious men, capable of extreme violence and worse. Your self-accusations of complicity and stupidity are completely unfounded. Did you not just recently take me to task for thinking in this way, arguing rightfully that a woman should be able to dress howsoever she pleases, and not be held accountable for the reactions of those too intemperate and libidinous as to be able to keep a proper check on their salacity?"

"Mayhap you are right, Roger."

"I am right. You need feel no blame attaches to you for this. None at all! And, you must be certain that we had no choice but to resist these scoundrels - for, even had we acted so meekly as to acquiesce to their demands, we would most surely have been subjected to bloody murder ourselves, or at best left badly beaten and naked in the ditch."

"I know. Please believe me when I say that I am grateful that we are safe, and I am glad that you were with me, my dearest," Lizzie said, touching my hand. "I have never before witnessed anyone fight to the death in the way that you did. It was both terrible and magnificent in equal measure."

I was, of course, flattered - for who does not enjoy being thought a veritable paladin among men. The poor girl wasn't to know that I had been in as much of a funk as she, after all. And, truth to tell, I was still in some way affected by our ordeal myself, with murderous footpads running roughshod through my dreams on many a night. A drink or two before retiring each evening seemed to help though, and therefore, in those times of torment, I was like to be found in the kitchen of the Anchor, imbibing the excellent local ale and swapping tales with some of Sally Dowsett's other customers.

There were usually a good half dozen or so people drinking at the Anchor on any given evening. Those two old cuffs, Cuddy Smith and Ned Symonds, were regulars, of course, and from time to time their company was supplemented by a colourful cast of supporting players. Aaron Rolfe, the blacksmith, was, as you might expect, a stocky, tough looking cove with shoulders like a bull, hands like shovels, and a permanent spark in his throat that required constant quenching. Rolfe's favoured messmate was Edward Sawkins, the butcher, a tall, lanky fellow with a pronounced squint. Sawkins appeared to admire Rolfe greatly, and the toadying little bugger hung on his every word. Hugh Nichols, the miller, and John Salmon, the apothecary, would also call in, and sometimes even Dr Lipscomb would grace the inn with his presence. Joseph Lipscomb was another Scotchman, dour and serious for the most part, but also possessed of a droll, dry wit that was known to surface from time to time to the amusement of all. Add to these, two or three labourers from Canewdon Hall Farm and a couple of brothers of the bung who worked in the malt house (fine fellows these, for where would the rest of us have been without them, eh?) and you have a typical soirée at the Anchor - and I loved it. There was no side to these people, you see? Life in Canewdon seemed to involve a unique kind of isolation from the rest of the world, with everyone knowing and being known by everyone, and with everyone knowing quite clearly their proper station in life.

Not that there wasn't some hardship, mind you, and my nights in the kitchen brought the plight of some of the poorest folk in the village into sharp relief.

"'Arvest's lookin' a bit more promising this year," said Cuddy one evening, taking a pull at his long pipe and blowing a cloud of smoke up to the ceiling.

That the state of the harvest should be a perennial topic in village conversation was eminently understandable. Almost the whole community, including the women and the children, would be closely involved in bringing in the crops and, quite literally, lives depended on the harvest's success.

"I hope so, Cuddy," I replied. "I heard that Nate Saunders was saying the other day that black stem rust has been seen in some of the fields."

"Aye, that it 'as," says Cuddy. "But the Reeve 'as been quick to get down to sortin' it out, so there's 'igh 'opes. Sal..! Can we get another nip of ale over 'ere m'darlin?"

"Ah, But it's not just the 'arvest that needs sorting,

though, is it, Cuddy?" put in Aaron Rolfe. "The Gov'ment needs to do sommink about the rising prices. Everythin' is getting so dear, that we can 'ardly live."

"That's right Aaron," Rolfe's loyal lieutenant, Sawkins, agreed. "Bread's so expensive to start with and, even if we do find a bit of extra money from somewhere, it's well-nigh impossible to buy a little milk or butter these days because so many smallholders have been forced off the land by them that seeks to enclose the common fields and meadows."

"I fear the Government will only go so far to help in this," I said, taking a draught. "They have offered bounties on imported wheat, and forbidden the distillation of spirits from grain. They are also prosecuting food speculators and fraudulent bakers, and have even proscribed the use of hair powder by the army. But all this, though well meant, only skates around the edges of the problem."

"Surely, more can be done," said Rolfe, bitterly. "There are people in the village who are near starving, dammit! Why, Cap'n, old John Appleby an' his son Walter got so bad that they 'ad to be taken in to that new workhouse just last week. There are nigh on two dozen poor souls in there now, and six of 'em dropped off the perch since Christmas last."

"An' then there was that business with 'Arry Watson's wife and that little babe o' theirs," Cuddy put in. "They was livin' in the workhouse 'til they got sold at Rayleigh market for a shillin'. Mind you, I s'pose the vicar did pay the cost of the journey. And 'e stumped up the price of a wedding dinner for 'em, as well, though there's some that might say that's the least 'e could 'a' done given the circumstances, if y'know what I mean. Heh, heh, heh..." the old buffer added, sniggering and touching a conspiratorial finger to the side of his nose.

"It's no wonder there's been trouble over at Saffron Waldron," growled Sawkins. "An' other places, besides. Down at Portsea Island, for one, where I 'eard a great crowd of 5,000 people gathered to march on the mayor's 'ouse, breaking windows and attacking baker's shops - the mob was only broken up when the bloody militia fired into 'em. But, maybe that's the only way. Maybe we all ought'a take matters into our own 'ands like them Frogs did, so that the Gov'ment might finally be made to take notice of us."

"Enough of that Jacobin trumpery!" snapped Cuddy, slapping his empty pot down on to the table. "Our Gov'ment might not be perfect but I'd not change it for the rabble they 'ave over in France. Over there no-one's safe, they murder and they rob whoever they will, 'an all dressed up in the name of freedom."

"All I'm sayin' is why should we always be grubbin' around for a morsel to eat while some folks lord it over us in their fancy carriages, feedin' on the fat of the land?"

Dangerous talk this, I thought, so, while Sal set down more ale for us, I set to nipping it in the bud.

"For sure," says I, in my best quarterdeck tone. "Things are dear, but riot and civil unrest is not the answer. There is much to be said for the spirit behind the revolution, I'll allow, but mob rule only leads to anarchy and terror - and the mere substitution of one ruling class with another. It is better that we continue as we are: free-born Englishmen, whose liberty is protected by a parliamentary monarchy, the rule of law and a social order that encourages beneficence towards the poor."

"Well said, Cap'n," agreed Cuddy. "'Ave you not yourself benefitted from the vicar's charitable collections, Edward Sawkins?"

"I s'pose I 'ave, at that," said Sawkins, reluctantly. "As you say, everythin' would be so much worse if the reverend, bless 'is soul, were not to pass round the money 'e collects from the squire and some of the other worthies 'ereabouts."

Our talk rambled on, as it usually did, through another couple of drinks, and I began to understand quite how much life in the village revolved around, and was controlled by, the church. The Reverend Gildersleeve seemed to have a great deal of power. Once a month he chaired vestry meetings with the more wealthy members of the parish, at which minor law and order offences were dealt with and constables were appointed. Decisions were also made in the vestry regarding the upkeep of the roads and, most importantly, the maintenance of the poor. It seemed that, by this means, the vicar was empowered to authorise payment of outdoor relief and various other monies for clothes, wood, medical attention and burial. He arranged for the employment of Dr Lipscomb, and was even responsible for the conversion of Pond House into the parish workhouse.

One night in the Anchor's kitchen our discourse turned to the character of the reverend himself. I was a trifle foxed, I'll admit, but I remember Cuddy and Ned being present and, notably, Dr Lipscomb had also called in to wet his whistle. We were seated by the hearth and Ned was waxing lyrical about the vicar's general good qualities.

"'E's a fine gentleman is the reverend," says this venerable old man of the world. "'E truly cares for all the people 'round 'ere, 'e does, and e's kind an' generous to a fault. Cuddy, d'ye mind the time 'e gave young Will Salmon arf a crown when 'e went to look f'work down Rochford way? An' that time 'e paid Susan Cook free 'n' six a week for nursing Martha Denny when she 'ad the fever?

"'E's paid Susan Cook for more than that, on occasion, I'll warrant," commented Cuddy, winking suggestively at the doctor.

"Och, Mr Smith," says our Sandy Sawbones, not unkindly. "Y'are naught but a wicked auld rummelieguts. Haud yer wheesht maun!"

Lipscomb was a Highland man and when he had taken a drink or two he was wont to lapse into his native brogue.

As this was not the first time Cuddy had intimated that Gildersleeve might be a trifle wrapped up in the tail of his mother's smock, I thought that I might venture to press the matter.

"Does the reverend have a weakness for the ladies?" I asked innocently.

"Well noo," replied the doctor. "Let's say oor vicar is sometimes prone to be a wee bit daft, especially where the young maids are concerned."

"Heh, heh," Cuddy chortled. "'E is f'sure. There's many a maid in the village can testify to that."

"He certainly has an unusual line in sermons," I said. "I recall in my first week here he preached a startling ovation in praise of dancing the feather bed jig."

"Aye," Lipscomb nodded. "That's one of his favourites, right enough."

"And, do you know, he behaved quite scandalously toward Miss Saunders at the Hall the other week?" I added.

"I'd heard aboot that, and sorry I was tae hear it too. But I fear ye must forgive the maun his foibles, Mr Ellis," the doctor urged. "He is, as Ned says, a fine maun f'all that. And he has an awfy good store of lurid tales concernin' spreets and bousiemen, y'ken?"

"Oh, most certainly I ken," I said. "I've been privy to some of his tales."

"Jings! Heh! The maun'll tell them to any who'll

listen, even the wemen an' the bairns, if he's able," Lipscomb laughed.

"Well, I for one do not approve of the reverend's stories," I announced, distainfully. "And, fine man though he may be, I'm afraid that I cannot find much that is praiseworthy in the vicar's general demeanour. He strikes me as a duddering rake who takes undue delight in his own outrageous habits."

I think my friends may well have been taken aback by my last utterance, judging by the looks I received, but I was very lushy by then and so paid them no heed.

"Gentlemen," I said, rising unsteadily to my feet. "I am for my bed so I shall bid you all a good night. Good night Doctor… Mr Smith… Mr Symonds…"

And with that I weaved my way to the stairs, with some small assistance provided by the kitchen furniture, and ascended to my room.

Lizzie and I continued our meetings and our relationship grew ever stronger. I was, however, becoming increasingly concerned at some of her behaviour. I supposed it must have been a further consequence of her ordeal and therefore perfectly excusable, but it seemed to me that the dear girl was showing an increasing lack of inhibitions when we were both together.

The weather improving somewhat, we two took a walk through the churchyard and then down the west slope of Beacon Hill and across the meadow. The sky was a deep blue, broken only by the occasional white fluffy cloud, and I had therefore ventured out in shirtsleeves whilst Lizzie had donned a light summer gown and neck handkerchief, topped off with a wide brimmed straw hat trimmed with ears of wheat. In order to allay some of Lizzie's (and, indeed, my own) natural trepidation on venturing out again alone, I had thought it prudent to carry a fowling piece borrowed from Lizzie's father, with powder and shot slung in a bag across my shoulder so that I looked every inch the country sportsman. After a while we sat down together on a small grassy knoll in the shade of a tall dogwood tree to catch our breath. I laid down my arms and Lizzie kicked off her shoes, removed her hat, and began to fan herself.

"Is it not a most beautiful day, Roger?" she said, looking up at the sky. "Such a day as this fairly carries all trouble away."

"It is a tonic, certainly. As should this be," I replied with a smile, rummaging through my bag to draw out a small stoneware flagon of cider that I had purchased from Sal that morning. "Would you care for a sip?"

"I think I would like that very much, thank you, sir" Lizzie said, sweetly.

We both took a draught and settled back, enjoying the sunshine. Lizzie closed her eyes and I cast an admiring glance over her as she lay, delighting in her beauty, from the delicate features of her face, over the gentle rise and fall of her bosom and down to her dainty bare feet. Suddenly, Lizzie's eyes opened, fair catching me in the act of gazing fondly at her.

"Mmm, do you like what you see?" she murmured softly.

"Er... I'm sorry Lizzie...," I stammered. "It is most impolite to stare at you so. I do beg your forgiveness."

"You are forgiven," Lizzie turned on to her side and propped herself up on her arm, facing me. "In light of recent events, I could not possibly reproach my gallant knight for any misdemeanour he may think to commit."

"I am pleased to hear it," I said. "I would not wish to embarrass you in any way, or cause you hurt. And on that very note, I must ask you, Lizzie, how are you feeling, my dear? Have you yet come to better terms with our recent experience?"

"I am beginning to feel that I have, Roger. My mind is more at ease, certainly - though I do still have some bruises here and there."

"You do? I hope that they are not too serious. Have you obtained salves or ointments from Dr Lipscomb?"

"No, no salves, Roger, nor ointments. My injuries are not so grave as to discommode me in any way. Look here, I will show you. What do you think?"

And with that Lizzie reached down to the hem of her dress and unashamedly drew it up to her hip. She wore no stockings and her long shapely limb was thus exposed, completely bare, to my regard. I was transfixed.

"Here at the top. Can you see?" Lizzie asked, clearly unabashed. "Feel the little bump."

She took my hand in hers and slowly guided it up, lightly brushing the skin of her smooth silky thigh, to rest just below her waist. It didn't seem to me that there was any bruising, but I assumed there must have been.

"Move your hand around... no, more to the front... there, do you feel it now?" she purred.

And to be sure, I did feel something, but it definitely wasn't a bump or a bruise! Becoming strangely flushed, I hastily withdrew my fingers before they inadvertently explored too deeply.

"There's no need for shyness," Lizzie said quietly, looking up into my eyes. "I know you dashing young bucks are all the same - boasting to one another of prowess and proportions, but bashful as a dairymaid when the cards are dealt."

"Erm... perhaps we should be thinking of getting back, my dear. It's a long walk back in the sun."

"Hush, Roger," Lizzie chided gently. "There is no need for haste. Tell me, do you think that a maid might be able to find herself fully satisfied in your company? Satisfied... within herself, I mean...?"

I saw then that the minx had come to lay her hand upon *my* leg, and was moving on up to the buttons on the front of my breeches. Astonished by this shameless conduct, I nevertheless felt myself begin to stiffen in response.

"We must go," I blurted, scrambling to my feet and beginning to gather up my gun and bag. "Come along, Lizzie, up you get."

Lizzie laughed merrily and got to her feet, straightening and smoothing down her dress as she did so.

"Very well, Roger, but I think we shall definitely have to take this matter properly... in hand... on some other occasion. And that right soon. Let's get off, then... you are right, it *is* a long way to go in the sun, after all."

My thoughts on the way back were confused, to say the least. I would not have believed that my Lizzie could attempt such an overt seduction, for make no mistake, I was not so *naïve* as to fail to realise that such wiles had been practised upon me, and in the open air too, where we might have been surprised at any moment. She was such a dear, sweet thing. It must surely have been a further aberration caused by our recent trials. I was, i'faith, starting to develop exceeding strong feelings for the girl and such perceived wantonness did not sit well with the flawless picture I had of her in my head. I tried to put the whole episode from my mind, but found that course to be nigh on impossible.

Even later, as I lay in bed, I could not help but

relive the entire experience and, I am ashamed to say, I began to regret calling the matter to a close so abruptly. Lizzie's beauty haunted me and in my mind I felt once more the feel of her skin and the touch of her hand. And what if someone had chanced to come upon us? The very notion of being thus observed was at once both appalling and inexplicably stimulating. My thoughts were in turmoil. I found myself becoming more and more aroused 'til mine own hand closed around me in imitation of my love's, and at length I subsided into guilty relief. Next time I will be better prepared, I told myself. I'll not shy away like a frightened boy again, damme if I will.

CHAPTER 7

It was about this time that Sir Henry, in another demonstration of his extreme wealth and generosity, got up a cricket match against the men of Little Stambridge, Canewdon's neighbouring parish, to compete for a purse of a guinea per man. The match took place on the Green, a delightful area of greensward to the south of the village bounded by trees and hedgerows and overlooked by the imposing tower of St Nicholas' church to the north-west and the creaking sails of the old mill to the east. I was co-opted on to the Canewdon eleven, taking my place alongside the squire himself, Mr Saunders, Aaron Rolfe and my two acquaintances from the malt house. Hugh Nichols the miller, was also in the side, as was the cooper and his apprentice, one of the footmen from the Hall and Sir Henry's coachman, James. Dr Lipscomb, being a Scotchman, did not care much for cricket, but had found himself persuaded to stand together with Cuddy Smith as umpires.

THE MOON DANCERS

The men of Little Stambridge, a crew of boisterous young men, arrived at around ten in the morning armed with a selection of curved and straight bats. It being a prodigious fine day, the greater part of the village had turned out to witness the contest and Sal had set up a lucrative makeshift tavern on the Green providing food and copious amounts of ale to spectators and players alike. By the time wickets were set up and the contest got under way there was, therefore, a prevailing atmosphere of merriment all around.

"So," pipes up the leader of the opposing forces, addressing our umpires. "We play by Stambridge rules, hey?"

"We most certainly do not, laddie," Dr Lipscomb retorted. "Y'are on Canewdon turf and so its Canewdon rules or nothing. Tek it or leave it, maun."

After some wrangling, the Stambridge man, a spotty little cub of about eighteen, finally agreed to our governance; a coin was tossed and, winning, he elected to put his side in to bat. For me this meant a lengthy spell lurking around in the outfield while Stambridge knocked the ball about and the scorers sat on a tump cutting the steadily increasing tally onto short sticks with their knives. Eventually, after what seemed an age, their last man was dismissed when, slashing away, he propelled the ball straight down the throat one of our scouts who accepted it with grateful, outstretched hands. A great roar went up from the assembled multitude to greet this prodigious feat and the

Stambridge rear-guard slunk dejectedly off the field. Altogether, they had notched up a hundred and twelve runs between them.

Thereafter, it was Canewdon's turn to defend the wicket and I was, perhaps unwisely, paired with the squire to open our account, Canewdon rules dictating that a batsman should be stationed at either end. At first, I dealt with the onslaught quite handily, delivered as it was at great speed by a large, thickset bully with naught but murder in his eyes, and I made a couple of good runs before handing the strike to Sir Henry. The squire took his guard and prepared to receive fire from the second of Stambridge's bowlers. The ball was pitched up waist high and Sir Henry flashed his bat at it, sending it bouncing and fizzing along the grass. We took one and, seeing the ball fumbled by a Stambridge fieldsman, I rashly called for another, charging full tilt back the way I had come. Before I had travelled very far, I noticed that Sir Henry had not heeded my call and was still standing, rooted firmly to his crease. Blind panic seized me and I turned to fly back to safety, only to trip and fall ignominiously at the very base of my wicket, scattering the sticks all around. Where the ball was I had no idea.

"Yerrout!" chorused the Stambridge men as I sat amongst the wreckage - an opinion that Dr Lipscomb and Cuddy Smith could only endorse.

Peals of laughter erupted around me as I picked myself up and walked off the field as calmly as I could. Aaron Rolfe was next man in, and on passing he looked at me with barely concealed contempt and made an audible tutting sound. Bloody stupid game, I thought as I regained the anonymity of the crowd. There was nothing for it but to chuck my bat, obtain another pint from Sal, and go forth to seek out Lizzie in the hope of soliciting some comfort in my hour of distress and sadness. I found her, annoyingly, in the company of the Reverend Gildersleeve.

"Rev'rend…" I nodded curtly as I approached. "Lizzie…"

"Ah, our gallant Hector is returned from the fray," said the vicar with a beaming smile. "How did you fare, Mr Ellis - went the day well?"

"Not especially," I answered, thinking that the disingenuous little bugger knew full well how I had fared for he could not have failed to observe the great amusement my clownish sporting endeavours had sparked.

"Take heart, sir," the vicar replied. "As it is said, all these things are sent to try us - and did not St. Paul himself comfort the Corinthians by telling them that God would not let you be tested beyond your strength? Take heart, indeed, for look, Mr Rolfe has taken up our cause most mightily. I see that he has added a dozen more runs already."

Fuck Mr Rolfe, I thought, fuck the Corinthians, and fuck you too. I was about to say as much (albeit more politely) when, luckily before I could articulate my sentiments, Lizzie stepped in to rescue me.

"You did very well, Roger. You were simply in receipt of some awfully bad luck," Lizzie said soothingly. "Come; let us sit awhile in the shade to relax. If, that is, you will excuse us, Reverend?"

"Why of course, my dear, I was hoping to obtain a closer view of the contest in any case. So please do run along, the pair of you, and do not think to mind me, for sure."

Lizzie and I moved through the crowd and away to the far corner of the Green where we sought out some shade and sat down. Lizzie was again wearing her summer dress and I watched her arrange its folds carefully around her as she sat.

"I've always hated cricket," I said miserably. "I mean, it's all fine as fivepence being a spectator, but playing the game seems to invariably bring out the worst in people."

"Do not trouble yourself overmuch, Roger. People have short memories. They will have other things to occupy them ere long, especially when all the hard work begins out in the fields."

"I don't much like that bloody vicar, either," I added churlishly. "He's altogether too familiar. What was he saying to you just then? Something he shouldn't, I'll warrant. Or was he telling more of his monstrous stories?"

"Why, Roger, I do believe you are becoming jealous! You have no need to worry on that account - no need at all. I have no special regard for the

Reverend Gildersleeve and, though he is prone to act somewhat indelicately on occasion, I am well able to cope with his eccentricities, believe you me. And besides, some of his tales can be somewhat thought provoking."

"H'rumph!" I puffed, becoming vexed. "In what way are they thought provoking, may I ask?"

"Well, I had not intended to tell you of this just yet, but since you ask, some while ago the reverend provided me with a description of how the people of antiquity would sometimes practice mysterious incantations to attract friendship and love."

"Love spells, Lizzie?" I said, incredulously. "Surely you place no store in such silly notions?"

"Oh, I know these things to be only old wives' tales, certainly. But I was tempted - let us say by the spirit of scientifical experimentation - to try something of the sort myself."

Lost for words, I could only listen as Lizzie continued; in a quiet whisper that only I could hear.

"This last midsummer night, during the time of the waxing crescent moon, I determined to carry out an experiment which, if successful, would supposedly reveal my true love to me. The essence, or shall I say the bare bones, of the incantation I had heard from the reverend, but I nevertheless found it necessary to add some of the fine detail from my own imagination. The reverend told me, for instance, that the old people believed that the naked body represented truth, and also that becoming naked was a sign of true freedom. So, that night I therefore rose from my bed and divested myself of all my nightclothes, anointing my whole body with rosewater to cool, smooth and calm my skin."

Entranced by the images conjured in my mind, I noticed that my breath was quickening and my heart was beginning to beat faster. I swallowed hard and shivered slightly as Lizzie went on with her tale.

"Having previously placed a small metal dish on the hearth, I knelt and burnt within it some rose petals and some cinnamon, breathing in the warm, sensual smell to heighten my senses and bring success to my undertaking. Then, after allowing some time for the potency of my feelings to build up I spoke the words of the incantation to the Angel of Venus, calling on the Goddess to fill me with a love that I might share with one with whom I will join together in a loving union."

"And was anything disclosed to you?" I breathed.

And, despite myself, I had to know the answer to this. For though I knew I should be shocked, I had in truth become completely drawn in to Lizzie's narrative, and at the back of my mind I dared hope that the true love to whom she referred might somehow be revealed to be mine own self.

"I think perhaps something was," said Lizzie, fixing me with an intense stare. "After I had breathed in the scent of the rose and the cinnamon for some while I felt a tingling sensation start to spread over me, causing the hairs on my body to stiffen and raising small bumps all over my flesh. I became aware of a most pleasant tightening deep within my loins and also the beginnings of a warm feeling rising up from that same honeyed location, now moist to the touch. A picture then formed in my mind. It was indistinct at first but, as the energy built and I came to speak the words, my body tensed, my back arched, and my toes curled. And, just when I thought that I could endure no more... suddenly all the tension was released, pulsing throughout my very being. I felt an overwhelming feeling of release wash over me, and I could see..."

"See what, Lizzie? Whom did you see? I gasped.

"I saw you, Roger," and, so saying, Lizzie leant closer to me and our lips met in a long, lingering, euphoric kiss.

Canewdon won the match by two wickets, the squire's coachman gaining the winning runs after larruping the ball over the boundary and into the hedge. The crowd was elated, lifting the man bodily onto broad shoulders and carrying him off the field in triumph. I'm afraid that, given what I had heard, and its sweet aftermath, I couldn't care less, although I do remember being pleasantly aware that I was now a guinea better off.

The next day I fell to pondering seriously over my relationship with Lizzie. Did she love me? Did I love her? Or was our attraction merely physical, a manifestation of mutual lust? For sure, I was experiencing an irresistible desire to be close to her, and I had, as I thought, an irrefutable willingness to place her well-being and happiness above my own. But, were these feelings simply driven by passion? Had lust blurred my senses so that I could not see Lizzie for who she truly was? That I wanted her, there was no doubt. I longed to feel her firm, supple body in my arms, to caress the curve of her breast and apply my lips not only to her upturned face but also to the gentle roundness of her belly and the delicate wispy mound that I imagined, and indeed had once fleetingly encountered, lying below. I wanted more than anything to possess her fully, to feel the smooth, encompassing, embracing depth of her, and to feel her melt against me in glorious ecstasy. However, I was worried too. Were these but base and unworthy feelings that served only to evidence a lack of respect or courtesy toward my love? Did my desires do nothing but place me firmly among the ranks of those licentious, hedonistic libertines that I professed to despise? My mind was in turmoil and I needed to get away on my own to clear my head. One thing was certain though; this was turning out to be a bloody unusual summer!

In an effort to think more clearly, I decided therefore to take a long walk up and over Butts Hill, across the South Fambridge Marshes via the various raised causeways that afforded access to that desolate place, and along the sea wall that bounded the River Crouch at Raypits Reach. In contrast to the previous day's bright sunshine, the sky was overcast and brooding when I set out on my journey, although the wild landscape still remained oddly beguiling.

Hummocky grassland, interlaced with fleets and creeks, was filled with reeds, sedge, and spring whitlow-grass; and sea wormwood and golden samphire thrived in the saltmarsh mud. Numerous wildfowl were all around, and skylarks and marsh harriers swooped over the grassland. My mood improved almost immediately as I walked and I soon found my thoughts becoming less disturbing, my mind turning instead to happy contemplation of Lizzie's enchanting personality and startlingly good looks. I could only wonder what she saw in a salty old sea-dog like me, but I was glad she did see something to her liking. I knew that we had formed a deep emotional bond over this last two months and that we had a shared affection - and yes, we did both have a deeper, as yet unfulfilled, need for each other which we could hope that one day might be finally satisfied. Perhaps this was love, after all. In any case, it pleased me to think so, and it pleased me to be able to place Lizzie securely on a pedestal that at once acknowledged and transcended sexuality, allowing me to continue in my worship of her as a paragon of maidenly innocence.

After a while it came on to rain. Not just a light summer shower, mark you, but a sudden, stinging deluge that, though it was over almost as soon as it started, left me soaked through, and left the ground sodden and glistening with pools of surface water. I trudged on, thinking to dry out along the way. My boots became caked in sticky mud which somehow spread itself up my legs and even onto my coat-tails. Then I slipped, and slid down the side of the causeway, reaching out with my hands to break my fall, and finishing up on my arse, plastered in mud. That was enough for me. Regaining the causeway, I turned and headed for home. Strange to say, my mood was still relatively light on that long drag back, but by the time I returned to the Anchor I was starting to feel most unwell.

And sure enough, that night I was as queer as Dick's hatband. All of my muscles ached and I had the fever and the chills in turn. I was pumping ship regularly and my head hurt like the Devil. When Sal saw me she took fright instantly and straightway called for the services of Dr Lipscomb.

"Ah, laddie," said the doctor, on being admitted to my room. "Ye don't look too well at all. What's being the matter with ye, hey?"

"I was hoping you might be able to help with that," I replied feebly.

"Och, it's good to see that ye still have your sense of humour, so it is. C'mon noo, what are ye symptoms?"

"Fever; chills; muscle aches; headache; cough; nausea; vomiting; and loss of appetite, Doctor."

"Nothin' too bad then," he pronounced. "Let's have a look at ye."

Dr Lipscomb fished out his watch and took hold of my wrist, timing my pulse beats. He then bade me hold my breath and began striking my chest with his fingers.

"Hmm, sounds healthy, like a cloth-covered drum," he muttered, and then, placing his hand on my forehead, continued. "Ye're very hot, definitely. Sal says ye were out on the marsh, yesterday and came back covered in all kinds of dung and shite. Is that right?"

"Yes it is, Doctor. I got soaked through and fell up to my middle in the mud."

"Well, I'll ask ye to provide me with a sample o'your pish, just to make sure, but I'll lay odds that ye have a case of the Rat Catcher's Yellows."

"What's that," I asked.

"It's a malady caused by exposure to mud and to wet vegetation that has been contaminated with animal urine, my boy. Ye're lucky in that ye seem only to have a mild case. In severe cases the disease has been known to spread to the patient's liver, kidneys, and other major organs, resulting in a most unpleasant journey unto death."

"Christ on his cross!" I croaked.

"Och, dinnae fash. Ye've nothing to worry aboot. Ye'll find that ye have a wee dose of an influenza-like illness for a few days, but with proper treatment ye'll be as fine as fippence and as neat as ninepence in no time, as my old ma used tae say."

"Tell me what's to be done, Doctor, and I'll do it. Whatever it is, it has to be better than feeling like this."

"Well, I prescribe plenty of rest, certainly," said the worthy physician. "But apart from that, I think we shall have recourse to the poppy. Have you heard of the drug, laudanum? It is but a mixture of opium and alcohol but is amazingly effective. In fact, so efficacious is this wonderful tincture in curing disease that I have come to prefer it before all other lesser drugs and remedies available to me. I shall leave ye a small vial and would entreat ye to imbibe ten drops each day, mixed with wine. It is a very bitter medicine to the taste, but if ye will but follow my instructions in this I guarantee that ye will be most speedily returned to full health within days."

The laudanum was bitter indeed, though after a while my condition did appear to be improving. The treatment was not without side-effects, however. I found my moods changing frequently, shifting in turn from feelings of sadness to extreme well-being or elation. My nightmares increased in frequency and became more lurid, with images of battle intermingling with highway robbers and acts of witchcraft in my mind. One night, to give an instance, I recall dreaming that Lizzie had somehow been transported aboard *Amazone* and was being menaced by a gang of leering French sailors intent on ravishment. My feeble attempts to rescue her were thwarted by the footpads, Sourface and Ratty, who threatened me with enormous cricket bats, and in the event Lizzie was only saved by the rotten Reverend Gildersleeve who seized hold of her from behind and carried her up into the air to hover, with arched back and outstretched arms, above the *Amazone's* mizzen peak.

To begin with, Sal brought my meals to my room and sometimes sat with me while I dozed, for which I was very grateful. Lizzie had asked to visit but I had declined politely, not wishing her to see me laid so low. I think it was just over a week before I had strength enough to rise from my bed to regain the warmth and conviviality of the Anchor's kitchen.

"Good t'see yer up an' about again, Cap'n," called Cuddy Smith, as I descended the stair.

"Aye," agreed Ned Symonds with a broad grin. "We was worried about yer, sir, an' right glad we are that you're on the mend - even though yer do still look like a moving dunghill."

"Thank you, gentlemen," I responded. "And right glad I am to see you too."

"Come Cap'n, sit yerself down 'ere and take a pot of malt liquor wiv us," urged Cuddy, steering me to a seat by the fireplace. "A good strong brew'll set yer to rights, t'be sure. Sal! A mug o'Pharaoh for the Cap'n, quick as y'like."

And so I sat down, Sal brought over the heady concoction and I took a sip, savouring the taste. It felt good to be drinking something more flavoursome than water once again and I drained the pot, calling for another for myself and for my companions. Soon, I was snoring, fast asleep in the chair.

CHAPTER 8

I awoke with a start. It was now late into the evening but nevertheless the Anchor's kitchen was still quite full of life. Peering blearily around me I could see that Cuddy and Ned were there, of course, and there were half a dozen or so others seated around the room. There was a general low hum of conversation, and in the corner someone was singing softly in a mellifluous baritone. I was still feeling somewhat half seas over and I was therefore only half listening to the song.

The lark in the morning, she rises off her nest,
And she goes up all in the air with the dew
upon her breast,
Like the jolly ploughboy she whistles and she
sings,
And she comes home each evening with the
dew all on her wings.

Oh, Roger the ploughboy, he is a bonnie
blade,

He goes whistling and singing down by
yonder lonely glade,
He's met with dark-eyed Susan, she's
handsome I declare,
And she's far more enticing than the birds all
in the air...

Somewhere in my mind I registered that the ploughboy of the song shared my name, but thought nothing of it as the intonation worked its soft, calming effect on me. I was beginning to drift off again when I became aware that there was some commotion at the door. One of the village lads had entered the kitchen in a state of high agitation.

"Oh, Mrs Dowsett, come quick, its Tommy, we've lost 'im," cried the youth. "We was up at the church an' we got scared, an' now we can't find 'im."

"Calm down, Billy, calm down," urged Sal. "Tell me, what's amiss?"

"It's not our fault, Mrs Dowsett," sniffed Billy, who was one of those ferrety-faced children that appear much older than their years.

"I'm sure it wasn't, dear, but you must tell me what happened, all the same."

"It's that ol' 'ighwayman that the Cap'n shot a while back," Billy blurted. "The reverend, 'e told us that 'cause 'e were such a bad man 'is ghost could be made to guard all the other graves up at the churchyard. 'E said that all it needed were for some people to go up there and dance around the

125

'ighwayman's stone seven times to make sure that 'is spirit stayed unquiet."

"And is that what you were doing, Bill?"

"Aye, we thought to go up to the church tonight to do it, an' so we all arranged to meet in Church Lane afore goin' on up to the west gate. But when we got there, there was a most awful 'ubbub broke out. Loud noises, like someone chopping wood, an' an 'orrible screeching sound coming from the church tower. We were afraid f'our lives, Missus, so we cut an' run, as fast as we could. Me 'n' Sam ran back down Church Lane, but the others, including Tom, scattered all over the place."

That bloody vicar again, I thought, is there no end to his mischief? By this time some of Sal's other customers had gathered around Billy. I left my chair and walked over to join them.

"Do you know where Tom went, son," I asked.

"No, Cap'n," said Billy. "All the rest of us met up again on the Green, but there was no sign of Tom. We called after 'im 'till our voices were 'oarse, but wherever 'e is 'e paid us no 'eed."

"Don't worry, he won't have gone far, I'll warrant," says I, turning to the others and assuming command. "Come on lads, who's with me? Let's get out there and find the boy. Sal, you stay here with Billy, this won't take long, I'm sure. We'll soon have him back, safe and sound."

Four of the younger men volunteered to join me

and as we left the inn to take up the search, I could hear that one of those who had stayed behind had again taken up the song.

> As they were coming home, one evening from
> the town,
> With the meadows being green and the grass
> it all cut down,
> And as they chanced to stumble, all in the
> new mown hay,
> 'It's love me now or never,' this bonnie lass
> did say…

"Spread out, lads," I ordered. "Let's try to cover as much ground as possible. Two of you head down towards the Green and the other two along the road to the Hall. I'll get up to the churchyard and look there. If we draw a blank we'll regroup here and spread the search wider."

It was a clear, warm, night and a mite humid so that I could feel the sweat breaking out on my forehead as I trotted up the hill and entered the churchyard. Moonlight illuminated the ancient church so that it loomed large over its environs and cast dark shadows behind.

"Tom!" I called. "Are you here, boy?"

No answer. I scanned the area just within the east gate and looked along the path that lay adjacent to the south side of the church. I then doubled back and entered the stygian blackness of the north side.

"Tom!" I called again.

Nothing. Then a movement below the north wall, where it adjoined the tower.

"Tom, is that you?"

And there he was, crouched low and pressed against the furthest buttress of the wall at the bottom of a gentle slope. He appeared to be frightened out of his wits.

"There you are, Tom," I said gently as I extended a hand to help him to his feet. "Come on lad, your ma's waiting for you back at the inn."

And then there came a sudden noise to my right. I instinctively turned, and as luck would have it, at the same time Tom took it into his head to pull sharply away from me and sprint for home as fast as he could. I felt my feet slip on the greasy, damp grass and I fell, landing flat on my back.

The impact knocked the breath from my body and as my head connected with the turf I experienced a sharp crackling sensation and pinpoints of light flashed behind my eyes. I lay on my back for a while whilst I recovered my wits, wondering why it was that, of late, I seemed to be ending up arsy varsey more often than a light-heeled wench, and whether it might actually be high time I invested in a good new pair of topboots. When I finally sat up my head span alarmingly and I thought I was like to cast up my accounts onto the grass, but the sensation passed soon enough and I was able to regain my feet. Once more, I heard noises, seemingly emanating from the open space to the west of the tower. I also now noticed that an orange light was glowing in the middle distance, surely presaging a large lanthorn or else a fire, set to light up the far end of the churchyard. I moved gingerly to the corner of the tower and peered round. Before me there was indeed a fire, burning brightly and casting flickering shadows upon the wall as a group of five figures moved slowly in a circle around the flames. As I watched, the figures began to dance and sway. Their pace increased as one of them began beating time on a calfskin fiddle. What in Heaven's name had I come upon? Could these people really be the witches that loomed so large in the tales that had been told in the village for all these years?

I could see that most, but not all, of the dancers were female, and all were loosely clad in white shifts, fastened at the shoulder with large ornate brooches. The light of the fire shone through the thin material of these flimsy garments causing the shape of the dancer's bodies to be outlined in sharp relief as they capered and leapt into the air. After a while, the rhythmic cadence of the drum was joined by the lilting notes of an oaten pipe and I looked beyond the fire to see that the tune was being played by a single piper, who was perched on the flat top of an ancient table tomb. This outlandish minstrel was dressed in a long dark robe, the folds of which provided a sombre drapery around his makeshift throne, and upon his head he wore a cap adorned with the antlers of a young deer. Shadows played across the face of the piper so that his features were more often shrouded in darkness, but when the light of the fire was fully cast upon him, his identity was plain to see - and I knew him - I knew him immediately. In fact, I think I would have known him even had his visage not been so revealed to me by the flames. Gildersleeve! The bastard was evidently playing Pan to this misguided crew of moon-struck lunatics for some bizarre or perverted purpose that I could not even begin to guess at.

Upon discerning that it was the detestable Reverend Gildersleeve who was the conductor of this shameful performance, I felt compelled to creep further forward to gain a better view. As I did so the music stopped abruptly and the dancers ceased their gyrations. I stood, rooted to the spot. Almost as one the dancers turned towards me and fanned out around the fire to form a half-circle directly to my front, so that, with the huge wooden Devil's door of the tower at my back, I was effectively surrounded. One of the dancers stepped forward to approach me and, to my utter dismay, I saw that it was Lizzie! I could not believe what I was seeing - my Lizzie, a part of this depraved and deplorable ritual? It could not be true. Yet it was true -she was standing before me in the firelight, her beautiful shape silhouetted through her gossamer sark. I knew not what to do, nor what to say. Lizzie beckoned me to her and I could only obey, walking slowly into the centre of the arc.

"Enter the circle my dear one," Lizzie whispered. "Enter the circle in perfect love and in perfect trust," she said, taking my hands and turning me, so that my back was to the fire and she was herself thus fully irradiated by the light of the flames.

With her eyes fixed firmly upon me she reached her hand up to her shoulder and unfastened the clasp that held her shift in place, letting the garment fall to the ground to reveal her nakedness. I could scarcely breathe, my eyes drinking in her exquisite glamour, from the elegance of her shoulders and the curve of her breasts, crowned with their delicate pink nipples, down, to her slim waist and on to the curvaceous hips that bounded that glorious triangle of downy hair which nestled between her lustrous thighs. I felt once more the prickle of sweat breaking out on my forehead as she spoke again.

"Do not worry my love, nakedness merely symbolises truth. Enter the circle, Roger. Do whatever you will, but beware, for in the doing of it you must be sure to cause no harm."

The beat of the drum resumed and Lizzie started to swing her hips in time with the pulsating rhythm. In the background the sound of the pipe added its note and texture to the refrain. Slowly, as I watched, Lizzie let her hands range all over her body, cupping and caressing her breasts and rolling each nipple between thumb and forefinger before moving down to linger a moment upon her mount of Venus, first entwining her fingers in its auburn curls and then sliding them between her legs to gently part the luscious lips of that which lay betwixt. Raising her arms, she laid her hands on my shoulders, pushing me to my knees so that my eyes were directly level with that which was fast becoming the centre of my desires, and then, bending forward, she lightly brushed a hardened nipple across my lips causing a most thrilling sensation to pass over me. Around us the other members of the circle had now also joined in the dance. The music was rising to a crescendo and my head was spinning with excitement as Lizzie danced closer, her glistening skin and her sweet musky scent combining to inflame my passions. I felt giddy and my eyes lost focus as I pitched forward, unconscious upon the grass.

When I regained consciousness I was lying in my bed back at the Anchor. Sal was sitting by my side holding my hand in hers and I could smell the scent of lavender oil in the air. I felt awful. My head throbbed, my mouth was dry, and I was cropsick in the stomach as from the effects of strong drink. At first I had no recollection of what had befallen me. And then it hit me like a thump on the back with a stone and I cried out in shock and in shame. Surely it couldn't be true. It must have been another one of my nightmares brought on by Lipscomb's infernal jallop - there could be no other explanation.

"Sal, what the Devil happened to me?" I croaked.

"Why sir," says Sal, smiling down at me beatifically. "You took such a tumble up at the church last night. Do you remember? You went up there looking for that young scamp, Tom. Well, he came home just after midnight and told us that you'd had a nasty accident and had knocked yourself out on the grass. Old Ned Symonds and Cuddy Smith were still in the kitchen so we three went up and fetched you home. You were in a bad way, lying there moaning and groaning hard by the wall of the church, but we got you up, and Ned and Cuddy managed to get your arms around their shoulders so as to carry you back down the High Street. We were half mad with worry about you sir, and it does my heart good to see you back with us again, truly it does."

"What about the witches, Sal? Did you see the witches?

"Witches, is it? Now, don't be a goosecap, sir. There are no witches, that's just a silly story. You've been having bad dreams, that's all. I've been watching you for hours and you've been tossing and turning all night, you poor thing."

All that day, and indeed the next day too, I was uncommon confused and could not come to terms with what I had experienced, or even determine whether or not any of it had truly happened at all. I therefore once more summoned Dr Lipscomb, to consult him upon the matter. When he arrived at my bedside I told him something of my dreams, although I took care to omit much of the fine detail and said nothing at all of Lizzie's part in them.

"I see," said the worthy water scriger, rummaging around in his bag in search of his ever ready urine flask. "Have these dreams become more frequent since ye have been taking the laudanum?"

"They have," I replied. "And they have become

more lucid. The dream that followed my accident in the churchyard was so vivid that it has caused me to think that it might actually have the ring of truth to it - but that I know is naught but abject folly."

"Aye, it is. However, a blow on the heid can do strange things to a body, ye ken? And I'm afraid tae say that opium-induced hallucinations are a rare yet significant side effect of laudanum treatment."

"What do you mean by hallucinations, Doctor?" I asked.

"Weel, laddie, y'see a hallucination is more than a dream or a nightmare. When we dream, the substance of oor dreams is often queer or exaggerated, like unto ye saw your enemies aboard ship waving their giant cricket bats, tae give ye an instance. But a hallucination, noo, that's a different kettle o'fish altogether. Hallucinations have the absolute ring o'truth aboot them and will feel very real indeed - and they don't occur when ye'are sleepin' but rather when ye are quite awake."

"So, you think I was having one of these hallucinations when I thought I saw the witches?"

"I would say that was highly probable. D'ye know, it's said that some o'these modern writers and poets will deliberately use laudanum to induce strange and wonderful visions so that they may use them to influence their wildest literary and artistic creations? Wheesht! I can only wonder what visions must have been conjured up in your heid when the effects of the drug were compounded by strong drink and a violent topper f'guid measure. Noo, if ye will just squeeze a drop o'pish into this bottle, we'll mek sure the colour, smell and taste are all as they should be and that ye're properly on the mend."

I knew it. Already befuddled by drink and drugs, my fall had brought on one of these blasted hallucinations. It must surely be the only explanation, I decided, after Dr Lipscomb had packed up his bag and departed. Witches and warlocks were merely the stuff of folklore and legend, a product of the superstitious imaginings of ignorant country people. To believe in witchcraft was simply irrational - there was no definitive evidence for such a belief and it could never be proven. In its fevered state, my drug fuelled mind had obviously processed the stories I had heard as a child, and shook them up with the ludicrous imaginings being pedalled around the village by the vicar to create a contemptible, dissolute fantasy that was no more real than the faerie stories of Charles Perrault or Marie-Catherine d'Aulnoy. And, even if my prurient unconscious fancies could be in any way countenanced, as for Lizzie being involved in such degenerate and orgiastic practices, well that was just unthinkable. Mark you, I wasn't so convinced about the Reverend Gildersleeve, it must be said.

CHAPTER 9

By the end of July, all around the village, fields of barley were beginning to change from green to gold and wheat was beginning to nod on the stem, thus prompting the farmers of Canewdon to start the long and arduous process of harvesting the crop. One bright morning, at Nathaniel Saunders' invitation, and with sickle in hand, I joined him and the labourers, men and women, in harvesting the first of the barley up at Canewdon Hall Farm. I was shown how to properly swing the sharp edge of my sickle as close to the ground as possible to ensure that I cut down the entire stalk, and then set to, working from one side of the crop to the other in large swinging motions. Once the stalks were cut, others followed behind tying the barley into narrow stooks for drying. It was backbreaking work and it was not long before painful blisters were raised on my palms. But it did me a power of good. After a few days, I felt fitter and stronger and my overall mood was lightened considerably. I was content - and I now had no doubt at all that what I remembered from the churchyard was merely a vision brought on by my fall and the effects of opium upon my mind.

We were uncommonly well fed as we worked. Before going out into the fields at around six in the morning, we would partake of bread, cheese, ale, and a few onions, and at nine we were given a hot breakfast. At around eleven, more bread and cheese was delivered to us by Mrs Saunders, Lizzie and some of the other ladies of the village, and at half past one we dined royally on beef or mutton, and plumb-pudding. Then at four the ladies again brought cheese and ale which we would consume whilst relaxing in the late afternoon sunshine.

During one such welcome respite I fell to conversing with some of my fellows.

"How do you think the crop is looking, George?" I asked one of the men.

"Not bad at all, sir, not bad at all - for the moment at least," George replied.

"Aye, for the moment," chipped in one of the others, a tall, burly cove humorously known as Little Ben, who, with labour always being in short supply at harvest time, had been brought over from Ashingdon with some other men. "We've 'ad just the right balance of sun an' rain so far, but, as you'll know sir, you being a seafarin' man an' all, the weather can change at any moment an' if'n we get a storm or two it can do us a lot of damage."

"The signs are good so far," I said, cutting a generous lump of cheese and slapping it down on an inch think chunk of bread. "But, in my experience, we should be sure to keep an eye on the shape and movement of the clouds, and on any changes in the temperature and the wind as well. That way we may be forewarned of bad weather and can get tarpaulins over the stooks to keep them dry if a storm comes."

"Right enough," says George. "But it's not only thunderstorms that we need to watch out for. If we get any kind of persistent rain at all it'll slow down the 'arvest and damage the grain."

"That's why we 'ave to work fast," declared Ben, draining his pot and making ready to get back to the grind. "So's we can get as much in as we can in as short a time as possible. C'mon Cap'n, eat up, there's no rest for the wicked y'know."

And work fast we did. Fortified by copious amounts of ale and cheese we worked both long and hard, so that by the second week of August we were well on the way to finishing the job. Some of the men were thus released to start bringing in the wheat, but for myself, I stayed on to reap the last of the barley, thinking it most satisfying to see out that which I had started. In truth, I enjoyed the challenge of pitting my strength against the demands of the soil and I was therefore happy to toil away alongside George, Ben, and the others well into the late summer evenings. And, after a hard day's work what better than a hot supper, good company and a pint or two in the kitchen of the

Anchor? Not much, to my mind, and so, once again, that was where I was to be found most nights.

"How are you faring with the corn, Dick?" I one night enquired of one of the Canewdon Hall Farm labourers who had shouldered his long scythe and gone along with Mr Saunders to begin cutting the wheat.

"Well enough, thankee, sir," Dick replied politely.

"There's been no reoccurrence of the black stem rust then?"

"No, sir, there 'as not. Though if'n the Reeve 'adn't acted so sharply, grubbin' out them barberry bushes, we'd 'ave 'ad an 'ole parcel o'trouble, f'sure, just like they've 'ad over Paglesham way."

"I didn't know that they had problems in Paglesham," I said. "Although I'll own that I am not one whit surprised. From what I hear, the people of that town are more concerned with evading the revenue officers and engaging in other such nefarious pursuits than they are with honest agrarian management."

"Well, I don't know so much about that there 'agrarian management', sir, but I knows they don't work their farms proper. And, aye, ye're in the right of it there. They're a black 'arted lot, 'tis true. An' maybe it's God's judgement upon 'em, for they'll suffer for their sins t'be sure. The black stem rust has took an 'eavy toll on their crop this season, and like as not, they won't recover from it. An' it could all 'ave been avoided, that's the rub. If'n they'd 'ave got at the

139

barberry like we did there would most likely 'ave been a lot less 'ungry mouths in the town come next winter."

"Amen to that, Dick," says I, piously. "Even though I suspect that their infernal resourcefulness will ensure that the wolf is kept from the door somehow."

After making short work of another pint, I found that I was in dire need of a leak. I therefore left the kitchen and made my way round to the muddy back wall of the inn, whereupon was erected a ramshackle wooden privy, partially illuminated by a couple of guttering lanthorns. Having taken my ease, I buttoned my breeches and headed back. As I went, I noticed Aaron Rolfe and Edward Sawkins leaning on a rail, taking a pipe together. They had evidently come out of the inn for some air and were deep in conversation. They did not see me and I made to pass by, but all at once I heard Rolfe laugh, long and loud.

"Aye, Ned," the blacksmith chortled. "That ol' snub Devil Gildersleeve, 'e's surely a prize buck fitch the way 'e moons over that young Miss Elizabeth, an' no mistake. She's no saint 'erself though, mind, a right game pullet, she is, 'anging on 'is every word and ready to join in all 'is gammon. Aye, an' play ol' gooseberry with 'im up at the churchyard late at night an' all."

I could not believe what I was hearing, how could that nazy rascal talk so foully of my Lizzie? Enraged, I accosted the two men and, swearing like a cutter, demanded to know what in blazes they were about.

"Christ!" spluttered Rolfe. "I'm sorry Cap'n we

ne'er saw you a'comin', I swear."

"That we didn't, sir," whined Sawkins, apologetically. "An' we didn't mean no 'arm by anythin', sir, truly we didn't."

"You damn Rogues!" I railed. "Don't you know not to speak of your betters in that despicable manner? Why, if I had you aboard ship I'd have you triced up to the grating for that - damme, I've a good mind to thrash you soundly myself, you ignorant fuckers!"

"Steady, sir, there's no need for this," said Rolfe, raising his palms and backing away slightly. "We don't want no trouble."

"The Devil, you don't!" I shouted back.

By now I was incandescent with rage and I hauled back a fist and let fly at the blacksmith with a wild swing. I connected squarely with the side of his big bullet head, the shock of the impact jarring my hand to the bone, and Rolfe dropped to one knee, rubbing the side of his face.

"You shouldn't 'ave done that, sir" he said quietly, getting slowly to his feet and shaking his head. "You really shouldn't 'ave done that at all."

Rolfe raised his fists and took a stance before me. I raised my guard too, and gingerly prepared to repel boarders. For a big man, Rolfe was bloody quick, his two fists snaking out in succession so that I was hard put to block the blows. He next tried to fib me, reaching out his left hand to take me by the hair so that he could belabour me with his right, but my guard proved sufficient to shrug him off and I managed to get in a couple of jabs of my own. Gad, though, it was like milling with Mendoza the Jew, and though I ducked and blocked for all I was worth, I finally succumbed to a stinging straight left that clipped my chin and sent me sprawling in the dirt. Seeing what he had done, Rolfe at once became the model of sporting contrition, fussing around me to make sure I had taken no serious damage, whilst Sawkins hovered in the background, looking most serious and sad.

"I'm right sorry to chalk you like that, Cap'n," Rolfe said, reaching down to help me up. "An' sorry I am to 'ave spoken that way about your sweetin' too. But you must know that some of the people 'round 'ere are not all as they might seem. If I were in your shoes, Cap'n I'd shift yer bob up to the parsonage an' ask the vicar about some of the nonsense he's been encouraging as of late."

Leaving me nursing a cut to my chin, and my injured pride, Rolfe and Sawkins went sheepishly back into the inn. Rolfe's words stayed with me, however, and rekindled the flames of jealousy and suspicion in my mind concerning the, by now hated, Reverend Gildersleeve and his louche attitude and attentions towards Lizzie. I had had enough, I decided. It was high time I had it out with the vile vicar and put an end to his sordid little games.

Despite the lateness of the hour, I grabbed one of the privy lanthorns and hurried to the parsonage, hammering rudely on the door, demanding entry. After a while the reverend appeared at one of the attic windows. He was dressed for bed, in a ruffled white linen nightshirt and white cotton cap.

"Who's there?" he called down, sharply. "What is amiss? Are you aware of the time, sir?

"Open up, Vicar," I growled. "For I have a serious bone to pick with you."

"Is that you, Mr Ellis? Whatever ails you, man? Wait but a moment and I will get Perkins to open the door. Perkins! Get up fellow, and let the Lieutenant in."

A few minutes later there was a rattling and scraping of locks and, with obvious reluctance, the vicar's elderly manservant admitted me to the house. Lighting the way with a tallow candle, Perkins ushered me directly into the parlour and, after deploying his own dip to light the sconces, left me to my own devices. The room was fairly modest and old-fashioned, dominated by a stone and brick fireplace, within which was set a cast iron hob-grate decorated with blue and white Delft tiles portraying stories from the Bible. The walls were clad with whitewashed pine panels, and an ancient oak gate-leg table and chairs stood in the corner. On one wall was hung a large tapestry which, I was not surprised to see, reproduced Breughel the Elder's *Offerings to Cybele*, with its chubby little nymphs and cherubs running around in a gesture of thanksgiving, thrusting all sorts of gifts of fruit, flowers and crops into the hands of a scantily clad goddess of nature.

Presently the vicar joined me, having donned a loose banyan and discarded his nightcap in favour of a tightly wound turban.

"What is the meaning of this intrusion, sir?" he said, sorely displeased at my trespassing upon his privacy so late in the evening with my bloody face, dirty, dishevelled clothes, and generally looking like I had been to an Irish wedding.

"I'll tell you the reason, Reverend," I spat. "Your behaviour towards Elizabeth Saunders has become of grave concern to me. I have seen with my own eyes the way you look at her and I know that you have been filling her head with silly, libidinous notions of witchery, spells, and Heaven knows what else."

"My dear boy, do be still, I pray you. I can assure you that I have no designs upon the young lady. And my stories are just that, stories - merely intended to entertain and pass the time. I mean no harm by them. Why, as for them being in any way 'libidinous', that is an absurd notion. Perhaps they could sometimes be described as slightly suggestive, but that is all."

"So, how do you explain the fact that your relationship with Miss Saunders is the talk of the village, sir?" I demanded. "I have just come from the Anchor where I overheard a conversation that, I must confess, painted you in an extremely bad light. Why, the persons concerned were suggesting, in no uncertain terms, that you and Miss Saunders are wont to engage in clandestine moonlight trysts - and that in your own churchyard, God dammit!"

"Please, Lieutenant, no blasphemy, I implore you," Gildersleeve said, calmly. "These allegations are foolish in the extreme, and I am convinced that any such conversation that may have been overheard was mere taproom bravado, no doubt fuelled by an excess of strong liquor."

Then he touched a grubby finger to his lips and paused for an instant, apparently thinking.

"But, nevertheless," he resumed, removing the digit from his lips and wagging it at me so as to emphasise a point. "I fear it may be in some way understandable."

"Understandable! Tell me, how so is it understandable, sirrah?

"Well, it is true that, some evenings, I do meet privately in the narthex with some of the members of the parish vestry committee, and it is true also that Elizabeth Saunders is one of this select group - as is her mother also. You see, we are most dreadfully worried that a repeat of last year's bad harvest would prove disastrous to the village, and we are therefore determined to do our best to ensure, by whatever means possible, that such an event does not occur again. And, should the worst befall us, despite our efforts, we are working to put measures in place whereby to mitigate some of the more ruinous effects that a shortage of grain would inevitably have upon the poorest among us. Therefore, though our meetings are simply to devise plans of an agricultural nature and to develop stratagems for the effective distribution of outdoor relief wherever we can, I suspect that the beef heads at the Anchor have gotten wind of them and, as is the way sometimes with country folk, have invested them with the whiff of scandal. And I do know right well that, to my eternal shame, sometimes my sermons and stories might serve to add fuel to flames of this particular ilk, encouraging shall we say… a more liberal… interpretation of my actions and beliefs - and for this I own that I am most truly sorry."

I opened my mouth to speak, but the vicar presented his palm towards me and continued on regardless.

"Please, do not seek to deny it, sir. I am fully aware that some of my preaching can on occasion appear somewhat, erm… radical… and whilst I am mostly tolerated in the pulpit some members of my congregation are wont to snigger behind my back and call me rakehell or debauchee. It was to counter this that I first began to tell my foolish tales, you know? In the hope that by so doing I might become more accepted by my flock. But it seems that this too has rebounded upon me. Oh, Mr Ellis, this is all most unfortunate, I agree, but we *must* excuse such behaviour. When people start to feel that what is happening in the world around them is beyond their ken or outside of their influence, spreading idle rumours, however improper, does seem to provide them with some rare comfort. Ah, and people are suffering so much of late. We must forever be ready to tolerate and to forgive, and in these troubled times so too must we be ready to do all we can to help - all we can."

Such was the vicar's sincerity; I could only believe that he spoke the truth and I almost began to feel that I should go easy on him. But I had seen him leering at Lizzie like a concupiscent goat, and I did know for a fact that he had been encouraging her to prance around her bedchamber in the middle of the night like a bare arsed Adamite. Despite this, however, I was once again struck by his apparent care and compassion towards those less fortunate, and I was impressed that he and others, including, it seemed, my dear Lizzie, would go so far out of their way in their desire to alleviate hardship and suffering in the village. Be damned if I'd let him off scot-free, though.

"Very well, Reverend," I said sternly. "I can appreciate that there is some measure of misunderstanding in this and so I will offer you my apologies for bursting in upon you in such an uncouth manner this evening."

"Which I am pleased to accept wholeheartedly, my boy," replied the vicar, sanctimoniously.

"But do not think that I in any way condone your unseemly attitude to Miss Saunders. It does you little credit as a man of the cloth to treat her no better than a common tavern wench, and I must demand that you desist, sir, lest I be forced to take further action."

And, leaving that vague threat in the air, I made to withdraw. But it seemed the vicar had not yet finished.

"I fear you do me wrong, Lieutenant," he said, laying his hand upon my arm. "I can but reiterate that I have no designs upon Elizabeth Saunders and I would most certainly not wish her to be in any way uncomfortable in my company. If I have made her so then I am deeply saddened by it. We work so closely, you see, and sometimes such familiarity makes one forget one's proper manners. Rest assured, sir, I will not be so forgetful of myself in future, and my dealings with Miss Saunders shall be naught but respectful. But wait, I have a notion that may appeal to you, and one that may also reassure you of my purest intentions. Mayhap you would consider joining us at our meetings in the narthex? I know you to be a learned man and a progressive one, and your erudition and experience would be a great asset to us in our endeavours. Do say that you will contemplate becoming one of our number, Mr Ellis. We would be delighted to be able to welcome you as an ex-officio member of the vestry committee for the duration of your stay with us."

"H'rumph," I snorted, clearing my throat. "I confess that the idea does appeal to me. I have come to feel quite a part of the community here of late and it would please me greatly to be able to contribute to the wellbeing of the village."

And it would please me greatly to keep a closer eye on you, my poxy, perverted parson, I thought.

"I shall consider your offer, Reverend, and I thank you for it. And now I will take my leave. Once again, please accept my apologies for disturbing you so violently, sir."

"Think nothing of it, Lieutenant. And I dare to hope that, in the event, much good will come of this inopportune meeting. Good night to you. Perkins will see you out. Perkins! The lieutenant is leaving us now. Pray see him to the door."

Dumped unceremoniously outside the door of the parsonage by a crotchety Perkins, I made my way back to the Anchor more content in my mind. I still didn't trust the Reverend Gildersleeve any further than I could spit, but his explanation and demeanour had satisfied me that he and Lizzie were not making the beast with two backs. I'faith, I found that I was not a little ashamed of thinking so ill of Lizzie. How could I have even imagined that she might contemplate having congress with that runty little swine? Such a thing was unthinkable. I could imagine her having congress with me, however, and I did, often. The images that had been conjured in my mind by the laudanum haunted me still, and the thought of Lizzie's delightfully provocative body, most gloriously displayed and writhing erotically before me in the firelight, fair maddened me with passion. At that moment I knew that, come what may, I must have her. She was fiercely her own woman and so I was sure by now that she must know whether or not she wanted me in turn. I therefore determined that, should the opportunity arise again, I would have no hesitation in casting aside my prissy, moralistic prudishness to take full advantage of whatever delicious favours my love might seek to bestow upon me.

CHAPTER 10

Next morning I awoke with a sore head, skinned knuckles and a swollen face, all of which caused some consternation when I appeared in the kitchen to break my fast.

"Mercy, Cap'n, whatever has happened to you now?" cried Sal when first she saw me.

"'Tis of no consequence, Sal," I said, stoically. "It is merely the result of a slight disagreement last night. There's no harm done, and I bear no grudges as a result."

"Sit you down and let me fetch some nutmeg and vinegar for your head, sir, and some wolf's bane for your cuts and bruises. And then you must tell me of all that has happened."

Sal hurried away and quickly returned with her salves, applying the wolf's bane unguent to my chin and gently stroking my head with the nutmeg and vinegar. Her soothing touch felt devilishly good after the rigours of the night. I relaxed in the chair and closed my eyes. As I sat, I fell to unburdening myself of some of my troubles.

"Sal," I said. "You must know I am sweet on Lizzie Saunders?"

"I think the whole of Canewdon knows that, sir," replied Sal, with a knowing look.

"No… I mean… properly sweet on her," I went on quietly. "Please do not breathe a word of this to anyone, but I think I love her."

"Oh, that's wonderful. Have you told her of this?"

"Not in so many words, Sal. But I shall, and right soon. But it grieves me that Lizzie appears to be the subject of some talk around the village concerning her relationship with Tom Gildersleeve. For sure, it is on that account that I came to blows with Aaron Rolfe last night. I heard him, Sal - outside by the rail - telling his spaniel, Sawkins, that Lizzie and Gildersleeve were wont to dance the blanket hornpipe together up at the church."

"Why, sir, that's just stupid talk, that is, and you should pay it no mind. Aaron Rolfe was ever a cod's head and is too full of himself by half. He has always been one who delights in the spreading of tittle-tattle and cares not who he injures in the process. And he seems to have gotten much worse lately, too. It's as if he's vexed by everyone and everything these days."

"Oh, I bear no grudge against Rolfe, Sal – or his mate. I fear there has been a lot to be angry about these past months," I said, sadly. "In fact, the vicar said as much to me when I confronted him about these rumours."

"What? You went to the vicar?" said Sal incredulously.

"I did. I got him out of his bed and demanded to know the truth about him and Lizzie. I was consumed with jealousy, you see?"

"Oh, sir, whatever possessed you…?"

"I know it was wrong of me, Sal, but I couldn't help myself. I think it was all to the good though. Gildersleeve was very contrite about the way he has been acting towards Lizzie recently and did convince me thoroughly that nothing sinful had ever taken place between them. He told me of the work they have been doing to improve the chances of a good crop this year and to help the poor people of the parish."

"He did?" said Sal, giving me what I thought to be quite a queer look. "Well, I suppose 'tis true there's many a poor soul about the village who has cause to be grateful for the vicar's charity."

"And I have decided that I want to assist in their endeavours. Gildersleeve has invited me onto the vestry committee, to work alongside him and Lizzie in distributing alms and suchlike, and I'm of a mind to take him up on his offer."

"Ah, distributing alms… of course… yes… I think that would be a most worthy thing to do, sir," Sal observed, quietly, beginning to clear away her potions.

"And I think that maybe you should discuss your decision with Miss Elizabeth, I am sure that she would be pleased to hear of it. I think also that she would be pleased to hear of your feelings for her."

"Do you *really* think so, Sal?"

"Yes, sir, I really do."

So, pausing only to make quick work of Sal's estimable bacon and eggs, I took myself off to pay a call on Lizzie. The maid, Susannah, once again showed me into the drawing room where, Mr Saunders already being at work supervising the bringing in of the corn for threshing, I was received by Lizzie and her mother. After the usual polite chit-chat, Mrs Saunders withdrew, leaving me alone with Lizzie. She looked wonderfully demure in a white linen cap and a loose, thigh length ivory linen shortgown, printed with an indigo floral pattern, which she wore with a single petticoat, and delicate ivory silk slippers.

Hearing her mother's footsteps receding into the hall the dear girl flew into my arms and kissed me full on the lips.

"Oh, Roger, what has happened to your face?" she asked anxiously. "Are you hurt?"

"A slight accident, nothing more," I reassured her, smiling. "You know what a clumsy gollumpus I can be."

We kissed again, more passionately this time, open mouthed and exploring each other with eager tongues. Breaking off, I gazed deep into the rich velvety brown pools of her eyes (they reminded me vaguely of old Hercules, truth to tell, but were none the less beautiful for all that) and I spoke softly to her.

"Lizzie... I love you..."

There, it was out, I had said that which I had never before said to another. I waited; terrified to see how my declaration had been received. Then, to my intense relief and overwhelming joy, the sweet *demoiselle* responded.

"And I you, Roger... I believe I have loved you ever since we were children together. You are so kind, and brave, and strong, and clever. Oh, I do so love you... please let me feel your kisses again, my darling..."

I drew her to me, closing my mouth over hers and feeling the warmth of her as she pressed hard up against me. I plucked at the topmost pin holding the front of her gown and, as she wore no stays, was able to easily slip my trembling hand inside to grasp one of the warm, soft and yielding mounds that nestled within.

"No my love, not now," Lizzie breathed, disengaging and stepping back slightly in order to rearrange her dress. "There will be time enough for that later, I promise. Now, come sit with me and tell me your news."

Seated on a walnut and leather *chaise longue* that had been set under the windows overlooking the garden, I provided Lizzie with a somewhat expurgated version of my meeting with the Reverend Gildersleeve.

"He spoke very highly of you Lizzie," I said. And he told me much about the compassionate and unselfish enterprises that he is undertaking with you and others to ensure the success of the harvest and to help the poor and needy."

"He told you that?" Lizzie seemed surprised. "He explained to you about our gatherings at the church, and what we do there?"

"Yes, he explained all, and I must say I am very impressed, and very interested in the whole thing. He has invited me to join with you at your next meeting, and I am pleased to tell you that I have determined to accept."

"Roger, this is most wonderful indeed. But, wait a while, so that I may make sure we are truly alone."

And with that, Lizzie rose and moved to the door. I watched as she peeped furtively through it and then quietly pulled it to. I own I was slightly nonplussed by this and wondered what to make of her behaviour - could she mean for us to resume our lovemaking? But no, having closed the door, Lizzie came back to sit beside me and went on, in a low voice.

"My dearest Roger, how I have longed for this, I am so happy that your wish is to join with us. Now we are together in this I have so much to explain to you, but you must promise me that you will not repeat to anyone that which I am about to tell you."

It was obviously a day for confidences, I thought, though I failed to see what could be so secret about a vestry meeting - mayhap it had something to do with the Freemasons or some such. I knew it to be a fact that the liberal principles espoused by that arcane brotherhood included both the furtherance of local government, and the practice of charitable endeavour.

"I promise, Lizzie," I said.

"Well, I'm not exactly sure how much Tom has told you, so I will start from the very beginning."

So, its Tom now, is it, thinks I. But I let it pass.

"I must tell you that the business in which we are involved is something that I think you might find difficult to accept, but it is nevertheless something with which you may find some sympathy - an idea that stretches back to a time long, long ago. Before even the advent of Christianity! Did you know that God had a wife, Roger? 'Tis true. It says as much in the Hebrew Scriptures. God's wife was called Asherah, and it is written in the *Book of Kings* that she was worshipped alongside God in his temple. And not only that, but it seems also that this Asherah is one and the same with the moon goddess that the ancient Greeks called Artemis and the Romans, Diana. She has even long been worshipped hereabouts, and that all through the mists of time, in her guise of the Great Mother - do you remember, I once told you of those curious stone statues that were found on the farm?"

"I remember. But, I don't understand, Lizzie. What has this to do with your work on the vestry committee?"

"Ah…" gasped Lizzie, biting her bottom lip, her eyes widening in realisation. "I begin to see that Tom has not perhaps furnished you with the whole truth. And that I may have misconstrued the substance and import of your discourse. But I have now embarked upon this tale and so needs must continue, trusting that, if you do truly love me as you say, you will understand. But first, I implore you; please say you will not think badly of me for this, Roger, please."

"Never in life, my dearest," I replied, earnestly. "On that I give my word."

However, I could only but stare in astonishment as Lizzie continued her narrative.

"You see, my religious beliefs are somewhat at odds with the more usual doctrines of the church, though it is true that they are closely connected," she said, solemnly. "This may shock you at first, but I believe that the world is governed not by one god alone, but rather by a pair of divine forces, the Goddess and the God."

"Christ on his cross!" I whispered, softly.

"Please, Roger, listen to what I have to say. The Goddess and the God are completely complementary in that their sacred union contributes to the continuance of life on earth, and demonstrates, without a doubt, the equal importance of both men and women in this world - which equality you well know to have always been central to my philosophies. And it seems there are others in Canewdon who are of a similar mind. It is because of this that I have become part of a small group of people from all around the village who are pleased to venerate femininity, the earth and nature as personified in the Goddess at the same time as we worship the orthodox male God, whom some call Yahweh or Allah and we ourselves call the Horned God. All of these things have been forgotten in modern Christianity, Roger - the Goddess is the true creator, whose boundless fertility is at the centre of all things and whose union with her husband ensures a bountiful harvest each year. Tom says that the poor crops we have seen of late can only be attributed to a failure in this holy congress. But he says too that it is possible, by what he calls a simple act of imitative magic, to compel the gods to renew their union and thus preserve the earth's fertility."

"Tom, says?"

"Yes. Tom. For it is Tom who is at the very centre of our group, or coven, as some of us are wont to call it in deference to those who have trodden this same path before us. Oh, Tom is so much more than a simple clergyman, Roger. He is our 'cunning man', and as such leads our meetings as the representative of the Horned God."

"But surely this is naught but witchcraft?" I spluttered.

"No, no! Not at all! We may indeed have recourse to some harmless practices that have been thus thought of in the past, but Tom has taught us all of this, and his teachings have helped us to see that it is all part of Holy

Writ. It is the true path. And it is plain that all of the Scriptures can be thus construed - saving those that were heavily edited by the men who first gathered them together in their misogynistic zeal, of course."

And at that point a shocking truth dawned upon me.

"Lizzie... You must tell me... Does this mean that what happened that night in the churchyard was not a vision, after all?"

"No, Roger it was not a vision. When you came to the churchyard in search of Tom Dowsett you inadvertently stumbled upon our *s'esbattre*, or as we say in English, our joyful frolic, a ritual we perform at full moon in praise of wholeness, motherhood and love. When you were seen by the others I felt compelled to involve you in the ceremony because of my deep feelings towards you. Feelings that, given your willing participation in the dance, I then knew must surely be reciprocated. And you were willing, were you not, Roger? Tell me you were pleased by that which you saw..."

I could not lie to her. Of course I was pleased with what I saw. Had not the thought of her dancing in the reddish yellow glow of the fire, whether real or imagined, lingered with me as a chimera ever since?

"I liked it right well, Lizzie," I confessed. "You are the most magnificent and irresistible creature I have ever seen. I love you, and long to hold and caress every line and curve of your body. But, what happened to me? How came I to be back at the inn?"

"You fainted, my love. Most likely as a result of the concussion that arose from the blow to your head. When you fell, everyone immediately became afraid for your safety and called a halt to the frolic so that you might be carried home. Once you had awoken we thought it best not to reveal the true facts of your experience to you just yet. But, now… now I think you may be ready… ready to join us in the dance. Please say you are, Roger…"

In truth, I did not know what to say. The idea of becoming a member of a witches' coven was both horrifying and ridiculous at the same time. But I did know that I wanted to love and to please Lizzie more than anything else in the world. And after all, it was probably no worse than all that silly nonsense perpetrated at the numerous so called Hell Fire Clubs that had proliferated since that damn fool Dashwood and his idiot friends first assuaged their hedonistic desires at Medmenham, over forty years ago. To blazes with it, I thought, it's high time I learned to live a little, in the same manner as everyone else!

"I think I am ready, Lizzie," I said. "When might the next meeting be held?"

"Oh that is truly marvellous!" Lizzie replied, clapping her hands together in that now familiar gesture of happiness. "Our next frolic is to be in less than two weeks' time and, as before, it will again take place in St Nicholas' churchyard. We shall meet at midnight on the thirtieth day of August - the night of the coming full moon. Oh, Roger, I am so happy that you have consented to join us in this. It will be so very special, you know? This time we will be directing our energy wholly towards maximising the yield from this year's crop, through the practice of that imitative magic that I have told you about. And as part of that I am to enter into a form of sacred marriage with the Horned God."

My eyebrows shot up.

"No, no…" said Lizzie, seeking to reassure me. "There is need to worry, my love, for the marriage will be symbolic only and, although the union will be carried out in a state of nature, you may be sure it will in no way involve any impropriety."

I recoiled at these *naïve* and innocent words, but before I could react further, Lizzie took hold of my arms and again sought to hold me close.

"Let us seal our bargain with another kiss," she beseeched.

So we did, and with several more besides. My hand once more explored beneath her shortgown and on this occasion was not repulsed. Neither were my lips denied as, upon laying bare her bounteous bosom, I applied them in conjunction with my fervent tongue in the raising of her delectable extremities. Becoming bolder, I dared to raise her petticoat and tenderly part her legs so as to insinuate my fingers into the sensuous dampness of Cupid's arbour and pay homage to that sweet spot situate therein. Lizzie's breathing became heavy and she stiffened, gasping in joyous abandon before eventually melting into my arms, a lock of hair escaping prettily from beneath her cap.

And all throughout I paid no heed to my love's revelation that she was about to enter into a strange and unearthly coupling with an eminent member of the Church of England masquerading as some preternatural horned spirit of the forest.

How Lizzie and I were left to ourselves and did not come to be interrupted in our passions I could not tell, but left to ourselves we were. After a little time we regained our composure and sat awhile smiling and holding hands as lovers do. It was not until later that night that the enormity of Lizzie's disclosure hit me - as hard as if I had been tipped another muzzler by Aaron Rolfe. I had been right about the vicar all along and I was willing to wager that he was manipulating Lizzie against her will. I was now sure that he had designs upon the girl and that this supposed 'sacred marriage' with the so called Horned God would in truth be far from symbolic. Well, I'll be damned if I'll let anything like that happen, I decided, there must be some way to stop the lecherous Levite and wrest Lizzie from his odious clutches.

To this end, I thought to reveal my suspicions to the squire, and so took myself off to the Hall to seek audience with him. Sir Henry received me in his study, where last I had stood following my adventure with the footpad who had waylaid me and Lizzie on the road to Paglesham. The squire greeted me cordially and bade me be seated, enquiring of the reason for my visit. As I launched into my denunciation of the Reverend Gildersleeve I was acutely aware that I must have a care in the telling of my story in order to ensure that Lizzie's honour be not compromised – and not to mention mine own.

"Sir Henry," I began. "I have come here on a most delicate errand concerning the conduct of the vicar of St Nicholas' and I pray that you will hear me out as I apprise you of his recent comportment with regard to Nathaniel Saunders' daughter, Elizabeth."

"Of course, Lieutenant," said the squire, fixing me with a quizzical stare. "Please do go on. It is my duty as squire, and as magistrate, to hear any concerns that you or others may have in relation to the appointed officers of the church."

"Thank you, Sir Henry. I am afraid that there may be no easy way to say this, but that I have reason to believe that the reverend harbours an inappropriate and impure desire for Miss Saunders, and that, in the furtherance of that desire, he has been filling her head with wild and unseemly accounts of witchcraft and sorcery, by which means he intends to draw her into some manner of perverted pagan ritual in the hope that he may thus assault her maidenhead and have his way with her."

"Good god, sir!" exclaimed the squire. "Do you have any idea what you are saying? These are preposterous allegations! Upon what evidence do you base these scandalous accusations, sir?"

"Rumours abound in the village of the vicar's penchant for young women, Sir Henry, and I have witnessed at first-hand how he makes sheep's eyes at Miss Saunders at every opportunity. Why, you must surely have seen for yourself how he ogled the poor girl when we dined at the Hall a few weeks' back. And, as for the stories, Miss Saunders has told me exactly what has been said to her, and for sure I have no reason to doubt her veracity."

"Rumours, Lieutenant?" Sir Henry thundered - plainly the interview was not going well. "What care I for rumours? Idle tittle-tattle spread by ignorant peasants. I'll have no truck with it, b'Gad! I will allow that the reverend has an eye for the ladies, but don't we all, sir, don't we all? Damme, Miss Saunders is uncommon attractive, is she not? And she is not above shamelessly flaunting her charms when opportunity arises. Who would blame the almighty himself were he to be tempted by such a saucy little minx, eh? Why, I know you to have designs upon her yourself, sir - don't bother to deny it. You spend half your days mooning over the wench and the other half trying to get under her skirts. No, I'll not hear of any of this. I refuse to countenance such things of the reverend, whom I know for certain to be a pious and godly cleric. Elizabeth Saunders is naught but a wanton young girl, and is undoubtedly making up wicked lies to gain revenge on the vicar for some or other minor perceived indiscretion."

"I, I'm sorry that you feel this way, Sir Henry," I

stammered, flinching in the face of the squire's unrelenting cannonade. "And I can see that you will allow me no credence in this case. I can only hope that you are proven right in your estimation of the vicar and that he is of such good character as you are wont to paint him."

"The vicar is a fine man, boy, and I'll thank you not to forget it. Now, I will hear no more of this. I am of a mind to excuse your excesses on this occasion for I know you to be a brave and honest lad at heart and I can only suppose that you are still suffering the effects of your illness and your fall. But, and mark me well on this, if you should repeat this scurrilous attack on the vicar's integrity, I will have you arraigned for false witness. You see if I don't. Now, be gone, sir, and be about your business."

Thus dismissed, I returned to the Anchor dispirited and downcast. It was certain that I would receive no official support in my attempts to thwart Gildersleeve's impious machinations and must therefore rely on my own mettle and take matters solely into mine own hands.

CHAPTER 11

Try as I might, I could not readily come up with a plan to break up Gildersleeve's jolly frolic and frustrate him in his efforts to deflower my Lizzie. My first thought was to deal directly with him and lend him such a polt in the nutmegs that would drive all thoughts of symbolic union with young girls in their birth-day suits right out of his scabby head. However, I knew from Sir Henry's reaction to my earlier assertions, that to do so would see me quickly fall foul of the law. Of course, I could always have recourse to the law myself. A letter dashed off quickly to the Bishop might see the vicar taken up under the Witchcraft Act, which legislation, although it abolished the crime of witchcraft itself, still considered the *pretence* of witchcraft an offence against our enlightened State.

But, despise him though I did, I could not bring myself to tread this path. The penalty for being found guilty of pretending to exercise or otherwise use witchcraft or sorcery was fine, imprisonment, and a lengthy spell in the pillory, and I would not in any conscience wish this latter fate upon any but the most evil of criminals. The purpose of the pillory was the public humiliation of the malefactor, but in practice, as well as being jeered at and mocked by the populace, those unfortunates so placed would be pelted with seven shades of shite and, more often than not, with more injurious missiles such as stones, bricks, or broken glass, so that they might eventually be maimed, blinded, or worse. Even Gildersleeve did not deserve that. There was, after all, an outside chance that the man was not as black hearted as I thought him, and that his half-witted encouragement of consensual nudity and symbolic ritual might not necessarily be predatory *per se*. You see, I still could not shake the belief that the vicar did truly care for those subject to his ministrations, or indeed the suspicion that he seriously thought that persuading people to dance his mutton headed jigs around the churchyard in the buff would somehow help the village survive the winter. So, there was nothing else for it. I had to play along with the charade for as long as possible hoping that, should it become necessary to extract Lizzie from the vicar's power, I would be able to soundly grasp the nettle and keep her from any harm.

To save my mind from dwelling upon these thoughts as I awaited the appointed evening of the frolic, I went once more to the farm to assist in the threshing and winnowing of the corn. This process was carried out in a massive timber barn wherein wooden boards had been affixed to the floor to allow the corn to be spread out, such wooden boards being considered less likely to cause bruising to the grain. The huge double doors at each end of the barn were opened to afford enough natural light by which to work, and a group of us, armed with flails, were put to work beating small quantities of the corn so as to knock the grain out from the husk. At first, in my agitated state, I most likely beat more furiously than my fellows found comfortable, swinging my two large sticks with such gusto that the swipple whirled dangerously around my shoulders causing a wide space to be cleared around me.

"Easy, lad," warned one of the other fellows in the barn, not unkindly. "Remember yer not settin' about them Frenchies now, y'know? Slow an' steady, that's the way of it. No use wearin' y'self out like that - we've a long way t'go."

After the grain had been threshed, the stalks were carefully raked away and the grain and chaff was put into sacks to be placed on a raised platform out of the reach of rats. What sort of rats, I wondered grumpily, black rats, grey rats, or mayhap its bloody cu-rats we should be looking out for? Later, the grain and chaff was separated by winnowing, whereby we tossed the mixture into the air so that the wind carried away the chaff while the grain fell back on to the threshing floor to be graded before being carted off to the mill. As I stared idly up at the dusty cloud of winnowing corn my eye was drawn to some curious circular marks that appeared to have been scratched deeply into the fabric of the building long ago. There were two circles, one inside the other, and in their centre a cross had been scored alongside the letter M.

"Them's witches marks," says another old cove, who had been watching me for some while. "They was placed 'ere when the barn was built. They ward off witches an' buggans, they do. The M in the middle stands fer the Virgin Mary."

Well, if that's their purpose, the marks are not doing much of a job, I thought privately, for if I am to believe all that I have heard lately, there's a witch in the making standing right here.

"Pfft," I sneered. "No such thing as witches…"

"Mind what you say, sir. Satan is ever at our elbow, 'e is," replied the old fellow. "An' y'should always be wary of the power of those that consort with 'im. The old 'uns' knew all about that, they did, an' that's why they carved these marks in the walls. Mark me well, the world then was full o'dangers, and it is still. Dangers that're both physical and spiritual. Take 'eed o'these marks, sir, an' don't you ever be scornful of 'em, fer they're put there to make it a safer place for us all."

"Yes, of course." I said guiltily. "I'm sorry, please do forgive me. It was wrong of me to scoff. I am ever quick to profess a great respect for, and tolerance of, all faiths and creeds, and so if I am to be true to myself in this assertion then I have no right to fly in the face of anyone's beliefs."

"Don't you worry none, sir, I know y'meant no 'arm by your words, f'sure. 'An maybe y'right anyways an' there ain't nuffin' in it after all. But I'd still advise you t'be wary all the same…"

With the threshing to occupy my hands, time passed quickly and before I knew it the day of the frolic was upon me. Lizzie had instructed me to arrive at the churchyard just before the stroke of midnight, when she and the others would be there to meet me. I was to wear loose clothing, she said, and I was to be sure that no one observed my leaving the Anchor to make my way to the rendezvous. Accordingly, that night I warily descended from my room clad only in a white linen shirt, breeches, low-heeled shoes, and woollen stockings, and being at pains to avoid the kitchen and its usual groggified occupants, exited the inn by way of the back door into the stable block. The night was warm, but I still felt a chill of anticipation as, rather than take the direct route along the High Street, I crossed the Green and from there entered Church Lane so as to approach the west gate of the churchyard. High above, the moon was casting its silvery light onto the tops of the trees, and on to the looming tower of St Nicholas, through a curtain of thin, patchy cloud. The nearer I came to the gate the more the moonlight combined with the reflected flames and sharp crackle of the fire that had been lit beneath the tower, investing the entire scene with an eldritch aura redolent of nothing less than an earthly manifestation of the ethereal realm of the Queen of Elphame herself. Despite my reservations I began to feel the excitement building within me. Gad, but this was an adventure, wasn't it just!

Those whom I took to be the other members of the coven were already present. All were dressed in simple white robes, the voluminous cowls of which had been pulled up over their heads and thus served to mask their faces. Two of them were marking the boundary of a wide circle around the fire with long straight blades, as I supposed, to create a magical or perhaps somehow sacred space. I entered and moved closer to the fire, taking stance just off to the side of the assembled acolytes. Not one of them appeared to pay me any mind whatsoever. The circle completed, all attention was fixed on the great wooden Devil door set into the base of the tower. Slowly, that ominous portal swung open and the black robed figure of the Reverend Gildersleeve stepped forward into the light. As before, Gildersleeve wore his horned cap, but this time he eschewed his oaten pipe, instead wielding a heavy black handled broadsword in his right hand and holding a curved, white hilted dagger, that was remarkably similar to the sickle I had used in the fields, in his left. In a loud, authoritative voice, and raising both weapons above his head, the self-styled 'Horned God' then called upon the members of the coven to enter the circle.

"Hear me!" he bellowed. "For I call upon you as did Thanatos call upon the Goddess on her journey to the underworld to solve the mysteries of life. Divest thy selves of thy clothing; lay aside thy ornaments; for naught but thine own selves may you bring with you into my domain."

I could scarce catch my breath as, obedient to the word of the Horned God, the five members of the coven threw off their robes and walked naked into the circle. It was then that I knew them - and I knew them right well. Tallest amongst them stood Sir Henry Spurgeon, the squire, his hair loose about his shoulders and his hard, muscular body clearly defined by the light of the fire. Beside him was his wife, Lady Mary, unashamedly displaying full breasts, gently rounded belly, and plump, yet still inviting, thighs. Then, astonishingly, there was Annie Saunders, her matronly form shaped by long years of motherhood and nurture. And Sally Dowsett too was within the circle, her long smooth limbs and well-formed bosom, already in part familiar to me, now completely revealed in all their glory. Finally, my gaze fell upon Lizzie, and I was once again struck by her sensuous beauty and the overt eroticism of her nubile young body. I noticed that I was shivering slightly, but not with the cold. This was forbidden fruit indeed, and I knew that I wanted to taste more of it.

Now entering the circle himself, the Horned God laid his sword and dagger upon the ground and beckoned Lizzie forward. I watched her intently as she approached to stand meekly before him, her head bowed submissively. I was vaguely aware that, by rights, I should act now to stop this unwholesome affair going further, but I was powerless to do more than look on slack-jawed and stupid, with a mixture of increasing arousal and expectation as the Horned God knelt to kiss her feet.

"Blessed be these feet that brought you to this path," he declared, rising and offering a hand to Lizzie. "Come take your place beside me as High Priestess and exalted representative of the Goddess, Asherah."

With Lizzie and Gildersleeve now side by side and facing the others across the fire, the Horned God addressed the meeting.

"Let us now consider the business that brings us together this night. First, I am told that we have a new postulant seeking admission as the sixth practitioner of our blessed order. Who is it that is to be welcomed into our midst? Who is it that seeks to understand the three overarching truths of our continued existence - birth, death and rebirth?'

At this, all eyes turned to me and I felt inexplicably compelled to move toward the fire.

"Strip him, and have him step lightly into the circle," commanded the Horned God.

I offered no resistance as Sal came to me, sublime, statuesque, and seductive in her nakedness, unlacing my shirt and sliding it off my shoulders. Annie Saunders crouched down to remove first my shoes and then my stockings, carefully folding them and setting them upon the sward while Sal unfastened the buttons

174

on my breeches and eased them unhurriedly down my hips, lingering appreciatively over my stiffening pintle. Finally, I stood tall and proud before them, as bare as they, revelling in the knowledge that my body, honed as it was from weeks of work on the farm, was plainly being looked upon with some favour.

Taking me by the arms, Sal and Annie propelled me gently into the circle.

"I am pleased to see you here at last, Roger," grinned Gildersleeve. "And, as is most evident, uncommon eager to play your part in our sacrament. Now, brothers and sisters, it is time! Let us begin the dance and by our actions call upon God and upon Asherah, his divine consort, to renew their holy congress and bring fresh fertility to the earth."

And, so speaking, the Horned God retreated from the circle and hopped up to take his seat on the table tomb, producing his pipe from somewhere deep inside the folds of his robe. Sir Henry cleared away the Horned God's weapons from the circle and Lady Mary began to beat a slow rhythm upon a small drum skin.

"Roger!" called Gildersleeve, loudly. "You may approach the Goddess."

I held out my hands to Lizzie and, smiling up at me, she took them in hers and drew me closer. I inclined my head and our lips touched in an electromagnetic apotheosis that would have been worthy of study by Signor Galvani.

"Now my love," she breathed. "Now is the time

to finish the dance…"

The beat of the drum and the swirl of the Horned God's pipe echoed around us as the coven began to move sunwise about the circle, slowly at first and then building to a frenzied crescendo as we leapt and cavorted round the flames. Suddenly the music ceased and we collapsed breathless on the turf.

After some moments I rose to sit upon my haunches and saw that Lizzie was close beside me. We embraced, feeling the heat of the fire and the warmth of our bodies as we settled to the task of exploring every inch of each other with hands and lips. Pausing a moment I saw that Sir Henry and Lady Mary were similarly engaged, stretched out on the floor with the squire's arse going like a Newcomen engine, and that Sal and Annie Saunders had also joined together in an ecstatic exhibition of Sapphic delight. Not being actively involved and still seated upon his tomb, Gildersleeve had hitched his robe up to his waist and was fumbling beneath as he observed the scene being played out before him. Mayhap he is stowing his pipe, I remember thinking, just before Lizzie reached up to once more enfold me in her arms. Pressing her mouth on mine she gently pulled me down beside her, our perspiration mingling with the dew on the grass to cause our limbs to slip and slide as I rolled over to lie between her lovely long legs. Guiding me up and in between, she locked those legs around me as I thrust away for all I was worth, caring not one jot for whosoever might be watching.

Eventually, our love being sated, we sat a while by the fire sharing tender kisses and caresses, sometimes catching a glimpse of the others as they too basked in the afterglow of their intercourse. I was perhaps conscious of a slight feeling of shame at what we had done, but overall I was enraptured by the experience. Whether it was the thrill of breaking the taboo that kept such excesses behind closed doors, the erotic potency of feeling that we might have been discovered at any time by other folk in the village, or the simple idea that to be watched in that way must surely be an affirmation of my good looks and sexuality, I did not know. It might well have been a combination of all three. But what I did know was that I could not wait to do it all over again.

Having recovered his two blades, the Horned God eventually re-entered the circle and there followed a tedious, pseudo-ecumenical litany of prayers to the divine couple, culminating in a bizarre vote of thanks for the harvest.

"Blessed are the Maiden, the Mother, and the Minerva," intoned Gildersleeve, raising his broadsword and dagger in the air. "Blessed are the Horned God and the divine Asherah! Great gods whose union brings life to all, we ask for your blessings on this night of moonlight and fire. As your gentle rain impregnates the earth and seeds grow in the warmth of the sun, we offer our prayers and our thanks to you for the continuing gift of fertility."

"Blessed be the sacred union!" responded the

coven in liturgy. "Blessed be those who have joined together this night!"

"So, brothers and sisters, who's for cakes and ale?" shouted the reverend, happily.

And with that, he led us back through the Devil door and into the church, where we dressed before gathering in the narthex to partake of ale, wine and feasting 'to honour the Goddess and her great abundance and richness' as Gildersleeve put it. I was welcomed profusely by everyone, Sal and Annie smiling broadly as they pressed Apple Charlotte and Ratafia biscuits into my hands, while Lady Mary filled my cup with ale. Even Sir Henry greeted me heartily, apologising for the rough treatment he had meted out the week before.

"I had no idea that you had the intention of joining with us, m'boy," he drawled. "Welcome aboard… shipmate! I'm right sorry to have put a flea in your ear the other day, but you took me somewhat by surprise, don't y'know? And d'you see now, y'had no reason to doubt the reverend's intentions towards your lady love, did ye? No, no reason at all, haw, haw!"

It was for all the world as if I were attending a genteel ladies' tea party and, in my euphoric state, I found that I had no shame in being amongst these people, despite having just engaged in the most intimate of acts in front of their very eyes. I said as much to Lizzie who seemed mightily pleased for me.

"Ah, Roger," she replied. "It is so wonderful to

hear you speak in this way. In becoming one with the Goddess you have truly transcended your innate desire for conformity and you will soon find that you have embarked upon a journey that will, in time, allow you to fully discover those parts within you that have hitherto been suppressed."

"You are right, Lizzie. Tonight I experienced such pleasure as I never have before and where once I was reserved and prudish, quick to find shame in the physical manifestations of love and sex, I can now see that such things are as essential a part of nature as I am myself."

"And if none are harmed by our actions, who is it that can raise a hand against us?"

"Yes, indeed. I confess that I can now more readily appreciate that tolerance and freedom to act, when tempered with responsibility of course, does seem to sit at the centre of all things. If what we do maximises pleasure, happiness and the greater good then mayhap it might be the case that we are actually morally obliged to continue with it. And so, if it is true that a symbolic sacred marriage will help ensure that the earth yields a bounteous harvest, we must surely be free to consummate that union, for without such freedom, and its natural expression in physical love, why, it may even be that the earth itself is like to die and, dare I say, perhaps all of mankind along with it."

You might well think that I was laying it on with a trowel but, having come this far in the performance, I was determined to give myself the best chance I could of being able to solicit an encore. Truth to tell, I would probably have acquiesced to a voyage to the moon and back in one of Monsieur Montgolfier's balloons if it would have helped get me back outside under the stars with Lizzie in my arms, even for just one more bout.

Whilst we were talking, the Reverend Gildersleeve joined us, sliding his arm around Lizzie's waist. I noticed that she did not resist.

"So, now you know all, young man," he said, ingratiatingly. "You have been of interest to us ever since you arrived in the eye of the storm, on the night our sister Biddy died. For some while now our dear Elizabeth, in fulfilment of her role as High Priestess, has been seeking to recruit you in Biddy's place as the sixth member of our order."

"I have, 'tis true," says Lizzie. "But you do forgive me for that, don't you, Roger? You are content to have been so artfully used? Please tell me that you are."

What could I say, other than that I was, at that moment at least, very content indeed?

"So, that poor woman I saw buried at the crossroads was a member of the coven too?" I asked the vicar. "Do you then know the reason for her so sadly taking her own life?"

"Yes, Biddy was one of us. But, in the interest of there being no secrets kept between us, I must tell you that she did not in truth commit suicide but instead died of a sudden infarction, brought on by infirmity. I am afraid that Sir Henry and I persuaded Joseph

Lipscomb to acquiesce in a verdict of suicide in order that Biddy might be buried at the crossroads."

"What?" I yelped, shocked to hear such a thing. "You brought in a false verdict? For what cause? Surely if Biddy Baker shared in your... er... our... belief in Asherah as the true consort of the Lord God you should never have allowed her mortal remains to have been treated in that dreadful way?"

"Sadly, our sister Biddy had strayed from the right hand path, Roger. That is to say the true path. She believed that her will was right to be done, no matter what the consequence, and she was also wont to rebel against the wider teachings of the church, preferring to adhere to her own personal credo, which I am afraid to say was itself simply a crude form of anarchy. She was, in short, what was once termed a black witch, ever ready to threaten or to curse, and as such the people of the village had the right to be protected against her, even in death."

"Good God!" I exclaimed.

"Roger," Lizzie interrupted quickly, lest our conversation take the same ugly turn as it had during dinner at Canewdon Hall. "Do you not see that this was your destiny? To stay with us and help cure the ills the poor people around us are suffering?"

And I think then that I did, and though it was certain that the vicar and I would never in life aspire to true comradeship, I therefore resigned myself to remaining in Canewdon as part of the coven, and doing as much as I possibly could to ensure a bountiful harvest each and every year. Especially if that meant that I could continue to tumble in the hay with my darling Lizzie.

CHAPTER 12

During the first, very hot, week of September the harvest was finally completed and the grain brought to the mill. Canewdon Mill was a fine post mill with roller reefed sails, built on a single-storey roundhouse and boasting an adjoining grain drying kiln. Like the workhouse, it been built only recently for the common benefit of the village at the behest of the vestry committee, and had been funded by money raised by voluntary subscriptions. Hugh Nichols, the miller, was also Canewdon's baker and, at times when there was little or no wind to mill, he operated a small, tidy bakehouse in the High Street. This year it seemed that the combination of fine weather and healthy crops (with perhaps some little spiritual help from the coven) would result in sufficient flour both to supply the village's own needs and provide surplus enough for Nichols to turn a fine profit from sales in Rayleigh, Rochford and beyond.

Suffice to say the end of the harvest was the source of great merrymaking. When the *cailleac*, or last sheaf, was left alone in the field, the men had fallen solemnly into line to harvest it by means of throwing sickles at it until it was cut - none there present wishing to be held solely accountable for angering John Barleycorn, the spirit of the corn, whom they believed resided therein. This last sheaf was then made into a large and elaborate corn doll, fashioned in in the shape of a ring terret, and carried in grand procession back to the Hall. Later, following the delivery of the last wagonload of grain to the mill, the squire provided a lavish supper for everyone who had helped in the harvest.

A long narrow table was placed on the lawn to the rear of the house and rich and poor alike sat down to dine regally on roast goose with sausage and apple stuffing, and fricassee of rabbit, washed down with cider, ale, and wine. In the centre of the groaning table sat the corn doll, a reminder, to me at least, that this would not be the last of the celebrations. You see, you can be sure that, for myself, I was looking forward three weeks to the twenty-eighth of September, the night of the Harvest Moon, whereupon the brothers and sisters of the coven would next meet to perform our Lammas dances and to give thanks for the harvest in our own special way.

Supper being cleared away there was music and dancing, and I was pleased to join Lizzie and her mother in several sets, including *Fickle Fanny*, *Cuckolds all a-row,* and *Epping Forest,* the latter involving much playfulness and kissing amongst all concerned. It was during a break from the dancing, however, that I became aware that Sir Henry had been accosted by an agitated looking fellow whose face I had not before seen. He appeared to be regaling the squire with some long story, accompanied by a great deal of hand waving and gesticulation. Quietening the man, Sir Henry took him in tow, the both steering in my direction.

"Roger," said the squire in a low voice, beckoning me to one side. "I have received grave news. Do not be alarmed, but it would seem that there has been a considerable amount of trouble in Paglesham, with rioting and other excesses likely to spread to Canewdon ere soon."

"How so, Sir Henry?" I asked. "What in Heaven's name has been happening?"

"This man has travelled post haste from Paglesham and tells me that a great number of people gathered there this morning, supposedly to remonstrate peacefully with Thomas Lamb and other landowners thereabouts concerning their management of this year's crops. However, it seems that certain agitators were claiming loudly that, owing to the farmers' undue laxity and negligence, the general populace were like to suffer extreme hardship and privation next year. As a result the mood of the mob turned and the gathering quickly became unruly."

"That's right, sir," put in the messenger. "They was all outside the Plough and Sail inn, where the farmers were shut up inside transacting their business. Shoutin' an' ollerin' fit to raise the Devil 'isself, they were. Then someone lobbed a brick through one of the windows and the crowd started to get nasty, 'ammerin' on the door and threatenin' blue murder. When they couldn't get in they moved on to the shops all around, breaking into the grocer's and the baker's to take whatever they wanted. Sam Perry, the baker, was sadly ill-used, 'e was - endin' up with is 'ead broke when 'e tried to keep 'em from firin' 'is bakery. Then someone started stirrin' 'em up even more, sayin' that you 'ad grain and flour aplenty stacked up in your mill, an' that it wasn't fair an' all when they 'ad nothin', an' that they shouldn't put up with it, an' should come over an' take their share. So a gang of 'em, two score or more, 'as set out to do 'is biddin', marchin' along the road from Paglesham, breakin' windows an' settin' fires as they go along. My sister an' 'er 'usband live 'ere in Canewdon, sir, an' I wouldn't want anythin' bad to 'appen to them, so I legged it over 'ere as quick as I could to tell you they was a'comin'."

"How far behind you are these ruffians?" I demanded.

"'Bout an 'our or so at least, sir, by my reckonin'. They're not 'urryin' their selves I don't think."

"Very well, I thank you for your timely warning, Mr…?"

"Cook, sir, Will Cook."

"You have done well, Mr Cook. Sir Henry, it

appears that we have a little time to prepare a warm welcome for these bullies. Pray you, rouse as many men as you can and get you down to the mill ready to read the Riot Act. I will see Lizzie and her mother safe home; then I will call out the constable and join you there."

As Sir Henry called an end to the festivities and began rounding up able volunteers, I hurried over to where Lizzie and Annie Saunders were sitting in order to apprise them of the situation.

"Please do not be afraid, ladies," I urged. "But it appears that some Yahoos from Paglesham are on their way here, bent on raiding the mill and stealing the stores of flour and grain. Sir Henry and I are getting some people together to prevent it but first I must get you home and out of harm's way. So, if you will but gather your things, we shall lose no time and be off."

"But what of Mr Saunders, Roger," Lizzie's mother asked, her voice trembling slightly. "Where is he? Is he not coming with us?"

"Mr Saunders is with the squire, madam. He intends to assist in the defence."

"Oh, Roger!" gasped Lizzie. "Father is too old for such things. You will keep him from harm, won't you?"

"Of course my dear, I will guard him with my life, as I guard you both. Now, quickly, we must be off, for once I have seen you safe I must fetch Willie Fisher and join the others at the mill."

Along with some others who were also heading

back to their homes, we hurried as fast as we could down the hill, and along the High Street, reaching the Saunders' house in just under fifteen minutes. I bade the ladies repair inside and urged them to make the place as secure as possible by barring the doors and closing the shutters on the windows, before dashing on to the Anchor and diving inside. Sal had not attended the harvest supper and was in the kitchen with, as usual, Cuddy Smith and Ned Symonds. Tom Dowsett was in the stables attending to Hercules.

"Quick, Sal!" I yelled. "Get Tom back indoors and get the place locked up. There's a mob coming across from Paglesham intent on ransacking the village. Cuddy… Ned…, get you away home and out of the way of any trouble. I'm off to find the constable by and by, and will be heading to the mill after that to see what can be done to stop them."

"Bugger that, Cap'n," says Cuddy. "We're with you, eh Ned?"

"Right you are, Cuddy," agreed Ned. "Let no one say that we ever ran shy of a fight!"

"Very well, off to the mill with you then," I said, somewhat reluctantly. "The Squire and the Reeve are on their way there now. Join with them and wait for me."

Taking the stairs two at a time I ran to my room and threw open my sea chest, rummaging around in it to find my uniform coat. A little show of authority might be all that's needed to tip the balance here I thought as I pulled it on and strapped my sword around my waist. Having reassured myself that the blade was loose in its scabbard, I rushed downstairs again and out in search of Constable Fisher.

Eventually, I arrived at the mill, with the constable puffing and blowing in my wake. There was a goodly crowd present, some armed with stout sticks, staves and clubs, and others hefting stones, half bricks and other missiles. Aaron Rolfe was there, wielding a large double pick hilt, and Sawkins, his crony, toted a singlestick, which was a type of wooden sword with a cup-shaped hilt of basket-work much used in competitive backsword play. Two or three of the squire's servants carried long arms and the squire himself had an expensive looking pistol jammed into the waistband of his breeches. All in all, they appeared as bloodthirsty a crew of cut-throats as had ever sailed the Spanish Main! Joseph Lipscomb had been had been called out to act as our surgeon and, surprisingly, I saw that the Reverend Gildersleeve had also rallied to the cause.

"Reverend," I hailed. "Surely this is no place for you?"

"Dammit, Lieutenant," the reverend snapped back. "I have every right to be here. No man will seek to rob me of my ten *per centum* while I live!"

Of course, I knew that Gildersleeve did have a stake in the game, for not only had he received a tenth of the price paid for the grain under the ancient Statute of Westminster but he was also entitled to a personal tithe on the profits made by the mill. And, even though the imposition of personal tithes was now exceeding rare, had not the vicar of Uttoxeter, only a few years back, instituted a successful action in the ecclesiastical court against one of his parishioners for non-payment of such a tithe? Mercenary old black fly, I thought, uncharitably, as I turned my attention to the proper organisation of the defences, for sure the greatest drawback on the harvest was the parson who pressed for his tithes.

Now, up until this moment you may well have thought me somewhat of a clown, blundering about and, more often than not, ending up falling head over heels and landing on my arse, but, and you can have my word on this, I was now in my element. Twelve years in the Service had rendered me well used to command and given me great confidence in my skill at arms. I knew that with a sword in my hand and good men at my back I could take on all comers. In the mill yard were parked two enormous four wheeled wagons, the sides of which were made up of ladders strapped in place to hold hay or grain, and I decided to use these to create a makeshift fortification or barricado, such as those so beloved by the Frogs during the revolution.

"You there!" I bellowed at a group of men standing idly by the door of the drying kiln. "Get those wagons out of the yard and haul them across to block the street. The rest of you, lay hold of anything you can carry and pile it up against the wagons to create a defensive wall. And make haste. The bastards will be upon us at any moment."

As the wagons were dragged ponderously into place and a whole assortment of household furniture, including chairs, dressers, mirror frames, and shutters, was brought out and heaped around them, Nichols the miller piped up in protest.

"Lieutenant Ellis, you can't do this! Sir Henry, stop them, they are tearing my mill apart!"

"Less of y'noise, sir," barked the squire. "Better y'lose a few sticks of furniture than we all lose our livelihoods, or worse. Carry on Mr Ellis. Is there anything I can do to assist you?"

"Make sure the barricado is anchored on the buildings either side of the street, Sir Henry, lest our friends seek to turn our flanks. Then I'd admire if you could help me muster the men behind it."

We took station upon the barricado just as the light was beginning to fade and the men of Paglesham hove into view, a great throng of thieves and rufflers, carrying lighted torches and armed *cap a pie* with wooden cudgels, long staves and other blunt instruments. Sighting our makeshift stockade, they pulled up short and fell to jeering and calling for us to get down out of the way so that they could gain access to what they considered should rightfully be theirs. Motioning for the squire to follow me, I drew my sword and stepped up on to one of the carts.

"Hear me now!" I yelled at the top of my voice. "In the name of the King I demand that you cease and desist in this mischief. Leave this place and return to your homes. The magistrate here will shortly read of the Riot Act, so be aware that any who hear it must disperse within the hour or be guilty of a felony punishable by death."

Dire warning, indeed. And one which elicited a chorus of worried rumblings on the part of the Paglesham men.

"Sir Henry, if you please…?"

The squire stepped forward onto the cart and, in a clear loud tone, started to recite the form of words that would authorise the use of force to disperse the crowd and indemnify those assisting with the dispersal in the event that any of them were injured or killed.

"Our sovereign lord the King chargeth and commandeth all persons, being assembled, immediately to disperse themselves, and peaceably to depart to their habitations, or to their lawful business, upon the pains contained in the Act made in the first year of King George, for preventing tumults and riotous assemblies. God save the King!"

At first, the ominous words of the proclamation stilled the crowd, but then one man, a small, scruffy, rodentian man, sang out.

"Look there, boys! That's the bugger who killed Jemmy Webb. 'Ush the cull, lads and lets 'ave at the corn!"

To my amazement, I saw that it was Ratty, my old adversary from the Paglesham Road. Evidently the man

Webb that he had cited was the sour faced man I had shot and who had been buried so unceremoniously at St Nicholas'. On hearing Ratty's call to arms the Paglesham men surged forward, only to be checked again as, on the squire's instruction, our musketeers loosed a ragged volley into the air above their heads.

"I warn you!" I roared. "Cease this folly now or face the consequences!"

"Fuck you!" Ratty shouted in reply. "Better to be shot than starved. Come on lads, scrag the cunts!"

This time our foes rushed forward in earnest and were met with a hail of beggars' bullets and brickbats which knocked over a few of them before they reached the barricado. Undeterred, torches were thrown, causing some of our number to be called to the task of extinguishing several small fires, and the Paglesham men started to climb and to pull at the lumber that we had hastily stacked in their path, so that we were soon engaged in some very unpleasant hand to hand fighting.

A man's face appeared over the side of the cart whereupon I was standing and I swung a boot at it, sending the man flying backwards into the press of bodies behind. Hands reached out to claw at my legs and a big, bald headed son of a bitch who had gained the deck of my wagon raised a cudgel with which to strike me down. I deflected the blow with my sword, its edge cutting deep into the shaft of the clumsy weapon, and wishing to avoid inflicting mortal injury, I smashed a straight left into the face of my assailant, feeling the cartilage of his nose crack under my knuckles. All around me, men were cursing and bawling and weapons were being plied as my motley crew of defenders fought desperately to throw back the assault. Two, then three more men made it on to the cart and I swung my blade in a wide arc to keep them at bay. They pressed forward nonetheless, screaming obscenities as they came, and I was therefore very relieved to see Hugh Nichols appear to my left, laying into them with a long shafted grain shovel by which means he forced the men back until they were finally put to flight by the appearance of Aaron Rolfe swinging his pick hilt.

Surveying the line, I could see that our barricado was proving a difficult obstacle to surmount, and that the Paglesham men were receiving the worst of the engagement. A few of the scoundrels had, however, breached our wall and two of them were grappling with Nathaniel Saunders. They had borne him to the ground and were raining blows upon him as he struggled to protect his head and face. Vaulting over the side of the cart I ran to the old man's aid, grabbing one of his attackers by the shoulder and spinning him around to face me. The man's head immediately snapped forward as he attempted to butt me full in the phyz, but he met only the knuckle guard of my sword as I rammed it into his snarling lips, breaking several teeth in the process. The second man then rounded on me and this time, being unable to deal with him by blunt force, I was compelled to drive an inch of steel into the fleshy part of his arm, causing him to yelp in pain, and to straightway turn to scramble back over the barricado from whence he came.

After satisfying myself that Lizzie's father had not suffered serious injury, I turned once more to the fray and saw that the enemy had melted away from the barricado and was now in full flight, with our lads cheering and flinging all sorts at them as they ran. The odd small fire was still burning amongst the scattered debris and we had suffered casualties, 'tis true, but at first glance what injuries we had taken appeared to be light. Some cuts and bruises and mayhap the odd broken bone here and there, but nothing more. And then I saw Cuddy Smith, lying propped against the wheel of one of the wagons, his gnarled hands clutching at his stomach as blood oozed through his fingers. Horrified, I sheathed my sword and rushed over to where he lay.

Ned Symonds, his constant companion, was kneeling beside him, unchecked tears streaming down his face.

"Oh, Cap'n," he sniffed. "Cuddy's 'urt real bad. It were that dirty little bastard 'oo were eggin' 'em on. 'E come at Cuddy with a great long knife - an' 'im with but a stick to defend 'isself with."

"Easy, Ned," I said, soothingly. "He'll be all right. Eh, Cuddy? It'll take more than a little scratch like this to see you off, won't it though?"

"No, Cap'n," wheezed Cuddy, wincing with the pain it caused him to speak. "I know I'm for peg trantrums this time. But I don't regret nothin', Master

Roger, nary I don't. It was a rare fight and you properly showed your mettle, so you did. Your ol' dad would 'ave been right proud of you…"

"Hush now, Cuddy," I whispered, tears now beginning to form in mine own eyes. "Dr Lipscomb will fix you up and you'll be back tiffing ale in the Anchor in no time."

"Y'are a kind lad, Master Roger, but I knows full well me time is up. But listen, I wants you to know somethin' afore I go. Come closer, son, and harken to me."

I leant in closer and Cuddy murmured into my ear so that only I could hear his words.

"Be careful with what you've gotten into, Cap'n," he croaked. "That ol' Devil walloper ain't the man 'e appears t'be. Ol' Biddy Baker didn't die of no natural causes, an' she didn't do 'erself in neither. Oh, she were an ol' witch, right enough, but she didn't deserve what the vicar done to 'er…"

Exhausted by the effort of speaking, Cuddy sank back and closed his eyes.

"What do you mean," I hissed at him. "Are you saying that Gildersleeve had something to do with Biddy Baker's death?"

But the old man did not answer. His eyelids opened and his eyes rolled back as, with a sharp rattle in his throat, he expired in front of me. I sat down heavily upon the ground, stunned, and not knowing what to make of Cuddy's dying utterances. But I was not allowed to rest long.

"Roger!" cried Nathaniel Saunders, hurrying over to seize and shake me by the shoulders. "They're attacking our house! Annie and Lizzie are inside. We must help them."

"Christ on his cross!" I exclaimed, jumping to my feet and dragging out my sword once again. "Ned, will you stay with Cuddy? Rolfe… Sawkins…will you come with us? The bastards are breaking into the Reeve's house and the women are in there."

And with that we were off, up and over the barricado and running at full tilt back along the street. On nearing the house we could see through the gathering gloom of the evening that, having failed in their attempts to breach either the front door or any of the windows, the villains had made their way round to the side and smashed down the wooden gate that opened into the garden. One of them had been posted by the wreckage, presumably to stand sentry, but before he could alert his fellows as to our presence I bludgeoned him brutally aside and led my small rescue party swiftly through to the back of the house. The drawing room windows had been kicked in and I could see people crowded inside. Annie Saunders and Susannah the maid were being held tightly by two of the housebreakers while a couple of others threw open cupboards and drawers in search of valuables.

Gathering ourselves outside the windows for but a second, we four burst into the room, screaming like banshees. One of the Paglesham men swung round, and then the others, as we tore into them, scattering them and sending them falling over themselves and fleeing for their lives back out into the garden and away through the ruined gate.

"Where's Lizzie?" I demanded, of no-one in particular.

"Oh, sir, she ran upstairs," quavered Susannah, who was the first to regain a modicum of her wits. "One of them went up after her. He had a big knife, sir. I think he means to murder her, I do."

Leaving Nathaniel Saunders to comfort his wife, I mounted the stairs as fast as I could, followed closely by Sawkins and Rolfe. As I reached the dark, cramped landing at the top I could hear the sounds of a scuffle behind the closed door of Lizzie's bedchamber. Without hesitation I slammed the heel of my boot onto the door, level with the latch. There was a loud crash as the jamb splintered and the heavy portal rocked violently back against its hinges, revealing a nightmarish scene within. The room was dimly lit by one or two candles that cast sinister, spectral shadows all around. Lizzie, clothes ripped and in disarray, had been forced down upon the bed and Ratty was atop her, pressing his long and bloodstained chive to her throat. The foul little bastard was in the act of unbuttoning his breeches as we burst in, but the shock of our entry caused him to recoil and he stood to meet us, his back to the wall like a cornered animal and his wicked blade extended before him.

"You again, is it sailor boy?" he snarled between

bared teeth. "I should'a finished yer on the road when I 'ad the chance. Fink you can take me do yer, cully? Come on then, let's see yer try."

Out of the corner of my eye I saw Aaron Rolfe start forward, slapping his pick handle into the palm of his hand.

"Leave him, Aaron," I said quietly. "This is my fight."

I took my guard, a stance drilled into me during countless hours of exercise aboard ship, sword up, point level with my left eye, right hand by my right breast, elbow half bent, and left forearm in rear. In response, Ratty dropped into a tight knife fighter's crouch, his weapon held shoulder-width and level with his waist so as to prevent himself from striking too wide. His off-hand he held vertically to protect his ribs, head, and neck. Grinning, he moved to one side so as to avoid meeting me head on and then suddenly threw himself at me, hand thrust out to buffet me in the chest whilst he struck upwards, lightning-fast, to stab at my neck. I flicked my blade over, feeling the knife glance off it, and then, instinctively, I cut to Ratty's right flank, the tip of my sword raking along his forearm, causing the knife to fall from his nerveless fingers and clatter on the rough boards. As he straightened, I drove my forehead into his face with enormous force, laying him flat out upon the floor. Standing over the fallen man with my point hovering at his throat I called over my shoulder to Sawkins and Rolfe.

"Get the shitten little arsehole on his feet, lads.

And get him over to the lock-up - Willie Fisher will open it up for you. We'll have the murdering bastard arraigned for what he has done this day and I give my oath that I'll be there to see him swing."

I aimed another cuff at Ratty's lolling head as the blacksmith and the butcher laid hold of him, dragging him roughly out of the room and down the stairs, leaking claret all the way. Lizzie, who throughout the brief fight had been huddled in terror against the headboard of the bed, now ran to me and buried her face in my chest. We spoke not a word, but simply clung to each other, waiting for the trauma to subside.

CHAPTER 13

Rayleigh Assizes were held quarterly at the sign of the Golden Lion at the top of Rayleigh High Street and, by happy co-incidence, the court was due to sit the following week. Sir Henry and Constable Fisher did not therefore tarry long in dispatching their prisoner for trial for the murder of the unfortunate Cuddy Smith under the justices' commission for gaol delivery. Ned Symonds and I were called, along with some other witnesses, to declare anything material to prove the felony and part of the evidence laid against the accused, one time oyster dredger John Kettle, as we now knew the man to be, was a short pre-trial confession that had been obtained by the squire and the constable whilst Kettle was being held in the Canewdon cage. By reason of Kettle having no access to counsel, very little enquiry was made into the circumstances of this confession and, accordingly, the jury were unanimous in finding the accused to be guilty as charged. Kettle stood, head bowed, face battered and bruised, as the presiding justice, resplendent in scarlet robe, black scarf and scarlet tippet, donned the black cap, a simple plain square made of black fabric that sat atop his plain bob-wig, to pronounce sentence.

"You shall be led from hence to the prison from whence you came," droned the judge dispassionately. "And from thence on the fifteenth day of September to a place of execution, and then and there you shall be hanged by the neck until you shall be dead, and afterwards your body shall be dissected and anatomised; and the Lord have mercy upon your soul."

The place of execution was to be Barling Gallows. The parish of Barling, around seven miles from Rochford, being notable for holding the legal right of *furca et fossa*, or gallows and pit, which allowed parishioners to hang men and, somewhat worryingly for me, drown witches.

Whilst in attendance at Cuddy's funeral service, which as a testament to the old man's popularity, saw a large proportion of the village turn out to pay their solemn respects, Mr Saunders sought to inform me that the family had determined upon travelling with me to see Kettle dance the hempen jig, and that he had, accordingly, imposed upon the squire to borrow his *calèche*, and his coachman, to make the twelve mile journey from Canewdon to Barling on the appointed day. We therefore gathered outside the Anchor at around half past eight of the clock on the morning of the fifteenth, ready to begin our journey.

There was a slight early morning nip in the air and,

the previous day having been bright and sunny, a thin mist lingered over the fields. With Mr and Mrs Saunders and Lizzie travelling in the carriage, space was tight, and would have been especially so were it to have come on to rain and thus caused all three to have recourse to shelter under the folding roof. I therefore elected to ride alongside, aboard the ever faithful Hercules, by which expediency I was also able to keep a sharp lookout for dangers on the road. As proof against such dangers I carried my popper in the pocket of my coat as usual, whilst the squire's coachman had been sent abroad heavily armed with two dragoon pistols and a flared, iron barrelled musketoon stowed under his dickey box. It took us around three hours to get to Barling and during that time I had ample opportunity to contemplate poor Cuddy's last words to me.

Could Gildersleeve truly have had a hand in Biddy Baker's death? If that were so, what purpose could he have had? Why, there was no denying that the reverend was uncommon strange for a clergyman - a liar, a lecher, and, I was beginning to suspect, a lover of filthy lucre into the bargain. His outlandish efforts to improve the harvest, if indeed they stemmed from anything other than his innate degeneracy or perversion, were likely as much motivated by fear for his tithes as for the suffering of his parishioners, I thought. But could he be a murderer? Biddy Baker was an impecunious widow woman, so monetary gain could not be considered a motive. Gildersleeve had confessed to thinking her a black witch, and mayhap this superstitious belief was strong enough in him for to wish to punish her - even unto death. I for one would not put it past him, but what evidence had I, the words of a dying man; spoke so soft that no other could hear him? And, if I was honest, those words were ambiguous enough. Biddy 'didn't deserve what the vicar done to her' Cuddy had said. That could mean anything, and might well simply be an allusion to Gildersleeve's collusion in the false verdict of suicide and the subsequent macabre treatment of the woman's corpse. But Cuddy had also asserted that Biddy had not perished through natural causes. I'faith, I did not know what to think, but I did know that I was growing stronger in my contempt and distrust of the vicar, even as I was being drawn further into his dangerous twilight world of theurgy and undeniably exhilarating sexuality.

We rolled into Barling a quarter before twelve, in time to join a large gathering at All Saints Church, assembled to witness the condemned man being brought from the small, ancient ragstone gaol hard by. Despite the press of the crowd, the height afforded by the floor of the *calèche* and Hercules' broad back afforded us an excellent view of the proceedings. On emerging from the gaol, the ordinary of the church placed a noose around Kettle's neck and two burly fellows dressed all in black pinioned his elbows in front of him before helping him up into the waiting cart whereupon he was to ride to his death, seated on his own coffin. Notwithstanding that such a day, though legally appointed for the felon's shame, is oft an opportunity for glory and admiration, Kettle shunned any gentlemanly pretence or bravado, appearing dressed in a shroud, burial cap tied under his chin, and with neither shoes nor stockings. He also kept his eyes shut, refusing to meet the gaze of the rabble that thronged about him as the cart moved off in procession. For rabble they were, though drawn from all sections of society, their very coming together with expectations influenced by past experience or newspaper reports, transforming them into a raucous, unruly mob.

Barling Gallows stood in a field near Mucking Hall, in a slight hollow on the side of a hill which allowed the condemned a last view of the surrounding countryside before they embarked upon their final voyage. The procession, led by John Hanson, the High Sheriff of the county who had been brought over from Great Bromley, was thus required to travel the road that led west from the church, past the mill, and on to the Hall a mile or so away. Hanson was mounted on a handsome black nag and was followed by the two burly coves that had brought Kettle out, and a body of constables who surrounded the cart armed with long pikes. Street vendors were pedalling gin, foodstuffs, last dying speeches, and broadside ballads to the crowd, who themselves showed but little pity for Kettle's plight as they followed the procession. The levity, laughing, cursing, and blaspheming of the mob increased all the more the closer we came to the fatal tree, a simple elevated beam beneath which the cart could be driven, so that by the time appointed for the execution of Kettle's sentence a carnival atmosphere prevailed all around. As the multitude fanned out into the field jostling for the best view of the grisly spectacle, our coachman manoeuvred the *calèche* around to the rear and I brought Hercules alongside, next to where Lizzie was seated. She was staring intently at the scaffold, her expression one of grim determination.

"Have you witnessed an execution before, Lizzie?" I asked her.

"No, Roger, I have not," she replied, evenly. "I confess that I have always found the idea distasteful. But this man fully deserves his fate. He has twice attacked us and has murdered one of your oldest friends. I wish he were to suffer worse than hanging, but if hanged he be I want to see it. I want to be sure that the wretch is dead and on his way to burn in the fires of Hell for what he has done to us."

"It will not be a pretty sight, I warn you."

"Nor should it be. This shall be retribution for his crimes, and a warning to all others that the wages of sin is death."

When the cart was drawn up beneath the gallows Kettle was temporarily allowed his liberty and permitted to stand, with the rope around his neck, to deliver his last address. Often felons would use this time to bewail their own awful fate, and beseech those present to take warning from their disgraceful and shameful end, but Kettle spoke very little, except to attempt to claim for himself a martyr's crown.

"My friends 'ear me!" the little man declaimed,

loudly. "Yer see what I am to suffer, and all for the sake of bread an' flour! I stand 'ere for want of sustenance. Poverty in our great nation 'as, alas, become a death sentence! Supposedly great men 'ave conspired together so that I an' many others cannot afford to buy food for our tables. An' now they 'ang me like a dog for doing that which was necessary for me to survive. 'Ave pity on me my friends, for my crimes are not mine alone. An' I 'opes that youse will all 'ave the goodness to grant me one request. The last request I shall ever make. I request that, from 'ere on, none of youse will ever eat of yer daily bread without remembering that which I suffered for the cost of it!"

"Ballocks," I hissed to myself, angrily. "So murder, housebreaking and attempted rape can be now justified by a hungry belly, can they? Make haste and turn the little bugger off before he stirs this lot up like he did those fools in Paglesham."

For indeed, the crowd were starting to murmur of injustice and tyranny, calling out in sympathy to the condemned man as the ordinary led them in the singing of Psalm 51, the *Hanging Song*.

> Have mercy upon me, O God, according to
> thy loving kindness: according unto the
> multitude of thy tender mercies blot out my
> transgressions,
> Wash me thoroughly from mine iniquity, and
> cleanse me from my sin.
>
> For I acknowledge my transgressions: and my
> sin is ever before me,

Against thee, thee only, have I sinned, and
done this evil in thy sight: that thou mightest
be justified when thou speakest, and be clear
when thou judgest.

Behold, I was shapen in iniquity; and in sin
did my mother conceive me,
Behold, thou desirest truth in the inward
parts: and in the hidden part thou shalt make
me to know wisdom.

Purge me with hyssop, and I shall be clean:
wash me, and I shall be whiter than snow…

The hangman renewed Kettle's bonds and pulled a
white cap over his face, before the singing at last came
to its conclusion and a loud cry of 'hats off' was heard.
As one, the crowd obeyed, and an awful silence
descended upon the field.

"Lord have mercy on us," shouted the hangman as
the cart lurched forward.

Kettle, determined to die game, launched himself
off the cart, giving two great kicks in the air in the hope
of breaking his own neck rather than submit to an
agonisingly slow, choking death. Mr and Mrs Saunders
and I watched this last act impassively, but Lizzie gave
a little yelp of fear and raised her hands to her face as,
failing in his designs, Kettle was left hanging and
jerking on the gallows until his demise could be
hastened by some persons rushing forward to pull on
his legs and thump his chest.

At this moment a unpleasant looking ballad-monger, who was lurking close by the *calèche,* began singing out his doggerel and waving his crudely printed sheets in our direction in an effort to solicit from us a penny or two for the purchase of a couple of dog eared copies of what was an apparently hastily written song - a song that he proclaimed to be *John Kettle's Lament.*

Come all good friends and countrymen and harken to my plea,
For I'll tell ye all just why it is that I am to hang upon this tree,
My crime was but to hunger and to seek for better diet,
To rise up against oppression, boys, by kicking up a riot.

My lads, ye are all hungry, but have little food to eat,
So pull down all the mills, boys, and snaffle all the meat,
I call upon ye, neighbours, no longer bide ye quiet,
And join ye all together for to kick up a bit of a riot.

For a riot is good sport, boys, as good as ever ye saw,
So, cry a fig for the judge, my lads, and another for the law…

I could see that Lizzie and her parents, on comprehending the dangerously seditious nature of the balladeer's ditty, had become visibly anxious for their safety. And rightly so, it seemed, for as the song continued I noted that a small knot of people was beginning to form around the carriage, jostling against the sides of the vehicle in what could only be described as an overtly threatening manner.

"Come, Roger, we must get away while we can," called Mr Saunders, sharply. "For who knows what may happen now, and I must say that I am inclined to fear the worst."

"I think you may be right," I agreed, urging Hercules forward so as to make a passage through the growing press of bodies ahead of us. "Let us be away as quick as we can. I have no wish for the ladies to be exposed to any danger. Make way there! Make way! James…! Whip up, sir and drive hard, man."

There was no doubt but that in this instance the better part of valour was most certainly discretion and, brushing off our little congregation so as to leave them sneering loudly in our wake, we set off along the road to Sutton and thence to Rochford at a great clip, with nary a word spoke between us as we reflected upon the afternoon's events. On reaching the town of Rochford, the hour being too late for us to press on to Canewdon, we sought shelter for the night at the Old Ship in North Street. The Old Ship was quite a grand place, built of high quality brick and boasting several large sash windows to the front and sides. On arrival we passed through the wide carriage arch to the stables, where a number of daisy kickers waited to take care of our horses, and entered the inn through a back door, receiving a warm welcome from the tavern keeper and his wife. Procuring three well-appointed rooms, a private dining room for the evening, and suitable accommodation for Sir Henry's coachman, we settled ourselves in before taking our seats to partake of a splendid meal consisting of thin cuts of tender grilled beef and veal, sprinkled liberally with breadcrumbs and served with potatoes on a silver dish, the whole accompanied by some excellent ale and a fine Bordeaux wine (you can be sure no questions were asked as to how that particular libation had found its way to our table, such provision having been contraband since the start of the war). As the wine flowed and we slowly came to relax once more, we fell to talking.

"Damn that fellow Kettle for his Jacobin cant," declared Mr Saunders, tucking into his beef. "Can you believe the man's effrontery in laying his bloody deeds at the feet of his betters?"

"There is intense hardship amongst the poor of this country, Father, as well you know," said Lizzie, helping herself to more potatoes. "But I do not allow that hardship be the root cause in this particular instance. Like his companion on the road, the man Kettle was a monster and I for one will not excuse his abominable actions on any such grounds."

"Aye," says I. "He was a dangerous man for sure, governed solely by his own greed and lusts. A madman, no less - but though deserving of a straight waistcoat in Bethlem he may have been, 'tis far better he be put to bed with a mattock and tucked up with a spade."

"Amen to that," agreed Mrs Saunders.

"It is, however, frightening, is it not, that a man like Kettle is able to stir up the kind of trouble that he did," put in her husband. "Damme, I curse the Frenchified politics that are ruining this country, for should the unrest we are lately seeing spread even further, I fear we may one day see another civil war."

"I trust that day will never come, sir," I said. "And, to be sure, if such an event were ever threatened, I feel sure that the overwhelming majority of free born Englishmen would remain united in their feeling for common morality and their contempt for revolutionary arrogance and destruction. Why, you need only consider our own good people of Canewdon to realise the extent of the common man's loyalty to the King and also to our traditional English values and beliefs."

"I pray that you are right, Roger," Lizzie concluded. "For the idea of a society swayed, nay, perhaps even governed, by avaricious and libidinous men the like of John Kettle fills me with abhorrence and is altogether too horrible a prospect to contemplate."

"Quite so, my dear, quite so," agreed her father, drinking deep of his wine. "Mmm, damn fine claret, is it not, Roger?"

"Indeed it is, Mr Saunders," I said grandly, raising my glass. "Will you take a drink with me, sir? Confusion to the minions of vice, and may reason be the pilot when passion blows the gale!"

"Your health, sir," responded Mr Saunders,

casting a cheerful glance in the direction of his daughter. "And, if you will allow me to borrow a form of words from your own noble profession, here's to the wind that blows, the ship that goes, and the lass that loves a sailor!"

"Oh, Father…" said Lizzie, colouring slightly and gazing downward most charmingly whilst the rest of the company joined in merry laughter.

I retired to my bedchamber that night weary and replete, shedding my clothes and sinking into the large feather bed lavishly caparisoned with linen sheets, blankets, quilts, curtains and valence. The night being a mite chilly, we had paid extra for firewood, so a crackling fire was burning in the hearth, spreading some welcome warmth and comfort all around the room. Suffice to say, I was happy, perhaps the happiest I had been for some time.

As I lay dozing I found myself awoken by a gentle rap upon the door. Thinking it to be a cinder garbler come to bank up the fire, or else the boot catcher looking to take my boots for cleaning, I sat up in bed and, pulling back the curtain, called for them to come in. The door opened and a slight figure entered the room. But it was no servant.

"Lizzie," I gasped. "What are you doing here? Is something amiss?"

"Hush, my love. There is nothing amiss, I assure you," whispered Lizzie, her voice low and sultry. "I am in sore need of company this night, for I find myself somewhat affected by that which we have witnessed."

Of course, my dear, I understand completely," I answered. "If you will but allow me a moment to find my shirt…"

"No, Roger, do not get up."

"Oh… er… yes… I see," I gulped, as, having quietly closed the door, Lizzie moved closer to the bed.

"May I get in?" she asked, shrugging her shoulders to allow her chemise to slip slowly and noiselessly to the floor.

I made no answer, simply drawing back the covers to allow Lizzie to slide in and nestle against me. I laid my hand upon her hip, running it up and over her voluptuous curves to cup her firm round breast. Her beautiful brown eyes looked up at me, smouldering with desire.

"Love me, Roger… please," she said.

And so I did. All that night we rolled in sport and play until, just before the dawn, Lizzie arose and kissed me tenderly before leaving to return to her own room. I couldn't help thinking that, had I known that was going to happen, we might have saved ourselves one and a kick for lodgings, not to mention another tuppence on top for firewood.

CHAPTER 14

The next week passed in a daze of glowing contentment. Now certain in the knowledge that Lizzie and I were very much in love, I began to consider the possibility of asking her parents whether they might give consent to our nuptials. I had heard lately from my prize agent in London that the combined prize money for the ships taken by our fleet on the first of June last had been confirmed to be a staggering £201,096, of which I myself was entitled to an, albeit relatively small, share by virtue of my having served aboard *Dione* under Lord Howe's command. This stroke of good fortune, when added to my reward for the capture of the *Amazone*, my lieutenant's half pay, and whatever dowry the Saunders' might be persuaded to part with, could well be enough pelf to set me and Lizzie up with a tidy little cottage in the village, complete with pink roses around the door to symbolise peace and our gratitude for it.

The thought of the Reverend Gildersleeve

presiding over our wedding did not fill me with as much joy though, but I supposed that if I wished to continue mine and Lizzie's involvement in his jolly frolics (and that I most certainly did) I would have to become more tolerant of the shady little spiritual flesh broker. For who knew, mayhap one day I might even take the vicar's place as Horned God, with Lizzie beside me as *my* priestess in the same way that she had stood at his side before we two launched into our intoxicating efforts to ensure the continued fecundity of the land. Be damned if I would countenance her attending to her devotions with any other young buck but me, mind.

One morning, as I sat in my room at the Anchor in contemplation of this idyllic rural prospect, young Tom appeared at the door.

"Beggin' y'pardon, Cap'n," he said, knuckling his forehead in imitation of a naval salute. "But there are two gentlemen t'see you downstairs."

"Thankee, Tom," I replied. "I wonder who they might be. Please do run and tell them that I shall be down shortly."

Tom scurried off back across the landing and down the stairs while I put on my coat and straightened my waistcoat before following him. A bit of a mystery, this, I thought. Who could have tracked me down to this isolated backwater? The mystery was soon to be solved, however, for on entering the kitchen, I was greeted by the beaming faces of Charlie Edwardes and Harry Felgate.

"Why, Charlie… Harry…!" I exclaimed, advancing upon them to pump the hand of each in turn. What a delightful surprise. Well met gentlemen, well met indeed!"

"'Tis good to see you, Roger," Charlie declared, clapping me heartily on the shoulder. "'Deed it is!"

"And looking right hale and hearty, too," chimed in Harry. "Country life must surely agree with you, old friend."

"I find that it does, and devilishly well, Harry," says I. "Come, sit you both down and bring your arses to anchor, you must be bone weary after your journey. Tom! Fetch some ale for my friends."

The three of us settled ourselves on a bench by the window. Harry was dressed in a dark grey coat and waistcoat, and wore a splendid pair of mahogany topped hunting boots that fair put my shabby specimens to shame. In contrast, Charlie was in full fig, resplendent in a spanking new blue and white naval lieutenant's uniform, though he too wore riding boots in place of his silver buckled shoes.

"Did you come up from Rayleigh by chaise?" I asked.

"No," said Charlie. "We hired a couple of prads from the coachmaster there. The boy has taken them round to the stables for us."

"Are you planning to stay, then?"

"Perhaps tonight, if there's room, we'll see… We

have taken lodgings at an inn in Rayleigh and stowed our dunnage there for the nonce."

Tom brought our ale to the table, along with some cold roast ham left over from breakfast, setting it down before us with a flourish.

"Ah, thank you. Lad," said Harry. "That is right welcome."

"So, tell me, what has been happening in London while I have been away?" I enquired, eager for news despite myself.

"Not very much, truth to tell, Roger," replied Charlie. "I declare, it has been altogether too damn hot in town lately for anyone to bother doing anything very much. But yes, this will interest you, especially given the nature of some of our discourse before you went away. It seems that fellow Blake has published a new book of allegorical verse, *The Book of Ahania*, he calls it, wherein he talks of something that he names as the Tree of Mystery and tells of the ritual nailing of a god-like figure to it. This sacred tree, he says, is closely connected with ancient Druidic and Norse mythology and he uses it in his poem to demonstrate that Christianity is but a continuation of older, pagan religions. Mark you, the poem may be a trifle indecorous for your taste, Roger, for the poet oft refers to of the joys of love freely given and received in a sexual embrace and, forsooth, makes much of the merits of unrestrained desire, sexual ecstasy and consequent fertility."

"And he has illustrated it with some very suggestive etchings, too," laughed Harry. "But, that's no more than we would expect, though, eh Roger? London's still the same sordid city it ever was. D'ye know, I hear that *la* Armistead, the paramour of that old puff-guts, Charles Fox, recently sent for a linen draper to bring her some Hollands, and as soon as the young fellow entered she cried 'Oh, sir, I find that you are a man fit for business indeed, for you no sooner look a lady in the face, but you have your yard in one hand, and are lifting up the linen with the other!'"

"Now Harry," Charlie scolded. "'Tis early in the day for such ribald jests, let us confine us to more philosophical conversation."

But, for some reason, I was finding Harry's japing far more amusing than I had hitherto and I began to chuckle rumbustiously.

"Heh, heh, heh. No, no, Charlie, let us not be so serious straight off the bat," I snorted. "It is no different out here in the country you know, Harry? Why, only the other day one of our local farmers was crossing his fields in the dusk of the evening when he spied a young ploughboy and his lass, very busy near a five bar gate. And when he called to them wanting to know what they were about the young man called back: 'No harm, Farmer, we are only going to *Prop-a-Gate*.'"

Harry and Charlie looked at one another in astonishment - for, in truth, they had never heard me make a joke before, even one as bad as that - and then they fair dissolved into such a fit of the giggles that I felt compelled to carry on. Why, I thought to myself, there must surely be something about the way I recount them.

"And not only that, gentlemen, listen, let me speak to you of our parson who, just happening to turn up against a house to make water one night last week, did not notice two young ladies looking out of a window close by him. That is, until he heard them tittering. When he asked these dells what made them so merry, one of them said to him: 'Oh Reverend, do not mind us for we are so easily amused, even by such a very little thing!'"

Well, make no mistake, I was mightily pleased with that one, and the three of us fell to laughing fit to burst. When we had recovered our composure, however, Charlie once more became serious.

"So, Roger," he said, putting his hand into his pocket and drawing out a document which I saw bore the fouled anchor seal of the Admiralty. "I think the time has come to tell you the reason for our visit this day. The ever parsimonious Mr Napean, in his desire to save on the cost of postage, has charged me to deliver this to you."

Charlie pushed the document across the table and I took it up, carefully breaking the seal. With mounting excitement, albeit tinged with an underlying sense of dread, I began to read.

By the Commissioners for executing the Office of the Lord High Admiral of Great Britain and Ireland

&c and of all His Majesty's Plantations &c.

To Lieut. Roger Alexander Ellis hereby appointed Lieutenant of His Majesty's Ship the Eros

By Virtue of the Power and Authority to us given We do hereby constitute and appoint you Lieutenant of His Majesty's Ship the Eros willing and requiring you forthwith to go on board and take upon you the Charge and Command of Lieutenant in her accordingly. Strictly Charging and Commanding all the Officers and Company belonging to the said ship subordinate to you to behave themselves jointly and severally in their respective Employments with all the Respect and Obedience unto you their said Lieutenant; And you likewise to observe and execute as well the General printed Instructions as what Orders and Directions you shall from time to time receive from your Captain or any other your superior Officers for His Majesty's service. Hereof nor you nor any of you may fail as you will answer the contrary at your peril. And for so doing this shall be your Warrant. Given under our hands and the Seal of the Office Admiralty this 18th day of September, 1795 in the 35th Year of His Majesty's Reign.

By Command of their Lordships

Spencer
Sir Charles Middleton, Bt,
Philip Stephens

So, I had at last been granted a berth. And a pay rise back up to five pounds twelve shillings a month!

221

But, welcome as this development would have been a few short months past, at that moment, I most certainly did not want it.

"I give you joy of your appointment, Roger," grinned Charlie. "The *Eros* is a trim little sixth rate of twenty-eight guns and she's lying at Woolwich Dockyard, waiting to be made ready for sea. I understand from Mr Napean that you are posted into her as second lieutenant - and, by reason of mine own commission being dated a mite later than yours; I am to be her third. Is that not grand? We are to be shipmates!"

"You don't look very pleased to hear the news, old chum," Harry said, quizzically. "Is something troubling you?"

"Oh, I am sorry, gentlemen," I responded. "It is, of course, wonderful news. But my circumstances are now much altered, and I fear I must decline the commission."

"What?" exclaimed Harry, suddenly becoming angry. "You cannot be serious! Don't y'know that there are at least a score of fellows hanging around the Admiralty who would give their eye teeth for such an opportunity, and me included. What ails you, man? It's a woman, isn't it? You have found yourself an eligible young chick-a-biddy and you can't bear to leave her. Is that it, hey?"

"I have become enamoured of a young woman from the village, Harry," I answered, stiffly. "And I'll thank you not to refer to her as a 'chick-a-biddy', if you please. Miss Elizabeth Saunders is an old friend of my youth with whom I have lately become reacquainted and I intend, should her parents be willing, to make her my wife."

"Surely that's no reason to pass up your commission, Roger," insisted Charlie, "There are plenty of married men in the Service, after all. If Miss Saunders loves you as you do her, I'll wager she would not wish you to turn your back on your career - not to mention your duty."

And, i'faith, there was the rub. To refuse this berth would undoubtedly be professional suicide, but that alone would be but a small price to pay for a life of conjugal bliss with my darling Lizzie. What was far more important was the fact that I would not only be failing in my personal duty to protect my prospective spouse and her family in time of war, but also in my duty to my country. Johnson may well have labelled patriotism as the last refuge of the scoundrel but, much as I did love Lizzie, I found that the call of patriotic duty was still strong within me. My country needed me. Was I not an officer in His Britannic Majesty's Navy, the only branch of the services in any way capable of protecting, why, not only old England, but also the rest of the world from the rapacious incursions of revolutionary France? The bloody soldiers couldn't do it - you only needed to look at the mess they had made in Holland to see that. Dammit, the country did not simply expect the Navy to be victorious; it was in desperate need of that victory for its very survival. It was right there in the words I had just read. 'Hereof nor you nor any of you may fail...' And for sure, I knew in my heart that I could not fail. I could not refuse this commission and in any way retain even a shred of my honour.

"You are right, of course, Charlie," I admitted sheepishly, after a pause. "I cannot, nor shall I, fail in my duty and we will ship together in the *Eros* ere long, have no fear of that. But first I must inform Miss Saunders of the situation and seek to allay such fears as she may have as to its consequences."

"Bravo, sir. That is well said," Harry was all smiles again, patting my arm reassuringly. "Best you get over to see her, then, soon as you can, hey? Your new captain will not be best pleased should you tarry too long."

"I am sure the lady will understand," added Charlie. "For, during these long years of endurance, has it not become the unfortunate lot of all wives and sweethearts to have to express their patriotic duty in the form of stoicism in the face of personal hardship?"

So, with a heavy heart and a mind in turmoil though fear of losing the sweet happiness I had gained with Lizzie over this truly unforgettable summer, I left Harry and Charlie in the kitchen of the Anchor and presented myself at the Saunders' house. Susannah showed me in and I found Mrs Saunders seated in the drawing room, working on some embroidery.

"Ah, Roger," said Lizzie's mother, looking up from her hoop. "If you have come seeking Lizzie, I am afraid she is not at home. She has taken herself off to the parsonage on vestry business, I believe."

"Oh, that is most regrettable, madam. I find that I have something to discuss with her that is of great import. Have you any notion of how soon she may return?"

"I am afraid not. She has not been gone longer than an hour or so. You may wait and take tea with me, if you wish. But if you need to speak with her as a matter of urgency, I am sure you will find a warm welcome at the parsonage."

I did not fancy meeting with Lizzie at the parsonage above half. But, I had to see her, and that right soon. And mayhap the vicar might be amenable to affording us some privacy in which to talk. I therefore took my leave of Mrs Saunders and set off along the High Street to find her daughter.

"I am afraid that the reverend is indisposed, sir," said Perkins on opening the vicar's front door. "He is engaged in, erm... vestry business... and cannot be disturbed."

"Nonsense, man," I barked, pushing past him and marching through into the parlour. "He'll see me - after all, I am a member of the vestry committee myself, don't y'know?"

"On your head be it, sir," warned Perkins dourly, as he followed in my wake.

I had scarce entered the parlour when I was joined by the vicar. Curiously for the middle of the day, the man entered pulling his banyan around him as he might have done had he just risen from his bed. He also wore no wig nor turban, and his mousey, short cut hair was ruffled.

"Roger, what are you doing here?" Gildersleeve demanded. "Did Perkins not inform you that I was not to be disturbed?"

"I have come to speak with Lizzie, Reverend. Mrs Saunders told me that she was here visiting you on a matter of parochial business."

"You are mistaken, sir. Elizabeth Saunders is not here. Now, if you would kindly withdraw, I would return to my bed, for I find myself, as you sailors say, distinctly under the weather bow this day."

Gildersleeve certainly did appear to be in a sweat and he was uncommon agitated. But I doubted he was unwell. And, as I looked around the room, I realised with increased trepidation that the bugger was lying to me about Lizzie. For there on the heavy oak table sat Lizzie's shepherdess hat and mitts, and draped across one of the chairs was her hooded travelling cloak. A pair of ladies' calfskin shoes lay discarded by the doorway, for all the world as if the wearer had kicked them off in her haste to leave the room.

"Damme Gildersleeve, I don't believe you," I said sharply. "Where is she? If you have harmed her in any way…"

"Don't be a fool; of course I have not harmed the girl."

"Lizzie! Are you here?" I shouted, running to the foot of the stairs. "Where are you?"

"I am here, Roger," said Lizzie, softly. "And I am quite safe."

She had appeared on the landing and was looking down at me. Like Gildersleeve, her hair was tousled and I was appalled to see that she was clad only in her shift.

"My God! Lizzie, what is the meaning of this? I gasped. "Surely you and he have not...?"

"Tom and I have been... enjoying each other's company... yes, my love. But is that such a terrible thing? It is but a fleeting pleasure, and no harm has been done to any by it."

"No harm's done? For God's sake! What of the harm done to me? I love you, Lizzie - how could you betray me so?"

"And I love you, Roger. You may be sure that this piddling dalliance does not alter anything between us. Nor should you consider yourself in any way harmed by what is but a simple expression of sexual desire between two people who are both free from commitment. Remember, we are not as yet wed, my darling, nor are we even betrothed and so, until then, as you must surely know, we are both free to do as we will."

"It is God's Law of Love, my son," the blasted vicar piped up sanctimoniously from behind me.

"You bastard!" I yelled, spinning round to face him. "You beshitten, bloody bastard!"

Backing away in the face of my fury, Gildersleeve retreated into the parlour, but I wanted his blood for this and so I followed, shoving him hard in the chest. Down he went, sprawling amongst the chairs and scrabbling desperately to escape me, his banyan flapping loose around his legs. Seeing him thus, I bore down upon him relentlessly; aiming a hefty kick at his exposed and unprotected nutmegs which saw him double up with pain.

"No, Roger, don't!" screamed Lizzie, flying down the stairs and laying hold of me in an effort to drag me off the vicar, who was now curled up, whimpering on the bare wooden floor. "There's no need for violence, really there isn't."

I stopped and reluctantly allowed myself to be pulled back. Lizzie, still radiantly beautiful in her *déshabillé*, took my hands in hers, and looked up at me imploringly. I felt a brief urge to take her in my arms, but some feeling deep inside me had died and I could only shake my head slowly in abject despair.

"Oh, Lizzie," I whispered. "How could you…?"

I fled from the parsonage in floods of tears, leaving a scene of devastation behind me that surely was of biblical proportions. Sprinting up Church Lane, I entered the churchyard and sat down heavily against the low stone wall. What an idiot I had been. How could I have let myself be gulled so completely by this parcel of moon-crazed Bedlamites? Lizzie's perfidy had caused the scales to fall from my eyes and I could now see clearly that I had been led along from the outset like a prize bull. Damme if I had not been brazenly seduced and manipulated into playing a part in the coven's depraved and orgiastic rituals by way of my own unexpectedly twisted desire. Why, I would wager that even my first tantalising encounter with Sally Dowsett had been part of their plan - some manner of test, if you will, designed to assess my suitability for the game. Well, I would be their plaything no longer. Rising to my feet, I mopped my eyes and tidied myself up before heading back down the road to the Anchor. I had more important business to deal with and the sooner I could get back to sea, the better. Nevertheless, I confess that I had begun to harbour a darkening desire to gain some small measure of revenge on these fat headed country bumpkins, and to wonder whether I might well be able to throw a final cat into the dovecote before I properly weighed anchor.

CHAPTER 15

I returned to the Anchor in high dudgeon and determined to be away from the accursed village of Canewdon as soon as could be managed. Charlie and Harry were anxious to hear the outcome of my interview with Lizzie, but I stayed reticent, merely indicating that things had gone well enough and that I was now of a mind to settle my account so that we could be on our way post haste. I therefore summoned Mrs Dowsett, informed her that I had been ordered to join my ship, and asked that she present me with my reckoning. I'll own that she did seem genuinely sorry to see me go.

"Oh, Cap'n," she said. "This is such sudden, and sorrowful, news. You will be sorely missed around the village, sir, for sure you will. Both I and young Tom have become so used to having you here, and I know that Miss Elizabeth will be beside herself to see you go. Have you told her? Does she know that you are off to sea?"

"Miss Saunders and I have spoken, Mrs Dowsett," I replied, dryly.

"Oh, less of the 'Mrs Dowsett' you silly man, its Sal to you, as it will ever be."

And with that she laid hold of me and, with more than a trace of a tear in her eye, planted a big wet buss upon my lips. I clung to her for a moment, in danger of breaking down once more myself, before giving up our embrace.

"I'll be off to prepare your bill directly sir," Sal sniffed, tugging on her apron and wiping her eyes with the back of her hand. "Just you wait here and I'll be back in a trice."

Harry and Charlie watched this scene with some amusement.

"Seems you're a popular man hereabouts, Roger," Harry commented, wryly. "I am beginning to wish that I had accompanied you on this jaunt of yours."

"H'rumph!" I rumbled in response, whilst privately thinking that it may have indeed been better had I not returned to this God forsaken village alone - or at all, for that matter.

When Sal returned I paid her what was owed, adding a little extra for Tom in gratitude for his service during my stay. I also arranged to take Hercules along the road as far as Rayleigh, explaining that I would charge the coachmaster there to send him back in the morning, along with a chaise to pick up my sea chest and other bits of luggage. While Tom was sent to bring the horses round to the front of the inn, I went upstairs, donned my uniform and sword, and, as usual, slipped my barker into the pocket of my greatcoat. As I looked around the room, memories of the last few months came flooding back and I was again hard put to keep myself under proper control. But my mind was made up and, with the venereal vicar presumably sat in his parlour nursing his scruffy ballocks; the die was well and truly cast.

We mounted outside the front door and I bade a final farewell to Sal and Tom. As I made to ride away, Sal put one hand on Hercules' bridle and reached up with her other to press a small piece of fabric into my palm. On it were a number of fantastical symbols embroidered in black on a white background.

"Keep this talisman about you, Cap'n," she whispered. "For it grants the possessor all the talents and knowledge of every art and will help protect you, no matter how far you roam from these shores."

"My thanks to you, Sal," I said, tucking her gift into my pocket. "Say goodbye to Ned and the others for me, won't you? They're good fellows all and I shall miss their company of an evening."

"I will, sir, don't fret. Farewell, Master Roger… And may the Gods go with you."

"And with you," I replied, tickling Hercules into motion with my heels. "Come on, old horse, time's getting on and we must be away."

We clattered into Rayleigh just before sunset.

Harry and Charlie were staying at the Crown, an inn situated at the opposite end of the High Street to the Golden Lion, which, as you will recall, I had visited to give evidence in the trial of John Kettle. The Crown was an altogether less imposing establishment but had space enough to accommodate me, nonetheless, though in all fairness I did find myself having to share a cot with Charlie.

Our dinner that night was of moderate quality, though in my miserable state I could do no more than toy with it. But no so with the ale and before long I was half cut, blurting out my entire sorry tale to my companions, save for one or two minor, inconsequential details, of course.

"Whisht!" exclaimed Charlie, when I eventually came to the end of my narrative. "I declare that I have never heard anything to rival this. I can hardly credit it. For sure, the possibility of the Lord God having a wife is an interesting notion which might well bear further study - and perhaps even a paper for the Edinburgh Philosophical Society - but the idea of otherwise respectable people dancing naked in the churchyard, and you yourself being cuckolded by an ordained minister who is wont to prance around wearing animal horns upon his head? Why, it beggars belief. *And* you say that you suspect the blackguard of murdering some old woman because he considered her to be a bana-bhuidseach dhubh... sorry... I mean to say a black witch?"

"Yes... tha's the way of it, my friend," I slurred,

throwing my head back to drain the dregs of my ale and slapping the empty pot down onto the table accompanied by a loud belch. "Cuddy Smith, the poor ol' sod who was killed in the fight with the Paglesham men, told me as much as he lay dyin' in the street. But I can't let him get away with it, y'know? Someone has to settle Gildersleeve's hash, and I swear I'm the man to do it. They're havin' another one of their bare arsed frolics on the night of the harvest moon, three days hence, an' I mean to break it up and call that bloody vicar out on his crimes."

"But what of joining the ship, Roger?" said Harry. "You and Charlie need to get down to Woolwich without delay."

"There's time enough for that," I answered. "If they say I'm late reportin' I'll tell 'em that I was in Rochford, or somewhere, on business an' so Charlie wasn't able to hand over my commission straight away."

"Might we not simply inform on the fellow," suggested Charlie. "A word in the right ear would set the yeomanry on his tail and see him in the dock for the pretence of witchcraft."

"There's definitely no time for all that palaver," I asserted. "An' besides, I've thought of doin' somethin' akin to that before an' I can't see how it could be achieved without exposin' Lizzie an' Sal, an' all of the others, to the risk of the pillory - an' even though they're all as mad as a bag of cats I'll not have that, nary I won't."

"Very well," declared Harry. "But you will not go after him alone, Roger. I'm with you."

"And I too," agreed Charlie. "But let us to our beds now and think on this again come the morrow, when with luck we shall all have clearer heads. For if we are going to serve your vicar out his just desserts, then 'tis best we plan carefully for it."

But, though we pondered over it all the following day and for the best part of the next, no clear plan presented itself to us. There was only one thing for it, we decided - we would ride up to St Nicholas' churchyard and intrude upon the coven's Lammas ceremony, whereupon I would denounce the reverend for a murderer in sight of all present and demand of the squire that justice be done. What might happen thereafter was anyone's guess.

Therefore, on Monday afternoon the three of us rode back to Canewdon. Hercules having been sent back to the Anchor on Saturday morning, I had hired a strapping bay gelding from the coachmaster. The horse was all of seventeen hands and came with a warrant that he would carry me through the fires of Hell itself, though in truth, for all his imposing appearance, he turned out to be quite a kindly old gentleman who provided me with a most welcome quiet ride. All three of us were in civilian clothes and, though I had left my sword at the Crown, I still toted my pistol. Harry and Charlie were similarly armed, with a pair of neat little breech loading turn-off guns being shared between them. We also brought three cheap tin lanthorns and some bread and cheese with us, this latter we consumed in a wood just outside Ashingdon as the sun started to set. While we ate, we watched the large, bright, flame coloured moonrise bathing the countryside around us in its early evening light. The moon grew smaller as it rose in the night sky, turning from orange to silver, the thin cirrostratus scudding across it diffusing its luminosity to form a halo and cause moonbeams to appear like steely lances held aloft by a host of spectral knights embarking upon an heroic quest in honour of their liege lord.

"Time we shoved off," I announced, with a nervous laugh. "If we make a move now we should reach the church just before the witching hour."

Charlie sprang aboard his nag while Harry gave me a boost up into the saddle before mounting his own prancer.

"It is the very error of the moon;" quoth Charlie. "She comes more nearer earth than she was wont, and makes men mad."

"Shakespeare?" asked Harry.

"It is."

"Thought so," said Harry, applying heels to his steed. "In that case, gentlemen, let us carry on in the spirit of the bard. 'Hark - the shrill trumpet sounds - to horse, away!'"

We cantered some way along the road before slowing to a walk as we neared the crossroads whereby lay the grave of the unfortunate Biddy Baker. There we dismounted once more, tethered the horses to the tall, weather-beaten fingerpost that stood at the side of the road, and bent to light the glims so that we might see our way better as we continued on foot up Church Lane. On reaching the parsonage, I called a halt and bade my companions douse their lights. In the distance we could discern the glow of the coven's fire and just make out the sound of drum and pipe floating on the air. Stealthily, we crept to the west gate of the churchyard and as we crouched down to peer in I heard Charlie draw a sharp intake of breath, and Harry emit a low whistle through his teeth. For the jolly frolic was in full swing.

Set up proudly upon the table tomb was the corn doll, brought from the harvest supper and now surrounded by lavish offerings of bread, cakes, and fruit. Propped against the tomb were Gildersleeve's broadsword and sickle, with the Horned God himself playing merrily on his oaten pipe and dancing a comical little jig beside them. Before him the members of the coven danced, stark naked, around the blaze, their bodies appearing first bathed in flickering orange light and then in dark silhouette as they circled the fire, twisting and turning in time with the music. After a while the music stopped, the Horned God forsook his pipe and took up his weapons, while his pursuivants gathered eagerly round to hear him give thanks for the harvest.

"Brothers and sisters!" he cried, raising his sword and sickle above his head to throw long, dark shadows against the rough wall of St Nicholas' tower. "Let us praise the divine Asherah! For it is thanks to her bounty that the harvest is safely gathered in and there is grain enough to feed us through the winter."

"Praise be to Asherah!" rejoined his outlandish congregation. "Praise be to the Harvest Mother!"

"And within that harvest is the very seed of rebirth and regeneration," bawled the Horned God, evidently warming to his task. "The present harvest holds at its heart the seed of all future harvests. That seed which returns deep into the earth to rest until it is ready to burst forth again in the spring. The Goddess is ripe and full this night, pregnant with the seed of John Barleycorn, the living spirit of the grain, within her."

Now or never, then, I thought as I stood and marched through the gate, Harry and Charlie following on behind. They were all there: Sir Henry, tall and muscular; Lady Mary, plump and flushed from her exertions; Sally Dowsett, lithe and handsome; homely Annie Saunders; and my Lizzie - radiant and beautiful, her bare skin appearing more healthy and glowing than ever before, her exquisite breasts more pronounced, her curves more rounded, and her inviting lips somehow more full than I remembered.

"Gildersleeve!" I bellowed, as if I were hailing the foretop in a howling gale. "Hold hard, man. Cease this unholy pretence at once."

"Roger," said Gildersleeve silkily, as I skirted the fire to face him head on. "I knew you would not be able to resist joining us. I'll wager the desire to renew your union with the fair Elizabeth and tup beneath the stars has proven too strong. Am I right, Lieutenant, do you wish to join us in one more dance?"

"Be still, sir!" I spat. "And hear what I have to say. You too, Sir Henry, for I fancy that my words may prove to be of uncommon interest to you, as our magistrate."

Sir Henry, though clad only in his birthday-suit, had puffed himself up and made to protest most haughtily, but I silenced him with a devilishly baleful look, and on seeing Charlie and Harry step into the light of the fire in support of my polemic, he and the other members of the coven shrank back, furtively casting around for their discarded robes.

"You are a thorough-paced villain, Glidersleeve," says I to the vicar. "And I charge you that you did murder Mrs Baker, the old woman of Butts Hill, damn your eyes!"

As I spoke these words a ripple of shock and disbelief ran through the churchyard and I heard gasps of surprise and general low mutterings emanate from the Horned God's minions as I continued.

"What say you, Gildersleeve? Do you deny it, sir?"

"I deny nothing, sir," growled the vicar, becoming angry and squaring up to me. "Thou shalt not suffer a witch to live, so sayeth the Lord. And make no mistake, Lieutenant Ellis, Biddy Baker was a malevolent, black-hearted beldam in league with the Devil and as such she had to die."

"My God, Tom!" cried out Sir Henry, clutching his robe about his loins like a Hindoo *dhoti*. "Murder was never part of our design. There can be no justification under our credo for such an act. To do what you will is not, and can never be, the whole of the law, man!"

"And what do you know of our law, sir?" Gildersleeve rasped, turning his anger upon the squire. "There is a rule of greater harm at play here. You and these other poor, deluded creatures are not witches, no matter what you think - but Biddy Baker was. She was a true witch: a charmer; and a caster of wicked incantations. One who consulted the spirits and sought oracles from the dead. And when I was summoned on the night of the storm to comfort her in her infirmity, I knew that my chance had come to rid our community of her evil forever. It took but a moment for me to hold a bolster over her ugly face and extinguish her life - and you should all be grateful that I did."

"Curse you for a murdering dog, Gildersleeve," I said, quietly. "You'll pay for this."

"Will I really, Lieutenant?" the vicar hissed back. "Do you not see that my actions were not dissimilar to your own when you were faced with the prospect of robbery and death on the road? Elizabeth was in mortal danger from a mean and dangerous rogue and you thought naught of ending that man's life to prevent any harm coming to her. You did not shy away from what needed to be done and you were quick to act where others may have hesitated out of fear for the consequences, notwithstanding that their deeds would nevertheless be to the greater good."

"Damme, you'll not liken me to a killer of defenceless old women! This talk of spells and witches is so much stuff and nonsense. Tales to frighten children. Superstitious fiddle-faddle that belongs in the past. There are no such things as witches and you damn well know it!"

"And yet you were pleased to play the witch when it suited you, Roger. You were happy to take Biddy Baker's place, to dance around the fire by the light of the moon, and to imitate the coitus of the Gods to help promote the harvest."

"Phew!" whistled Harry from behind me. "You didn't tell us that part of the tale."

"Genuine or no," continued Gildersleeve, his voice beginning to rise once again. "There have always been six witches in Canewdon and if you will not be the sixth another must stand in your stead. It is naught but fitting. As the corn is cut so John Barleycorn is cut down also. And, as you have shown yourself willing to be our John Barleycorn, so must you give up your life in order that others may be sustained, and so that the life of the community can continue."

Suddenly, things did not appear to bode well and, franticly, I started to back away from the crazed cleric as he raved at me, raising his sickle as if to strike me down where I stood.

"Death and rebirth!" Gildersleeve screamed as he came at me, scything his blade in a wide arc fit to take off my head with one massive swipe. "Everything dies in its season! Everything is reborn!"

And at that moment I had cause to be grateful for the muckworm in me who had begrudged the price of a new pair of topboots, for, as I scrambled back, my foot slipped once again on the wet grass and I landed full on my fundament, the vicar's wild swing passing harmlessly above my head. There was a scream and the flash-bang of a pistol, and Gildersleeve stood rooted to the spot, staring down at his chest as blood pumped and ran in a rivulet down the front of his dark robe to drip onto the turf at his feet. Then he fell, collapsing in a heap upon the ground to lie curled up like an unborn babe, legs kicking in pain.

"Roger...! Charlie...! Get away from here, now!" yelled Harry, his little breech loader still smoking in his hand. "I'll see this one out. There's none here will raise a hand against me with the threat of a charge of witchcraft and a spell in the pillory hanging over their heads, and I'll wager there will be witnesses enough among 'em later to swear that the madman sought to butcher you with that bloody great knife. Get you to the barky, lads, and God speed you on your way."

I rose quickly and looked over at Lizzie. She was huddled with the others, clinging to her mother, the pair holding their robes to their chests to cover their modesty. She met my gaze and I felt a sharp pang of regret for what might have been. Charlie called for me to hurry, and I confess that I was sore tempted to fly tantwivy, and leg it out of the churchyard and back down to the crossroads as fast as I could. But I could not, in all conscience, pike off and leave Harry to face these freakish people alone.

"Hold, Charlie," I commanded. "I'll not run!"

"Aye-aye, sir," said Charlie, responding with the correct and seamanlike reply on receiving an order from a senior officer. "So be it. Harry, this bugger yet lives, help me turn him over. Mayhap he'll recover enough for us to see him swing."

Charlie and Harry knelt to attend to Gildersleeve who was indeed still living, though I seriously doubted his chances overall, and I turned to face the coven.

"Ladies," I said. "I would suggest you repair to the narthex and get your clothes back on. The night air is turning chilly and I fear you may catch cold were you to stay stripped as you are."

With downcast eyes, the members of the coven made to return to the church.

"Not you, Sir Henry!" I snapped. "We have unfinished business, you and I."

To his credit, though half naked and draped in a bed sheet like a Bombay *pani-wallah*, the squire drew himself up to his full height to regain some semblance of dignity and looked me straight in the eye.

"Lieutenant Ellis," he said, with some pomposity. "I find that I must apologise for your treatment at the hands of our order. 'Tis true that we have had recourse to various underhanded stratagems to persuade you to join with us in our devotions, but violence has never been our intention. As you know, our moral code requires that we do no harm, and we believe that whatever we do, be it positive or negative, will come back to us in this life, three-fold. It is therefore of vital importance to us that we should always act with positivity and tolerance towards others. Gildersleeve has taken a step beyond the teachings of our faith - a step into the realm of darkness, if you will. And he has reaped his just reward. Have no fear, Roger, none here present will seek retribution against you, or your friends, and on that you have my word. But I would ask you to leave this place now and never return. Like the animals of the forest, we needs must withdraw to lick our wounds, and if we are to do that with any measure of success, we must be left to recover in peace."

"Very well, Sir Henry," I acquiesced, for indeed I was at a loss to say otherwise in the face of the squire's lordly affirmation of the equity of our situation. "We will be away directly. But pray get you hence to Dr Lipscomb. The vicar is in dire need of his services, though I doubt that even our esteemed doctor's ministrations will be enough to keep him in the land of the living for long. But for all that, bad cess to him I say, for in truth, the fellow does not deserve to live."

We left the churchyard then, and walked calmly, and in silence, back down the lane to the crossroads.

Regaining our horses we cantered off towards Ashingdon, only reining in once we felt we had put a reasonable enough distance between ourselves and the shadow of St Nicholas' church. Dawn was beginning to break, the gravid light of the new day turning the sky a deep blue, etched with streaks of orange and gold where the rays of the sun were diffused by thin cloud and haze. On the ground, the occasional large brown hare, startled by our passing, broke cover to run flat out across fields now devoid of crops.

"That was a damn close thing, Roger," said Charlie, as we rode three abreast along the road. "I had thought you to be expended there. That ridiculous fellow was like to dance away with the faeries and would have put an end to you, had you not had that lucky squelch. I'faith, I am reminded of that infernal piece of doggerel penned some while ago by my august fellow countryman, Mr Burns. What was it? Though they swore he was dead, 'John Barleycorn got up again, and sore surprised them all.'"

"You have the right of it, Charlie," I replied. "It was good fortune indeed that the bugger missed me with that cleaver. I have ever been a humpty-dumpty sort of a fellow, but I warrant I have had no cause to give such thanks for it until now."

As I said this, I surreptitiously felt in the pocket of my coat and closed my fingers around the little cloth talisman that Sal had given me. Mayhap there was nothing in it, but to be sure, I was grateful for any protection it might have afforded me this night.

"And thank you Harry," I said earnestly. "For without your timely intervention, I would be dead as mutton by now."

"Think nothing of it, old chum," replied Harry, smiling broadly. Always pleased to help. I say though, thinking on how you sent the old squire to fetch the doctor just now. Y'know, I once heard of a drunken surgeon who had killed most of his patients but still boasted himself a better man than the parson. For, said he, your cures maintain but yourself, but my cures maintain all the sextons in the town! Heh, heh, heh!"

"Gad, Harry, that is terrible," I groaned.

But, I had to laugh, despite my woes.

CHAPTER 16

The Royal Navy dockyard at Woolwich was a bustling place, alive with workmen busy not only upon the repair and refitting of warships of every class, but also in the constant expansion of the yard's buildings and facilities consequent upon the needs arising from the last three years of war. Charlie and I arrived on a dreary and overcast October afternoon that gave sure sign that the glorious late summer weather that we had seen throughout the previous month was finally at an end. We had travelled back to Aldgate with Harry by stage and then the two of us on, south of the river, to Woolwich by Hackney coach, a distance of some eight miles at a shilling per mile (four bob each, but I'll own it could have been worse). The Jarvis dropped us outside the Ravelin, otherwise known as the Barrack Tavern, a fancy new hostelry situated on Woolwich Common and much frequented by officers of the Royal Regiment of Artillery. There we settled ourselves before reporting to the Navy Board the next day.

Passing through the imposing Portland stone entrance gates, the fouled anchor reliefs upon their panelled piers proclaiming the presence of the Navy, and carrying on past the guard houses beyond, we entered the Dockyard on foot and made our way to the Clock House building wherein were housed the offices of the Yard's most senior officials. There we sought out the Master Attendant of the Dockyard, Richard Prowse, who would point us in the direction of the *Eros*. As was usual in the Service, gaining an audience with the likes of Mr Prowse necessitated a good deal of waiting around. This time in the anteroom that formed part of the suite of plain but well-proportioned rooms that comprised the Master Attendant's office. After a while, however, we were rewarded for our patience and were ushered into the presence of the great man himself.

Mr Prowse, a short, fairly unassuming fellow seated beneath a large window behind a plain mahogany desk piled with maps and other papers, rose to meet us.

"Good day to you, gentlemen," said he, friendly enough. "And what may I do for you?"

"Good day, sir," I answered. "We are lately arrived in Woolwich and are commissioned aboard the *Eros*, sixth rate."

"Ah, the *Eros*, is it. Lovely little ship she is. I give you joy of her, sirs. And I suppose you will be wanting to know where she lies?"

"If it please you, sir, yes," said Charlie. "We have been long on the road and I fear that we should have reported for duty some considerable time past. So, if you could confirm *Eros'* berthing for us we will make haste to repair on board."

"All in good time, gentlemen, all in good time," said Mr Prowse, shuffling through the papers on his desk. "First I need to take down some particulars, Record your arrival and suchlike. Sit you down, both of you; I will not keep you long."

Eventually, Mr Prowse informed us that our ship was to be found moored at the western end of Woolwich Reach and that we could, accordingly, approach her by boat from the public river stairs at the end of Hog Lane. Several watermen operated from Hog Lane, as did others on each of Woolwich's remaining four stairs, and we were thus able to engage a down at heels and out of elbows looking boatman to scull us out to *Eros* for tuppence.

As Mr Prowse had indicated, our ship was saucy indeed. A three-masted square rigger built to French lines, she sported both quarterdeck and fo'c'sle, was pierced for eleven long guns a side and carried chasers and carronades to boot. Her sides were painted pitch black with a white chequered strake running the length of her hull, set off by gilded stern and quarter galleries, and a jaunty little fat faerie fellow armed with bow and arrows at her beak. I loved her at first sight.

"Is she not beautiful, Charlie," I said, as we got closer.

"She is, Roger," Charlie replied, happily. "She'll do for me, right enough."

"Boat ahoy!" shouted someone aboard.

"*Eros!*" our boatman bellowed back, leaning on his single stern mounted oar and raising his hand to indicate the rank of his passengers and thus the number of side boys required to pipe them on board.

We fetched up alongside, bobbing in the water. Hitching my sword around me in order that it did not tangle in my legs, I reached out for the manropes to haul myself aboard, scrambling up the battens to the entry port. Charlie followed on behind. Once on deck we were met by a tall, imposing figure, evidently one of *Eros'* senior officers.

"Lieutenants Ellis and Edwardes, sir, come aboard to join," I said smartly, raising my right hand to my head in salute.

"Y'late," grunted our receiver, "Pertwee, first lieutenant. Now, let's get you off to the captain, the both of you, and look sharp. We've still a lot to do afore we can sail. Mr Jenkins! Show these officers aft, if you please."

"Aye aye, sir," chirruped a diminutive midshipman, most likely not much older than twelve. "If you will oblige me by coming this way, sirs…"

Midshipman Jenkins led us aft to the captain's cabin where the Marine sentry crashed the butt of his musket on the deck and announced us in a stentorious bellow."

"Enter," came a voice from within.

Captain William Radford, a short stout gentleman of early middle age, examined our commissions, pay and certificates through a quizzing glass. He wore a blue coat adorned with one of the new plain gold epaulettes on each shoulder, thus denoting that the wearer was of more than three year's post.

"Welcome aboard, gentlemen," he said, politely. "We have been expecting you for some time. Might I ask the reason for your delay?"

"I am sorry, sir," I replied. "But it is my fault entirely. Lieutenant Edwardes was required by the Admiralty to fetch me from the country, where I had been staying, but when he arrived at my lodgings I had, unfortunately, been called away on business and did not return for some few days."

"Away on business, were ye?" Radford asked. "Might I enquire what kind of business, Mr Ellis?"

"Parochial business, sir, I was acting as an unofficial member of the church vestry committee at Canewdon."

"Where?"

"Canewdon, sir. It is a small village in Essex."

"Ah, Essex... I see... the witch country, hey?"

"Some say, sir," I said, noncommittally.

"And, Mr Edwardes, you did not seek to follow, Mr Ellis in order to deliver your dispatch more speedily?"

251

"I did not, sir," answered Charlie. "Mr Ellis had travelled to Southend a day or so before my arrival, and I worried that we might pass each other on the road."

"Hmm, is that so? On parochial business, eh? Yes, I see…Very well, can't be helped, I suppose - civic duty and all that," said the Captain grudgingly, apparently suspicious but nevertheless happy to accept our lies at face value. "You are here now anyway. Mr Jenkins will take you to your cabins and help get your dunnage stowed. Thereafter, if you will kindly report to Mr Pertwee he will be pleased to assign you to your watches. I dare say he will be relieved to no longer have to keep a watch himself now that you have turned up. Might well improve his mood, hey?"

Eros was bound for the West Indies to join the fleet under Vice Admiral John Ford on the Jamaican Station and therefore needed to provision for a long voyage. Therefore, after about a fortnight aboard, spent familiarising myself with the workings of the ship and attending to various mundane tasks, I was required by Captain Radford to liaise with the Victualling Yard at Deptford to obtain, amongst other things, suitable supplies of livestock, salted meat, butter, bread, biscuit, cheese, peas, and fish. Somewhat felicitously, it was thought expedient for me to sleep ashore whilst engaged in this work so as to be handier for the Yard, and thus it was that I found myself, for the nonce, tucked up tight in the Ravelin whilst I conducted protracted negotiations with the Clerk of the Cutting House, the Clerk of the Dry Stores, and the Clerk of the Issues.

I had not been at the tavern more than a day or so when I received a visitor. It was early in the morning and I was seated at a table in the public room, poring over the inventories supplied to me by our purser, prior to heading off up to the Yard to see whether the hens I had purchased had arrived safely from Smithfield. If all was in order I would then make arrangements for them to be brought on board and delivered into the hands of the Duck Fucker, who looked after the ship's poultry.

"Harry!" I cried on seeing my caller ushered into the room by one of the tavern's mopsqueezers. "What are you doing here? How good it is to see you."

"It's good to see you too, Roger," said Harry. "I trust I find you well?"

"Tolerably well, my friend, yes. *Eros* is a fine ship and Charlie and I have been made right welcome. Our first is a miserable bugger mind, but you can't have everything, can you?"

"No, indeed you cannot," agreed Harry. Then, after a pause: "Roger, I must tell you, I am not here alone."

"Are you not?" I said, brightly. "Pray tell, who is it that accompanies you?"

And it was then that I saw her. Harry stood to one side and there, framed in the doorway was Lizzie - beautiful, darling Lizzie - dressed against the cold in a charming maroon coloured, fur trimmed pelisse worn over an ivory gown, her hands held in front of her waist and encased in a large fur muff. We stared at each other for some time before she let out a small sob and ran to embrace me.

"Oh, Roger, I am so, so sorry," she wept, burying her face in my shoulder. "How can you ever forgive me? I have treated you so very badly."

I could not deny it.

"I loved you Lizzie," I told her. "I most truly loved you. And I thought that you loved me. It fair broke my heart to see you with that odious man."

"I did love you, Roger, and I do still. Oh, I admit that at first I pursued you for the sake of our order, to seduce and enchant you so completely that you would join with us all the more readily, but when I came to really know you, I came to love you too. My relationship with Tom cannot in any way be compared with my relationship with you. I have no love or affection for Tom - our congress was an expression of our natural instinct, nothing more."

"Does Gildersleeve still live, then?" I asked, harshly."

"He does, but his life hangs by a thread. Dr Lipscomb removed the ball, for it had not travelled too deep, and dressed his wounds, but he remains gravely ill and it is feared that he may not last the month."

"So there is still hope."

Oh, there is," said Lizzie, misconstruing my comment completely. "Thank Heaven, there is always hope. But let us not stand here like this. Please let us be seated over by the fire, for there is more that I must say to you."

Harry left us then, to afford us more privacy as we sat together on one of the high backed oak benches that were positioned so as to create discrete boxes along the wall close to the hearth. The fire had been lit for a while to take the chill off the room but, as it was yet early in the day, there were no others present and we were able to talk freely. No sooner had we sat down when Lizzie hit me with another facer.

"Roger," she whispered. "I am with child."

"What!" I spluttered. "Surely not? Dammit, you'll not pin this on me, Lizzie. How do I know it's not Gildersleeve's child? I'll not stand Moses to any kid of his, damme if I will."

"Calm yourself, my love," Lizzie said, gently. "I have not come to lay the child at your door. It matters not to me who the father is, though by my troth I do entertain some hope that it might be you."

"But you cannot be certain, can you, Lizzie? You cannot deny that you lay with Gildersleeve at the same time that we were together. If the child were indisputably mine I would not hesitate to do my duty by you, but I will not simply accept the baby whether it be mine or not. It would not be fair on either of us, nor on the babe. Why, what might transpire if, after a year or so, the child so resembles Gildersleeve that it becomes impossible to deny its parentage? I could not abandon you, and we would be forced to live a lie for ever more - a lie that would be as transparent as a rock of solid crystal."

"I assure you, Roger, I do not wish for you to fulfil any imagined duty to me. I am resigned to the fact that the child will grow up as unaware of its parentage as I am myself at this very moment, and also believe me when I say that I regret nothing. Oh, I will admit that my behaviour has been both irresponsible and *naïve*, but, I ask you, who is it that can say that they have not behaved so at some time in their lives? I confess that I would have wished that you could have met this news with joy, and not with all the pain that I have created, and I also confess that my motive in coming here was to attempt reconciliation between us, if only for the sake of the child. But it is of no consequence. I declare that, no matter what, I will still love this poor babe and that even now I cannot in any way imagine my life without them."

"And should Gildersleeve recover and lay claim to the child? What then?"

"I have told you, I have no regard for Tom Gildersleeve. I would not entertain any such suit made on his behalf. And, in any event, Sir Henry will not allow Tom to remain in Canewdon after all he has done. He has sinned against our order and before the Gods."

"But there will be scandal, Lizzie. The child will be born a bastard."

"Oh no, there shall be no scandal. My parents will stand by me, as will Sir Henry and the others of the coven. The child will not suffer, far from it. Not for them the Foundling Hospital, my life upon it. Sir Henry is a very wealthy man. He will ensure that any child of mine shall lack for nothing. They will have the very best in life, as befits the divine child of the Goddess, and they shall live at peace with themselves and with the world around them. And, as for me, I am resolute in my belief that my body is mine to do with what I will. I feel no shame for what has happened, just love and thankfulness that I am able to bring new life into the world as part of the endless cycle of birth, death and rebirth."

We sat in silence for a while until Lizzie spoke again.

"But was it not a wonderful summer, Roger? Did we not have some marvellous times together?"

"Damme, Lizzie, I do believe that it was. And that we most certainly did."

We kissed for one last time, with tenderness rather than our previously accustomed passion, and bade each other farewell. Harry was waiting for us as we left the room.

"Thank you, Harry," I said. "I trust that I can rely on you to escort Miss Saunders safe home?"

"You may depend on it. I must tell you, Roger that I find Miss Saunders… Lizzie… a most pleasant companion and I have grown quite fond of her in these last few days since she and her maid sought me out at my place up in town to ask for help in finding you again."

"Miss Saunders is a very… er, likeable… young lady, Harry," I said, with a smile.

"Indeed she is. And I am in hopes that she may yet delay her return to the country for some short while in order that I may be able to show her something of the delights of the city."

"I am sure Miss Saunders would like that very much," I said.

"Yes, I would like that very much, Mr Felgate," agreed Lizzie.

"Why then, come, my dear," cried Harry, brightly. "I shall procure us a Hackney coach to take us back. And then we shall do something about finding suitable lodgings for you and Susannah. I'faith I swear we shall have such a devilishly good time, Damme if we don't."

I do believe you will, Harry, old trout, I thought as the pair headed arm in arm in the direction of the tavern yard in search of a conveyance. I do believe you will.

Eros sailed three weeks later. Leaving Woolwich at high tide under reefed tops'ls alone, we threaded our way slowly through the scores of ships and boats navigating the Thames and eventually emerged into the estuary to begin our journey to the Americas.

"Hands aloft to loose sail!" shouted Lieutenant

Pertwee, issuing the first in a flurry of commands designed to get *Eros* underway as she turned to point her bowsprit out to sea. "Tops'ls and t'gallants!"

The first lieutenant's call prompted a burst of ordered chaos as hands from both watches hurried to assemble inboard of the ratlines before laying aloft to clap on to the slings beneath the yards.

"Man the boom tricing-lines! Trice up, lay out!"

The topmen edged their way out on to the yards, toes clinging to the slings like so many monkeys, and, once all hands were in position, the captains of the tops raised their right arms each in turn as a signal to Mr Pertwee that the sails were ready to let fall.

"Loose and let fall!" bellowed the first lieutenant. "Shake reefs and haul out the bowlines!"

Men on deck then ran away with the bowlines, dragging them out to stretch the canvas as it fell, so that the sails hung square to catch the wind. As I was not directly engaged in this exercise, I stood at the taffrail and watched the huge sails boom and tauten as they filled, driving our little barky on through the waves.

"Lay in! Lay down from aloft!" screeched Pertwee, grinning from ear to ear and right pleased with the smart showing our ship had made.

After a while, I turned and looked back at the mud and sand of the Essex coastline slipping away behind us, thinking of Lizzie on her way back to London with good old dependable Harry. I wondered had I been too quick to renounce the child? Could I have made a good life for myself with Lizzie? But to do so would have necessitated a hasty wedding followed by a long separation, for *Eros* was like to be away for upwards of three years, during which time I would have been ever mindful of the temptations that might arise on shore for such an independent and free thinking a woman as my new wife. No, it was best that we parted. The exotic pleasures of the Caribbean lay ahead of me and I found that I was quite looking forward to experiencing them to the full. I would leave Lizzie in Harry's capable hands, I decided, and I would leave the babe safe, as I knew for certain, in the hands of the moon dancers of Canewdon.

EPILOGUE

Around two months later, *Eros* was anchored in Kingston Harbour. Our passage from England had taken fifty three days all told and, in recognition of the crew's exemplary behaviour during the voyage, Captain Radford had allowed the men free trade with the bumboats that brought fresh vegetables, supplies, doxies, and drink out to the ship, whilst at the same time the officers were permitted to taste the sweets of liberty on shore. Eager to make the most of this, I persuaded Charlie to come with me across the Palisadoes, a tombolo of sand joining Kingston to the Royal Navy Dockyard area of Port Royal, to explore what was left of the old town. A town once known as the wickedest city on earth; a den of buccaneers, whores, and blackbirders the likes of which had never been known either before or since. The pirate lair had been all but destroyed by an earthquake in the last century and now only a few streets remained. Nevertheless there was still a vibrancy about the town with street vendors and higglers eager to sell their wares, and harlots of every hue going publicly about to seduce those poor sailormen who wandered cup shot, having found their way into some of the likely looking taverns and grog shops of Lime Street.

It was into one of these taverns that I dragged Charlie. A two storey wooden framed building that had at its heart a single great room with enormous beams running across its low ceiling. A counter, from which drink was served, was situated in one corner and a large stone fireplace took up much of the wall at the far end. Various chairs, settles and stools were arranged about the room leaving an area of hard oak floor for dancing. It was a balmy evening and the place was full. Young bucks from the better parts of Kingston rubbed shoulders with Navy men and officers of the Royal Artillery and West India Regiment - and all were seemingly roaring drunk. Black Creole women, presumably slaves, were moving from table to table clearing pots whilst several *mulatto* ladies in various stages of undress openly flirted with the drinkers, laughingly allowing them to practice all kinds of liberty upon their persons.

"Are you certain that you want to stay here, Roger?" asked Charlie, incredulously. "This does not at all appear to be the type of establishment that you would wish to patronise."

"Live a little, Charlie," I replied, grinning and steering my friend towards the counter. "I find that I have hidden my light under a bushel for too long.

Come; let us get a drink inside us. It looks like a show is about to start."

I bought two pots of rum from the old Negro servant behind the counter and we elbowed our way through the pack to sit at a table close to the dance floor. Someone somewhere started to scrape at a fiddle as a line of dancers emerged on to the floor to the pulsing rhythm of a gumba. The dancers were all damnably handsome, near white *mustifino* girls who, as the tempo of the music slowly increased, swayed and shook their bodies in the wildly indecorous dance *à la mustee*. The effect was as intoxicating as the rum. The women danced with arms and legs splayed, their insubstantial shifts torn off short and knotted below the bust, the remainder cut low to reveal an expanse of quivering bosom. Their loose skirts they hitched up high to display shapely thighs and well-rounded rumps as they waggled and bounced to the beat of the drum.

"They throw pepper on the floor, y'know," said a sweating, red faced fellow next to me, nudging me in the ribs. "As soon as the wenches begin to warm, it rises and has such an effect upon their thighs and quim that it almost sets 'em mad and right easy to be debauched. Gingers 'em up better than a feague shoved up a horse's arse, it does!"

"Good to know," I acknowledged. "Thankee for the information."

"Think nothing of it, sir," nodded our new acquaintance, his dark blue jacket and red facings showing him to be a soldier. "Wilkins, Royal Artillery.

And you are?"

"Ellis, lately landed from the *Eros*. And this is Mr Edwardes."

"A pleasure to meet you, gentlemen. First time in Jamaica is it?

"It is."

"Ah, well, you'll find us a rum crowd. Generous and hospitable to a fault, and uncommon dedicated to hard drinking, dancing and swiving! Hedonism and libertinism - that's the way of it here, m'boy. You'll not want for a willing piece on this island, sir, and you can have m'word on that!"

"Excellent!" says I. "Damned if I won't fit right in."

The dance reached its final climax with the dancers kneeling supine upon the floor, legs apart and backs arched, shaking their cat-heads for all they were worth. And then they were up again, running squealing amongst the drinkers in search of willing arms and comfortable laps. Happily, I found myself approached by two particularly fetching specimens of Jamaican womanhood who draped themselves around me, fluttering impossibly long lashes and cooing seductively into my ears with that distinct patois native to the island.

"Hail dahlin' yuh lookin' fi a gud time?" says one, a beautiful, full breasted Juno, with dark hair, invitingly plump lips and almond eyes.

"Indeed I am m'dear," I replied, toying with the top of her shift and working it down to uncover one deliciously dark, hard nipple.

"Well, wi two girls cud show yuh di very best of times eff yuh willin', cap'um," trilled her companion, another raven haired lass who was of more delicate appearance and yet every bit as delectable.

"Why, I do believe you could," I said to the second girl, who had by now perched herself upon my knee and was allowing me to run a hand along the length of her well-muscled thigh.

"Di landlord here 'ave sum very comfortable rooms upstairs, dahlin'. Eff yuh wa wi cud tek yuh up tuh rest awhile wid wi. Yuh wudda like dat, dahlin'?" purred Juno, stroking my hair and planting a gentle kiss upon my lips.

"Capital idea!" I exclaimed. "An early night would do me good. Charlie, you don't mind if I leave you here with Mr Wilkins for a while, do you? It's just that I find myself suddenly overcome and in need of a short rest to pick myself up again."

"Er… of course, Roger," said Charlie, gaping at me open mouthed. Please do come to find me again when you are… er… quite rested."

"You may be sure of it, old chum. Now, ladies, shall we retire?"

Charlie watched me climb the stairs, yardarm to yardarm with my two dainty little merry arse Christians.

"Damme!" I heard him say as I went. "Had I not witnessed it with mine own eyes, I never would have believed it."

"It is the way of the island, sir. Oh, yes indeed, it is most definitely, the way of the island," declaimed Wilkins.

On reaching the landing I could hear that below us someone had taken to singing. It was a familiar song, but I could not quite place it. Damn pleasant it was though.

> When twenty long weeks they were over and
> were past,
> Her mammy asked the reason why she
> thickened round the waist,
> "It was the pretty ploughboy," this girl she
> then did say,
> For he asked me for to tumble, all in the new-
> mown hay.

> Here's a health to all you ploughboys
> wherever you may be,
> That like to have a bonnie lass a-sittin' on
> each knee,
> With a pint of good strong porter, ye'll whistle
> and ye'll sing,
> For the ploughboy is as happy as a prince or a
> king.

Juno opened a door that led to one of the tavern's bedchambers and the three of us went in. Far from being the 'comfortable room' that Juno had promised, this, albeit expansive (and I guessed, expensive), bedroom was Spartan indeed, it's only furniture consisting of a low, untidy bed, a small table upon which stood an old grey basin and a jug of cold water, two ramshackle chairs, and a chamber pot.

"Eh will cost yuh ah yellow bwoy tuh ave di both ah wi, dahlin'," said Juno, getting down to business. "A yuh criss fi dat now?"

"A guinea?" I replied. "Er… yes… I'm sure that will be fine."

"Den mek yuhself comfortable pan di bed now, cap'um," urged Juno, playfully. "While Susie an mi git stripped fah action, as yuh sailors mite seh."

"Duh yuh lakka tuh pree, sah?" asked Susie coquettishly, taking Juno by the hand. "Wi can put pan ah special lickkle show fi yuh, eff yuh waan."

"That would be splendid!" I answered. "Do carry on."

Then, to my great amusement, the two of them commenced to slowly and teasingly strip one another stark naked whilst I watched.

Susie was the first to begin, carefully untying the knot that served to hold Juno's shift in place and freeing the beautifully rounded orbs beneath. These she then fell to caressing tenderly, raising each proud nipple in turn by the ministrations of tongue and teeth. Scorning the effort required to untie Susie's flimsy shift, Juno countered by laying hold of Susie's plunging neckline in both hands and tearing it sharply down, splitting the garment in twain and pulling it off Susie's shoulders to pinion the smaller girl's arms behind her while she held her close and rained passionate kisses down upon her upturned face and creamy white neck. I could see that this was going to set me back the price of some new duds on top of the guinea I had already agreed to, but b'Gad, it was proving well worth it.

Susie's skirt was next to go by the board, the strings at her waist broken and the fabric tossed to the floor to expose her entirely to my inspection in a state of perfect nudity - which state it seemed Juno was determined to fully explore. Slowly and deliberately turning Susie around to face me, Juno gently bent her partner backwards so as to lift her bosom slightly and thrust her hips forward; this action facilitated by Susie herself stretching her arms up and behind her friend's neck. Thus positioned, Juno allowed her arms to snake about Susie's waist, her questing fingers travelling all over Susie's bowed body, stroking her breasts and her sweet upright nipples before moving down to part her legs and penetrate the irresistible dampness of her cunny, causing Susie to sigh and to moan, softly at first and then rising to a crescendo as she responded ecstatically to Juno's touch. Panting, Susie wriggled round to face her erstwhile succubus, now untying Juno's own skirt and dropping to her knees to clap on to Juno's ample buttocks and bury her face in the lush growth atop Cock Alley, working her tongue furiously to elicit from her lover that most joyous of reactions that she had herself only lately experienced.

"Christ on his cross!" I gasped in amazement. "I declare, I've never seen the like."

At length, breaking off at last from their lovemaking, both girls turned their attention back to me.

"Suh, cap'um mi tink wi a both ready fi yuh now," drawled Juno. "Wah duh yuh seh, Susie, dahlin'?"

"Oh, mi tink wi a," said her companion. "Di question a doah, a he ready fi us?"

Oh, but I was. Make no mistake about that.

"Tell me, ladies," I thought to enquire as the delightful pair finally came to settle on the bed and began to ease the clothes from my back. "I wonder, were either of you aware that God actually had a wife?"

AFTERWORD

So, Roger's tale has come to an end and as in all the best stories, our villain, the randy Reverend Gildersleeve, has got his just deserts. On top of that, Harry has got the girl (for now, at least), and there's no telling what Roger might get if he carries on the way he's going. But let's be clear, *none of this actually happened.* Oh, Canewdon is a real place, right enough, a small, quiet, out of the way village in south Essex, with an atmosphere all of its own and a long tradition of witchcraft. And its topography in the year 1795 was roughly as I have described. But, unless I'm sorely mistaken, there has never been a Reverend Gildersleeve at St Nicholas' church, Sir Henry Spurgeon never occupied Canewdon Hall, Sally Dowsett was never the landlady of the Anchor Inn, and the family of Nathaniel Saunders never lived in any of the houses in the High Street. Nor do I have any evidence for the existence of the other colourful characters I have invented to populate my fictitious version of the village.

Right, now we've got that straight, the question is can you believe anything you have just read? Well, historically, the tradition of witchcraft in Canewdon dates back to the late 16th century, when spinster Rose Pye was tried and acquitted on the charge of bewitching to death a twelve month old child and 'Goodwife' Cicily Makyn was excommunicated for carrying on the practice of witchcraft. Ever since then, it seems that a vast array of folktales and legends have grown up around the village, most of which centre on St Nicholas' church, and I confess that I have taken the liberty of borrowing one or two of these for the purposes of Roger's story.

In 1867, for example, Philip Benton, writing of the tower of St Nicholas' in his book *The History of Rochford Hundred* recorded that 'a tradition exists, and is believed by many, that so long as this steeple exists, there will always remain six witches in Canewdon', to which, in 1960, the folklorist Eric Maple, in his work *The Witches of Canewdon in Folklore*, added a postscript to the effect that 'every time a stone falls from the tower, one witch will die, and another will take her place'. In that same work Maple also tells of the legend that 'those who walk round the tower at midnight will be forced to dance with the witches'.

Other local legends refer to the crossroads in Canewdon where a witch is buried (thought to be the junction where Anchor Lane, Scotts Hall Road, Lark Hill Road and Church Lane converge) with Eric Maple once more contributing, in *The Dark World of Witches,* that the supposed witch who was interred there actually committed suicide and was therefore buried with a stake through her heart. And as for the shenanigans following the lonely burial of the fictitious footpad, Jemmy Webb, in Jessie K. Payne's 1987 book, *A Ghost Hunter's Guide to Essex,* the author contends that the children of Canewdon have long shown interest in the grave of a highwayman, who it is said was buried in the churchyard in 1795, and were once in the habit of entering the churchyard to dance around this grave seven times to ensure that the highwayman's spirit would remain 'unquiet' and would therefore be forced into standing guard over all of the other graves.

In his fictional narrative Roger refers to the Reverend Gildersleeve being thought of as a 'cunning man', and in this I have borrowed from the traditions of the Canewdon magician, George Pickingill and the cunning man of Haleigh, James Murrell. In the early 19th century Pickingill, was known as the 'Master of Witches' and, according to Bill Liddell, the author of *The Pickingill Papers* (1994), was the latest in a line of hereditary witches who had been priests of the Horned God since Saxon times. Pickingill was reputed to be able to use magic to heal both humans and animals and restore missing property, and was, apparently, not averse to threatening the odd curse or two as well. Murrell, Pickingill's contemporary, also claimed to be able to work magical cures, and to have the power to exorcise evil spirits and counter witchcraft. In addition, both men were supposed to have the ability to whistle up all six of the Canewdon witches and, as was reported in an article in *The Times* dated Tuesday, 27 January 1959, at one time the fear of witches was so great in the village that it prompted the people to enlist Murrell's assistance in exposing them. To this end Murrell petitioned the vicar, the Reverend William Atkinson, to allow him to exercise his power and make the witches show themselves by dancing round St Nicholas' churchyard. But the vicar steadfastly refused to cooperate because, some said, to do so would cause him to reveal the fact that his wife, Mary Ann, could be counted among their number.

With regard to some of the beliefs and rituals practiced by my imaginary Canewdon coven I have been somewhat influenced by the theological structure of the modern pagan religion, *Wicca*. As a duotheistic faith, *Wicca* involves the veneration of both a female Goddess and a male God (termed the Triple Goddess and the Horned God, respectively) and *Wiccan* celebrations involve both *Sabbats,* which concern the movements of the Sun, and *Esbats* (originally from the French *s'esbattre*, or 'joyful frolic') based around the cycles of the Moon. Traditionally too, many *Wiccan* ceremonies and rituals were performed naked, or 'skyclad', in order to promote equality between the participants and allow power to flow freely from the body, but it must be said that today's practitioners are more likely to keep their clothes on. Moreover, where some groups continue to practice ritualised sex magic through the Great Rite (whereby, in order to generate magical energy, the High Priest and Priestess call upon the God and Goddess to enter their bodies before they engage in sexual intercourse) this is now almost exclusively a symbolic ritual involving the immersion of a knife blade into a cup of wine to represent the penis entering the womb. Perhaps understandably, however, many *Wiccans* have sought to eradicate even this aspect of their practice in the face of rampant tabloid sensationalism and recent concerns around ritual abuse.

Wicca is essentially a reassuring and optimistic religion the practitioners of which, according to Wouter J Hanegraaff in his 1996 work *New Age Religion and Western Culture*, view themselves as 'a positive force against the powers of destruction which threaten the world'. The majority of *Wiccans* follow a code known as the *Wiccan Rede*, the central tenet of which is expressed as 'an [if] it harm none, do what ye will', Usually interpreted as allowing the freedom to act as one wishes provided that full responsibility is taken for any consequences and any harm to oneself or others is avoided, it is easy to see a correlation between the credo encapsulated in the *Wiccan Rede* and the 18th century Enlightenment philosophies of Jeremy Bentham, David Hume, and others - Bentham's core principle of classical utility, for example, stating that any action or behaviour can be considered right in so far as it promotes happiness or pleasure, and only wrong if it produces unhappiness or pain.

But what of the idea that God had a wife, where did that come from? Good question. In 1967, the Hungarian, Raphael Patai, was the first historian to suggest that God had a wife, Asherah, whom the *Book of Kings* indicates was worshiped alongside Yahweh in his temple in Jerusalem, and this theory has since been expanded by Francesca Stavrakopoulou, Professor of Hebrew Bible and Ancient Religion at the University of Exeter, in the BBC documentary series *The Bible's Buried Secrets.* Stavrakopoulou's contentions are based on ancient texts, amulets, and figurines unearthed in the ancient Canaanite coastal city of Ugarit in what is now modern-day Syria. All of these artefacts reveal that Asherah was a powerful fertility goddess, with both the Bible and an 8th century BC inscription on pottery found at Kuntillet 'Ajrud in the Sinai desert providing further evidence for the idea that Yahweh and Asherah were a divine couple. Admittedly, specific references to Asherah in the Old Testament are rare but, if you believe Aaron Brody, Professor of Bible and Archaeology at the University of California, this is only because they were mostly edited out by the men who originally gathered and subsequently transcribed the Bible's texts.

Because of this editorial intervention God's union with Asherah ended with the rise of monotheism in around the 5th century BC, and Asherah was swept aside in the same manner as other deities worshipped in ancient Israel - either being relegated to the serried ranks of the angels, or else rejected as being an abomination - resulting in two of the world's most important religions, Judaism and Christianity, coming to revolve around a single male deity. The question is therefore, did Asherah somehow survive the editing process to emerge again in the form of the Mother

Goddess of the witches, and is she thus able to offer a tangible link between modern mainstream religious beliefs and the fertility cults of our perhaps not so distant pagan ancestors?

Turning now to the, arguably more mundane, general historical context of the novel; the harvest of 1794, the first in a series of bad harvests, was followed by an exceptionally cold and wet winter which, when combined with high taxation and spiralling prices, resulted in widespread poverty and hardship across the country. As these few lines written at the time have it:

> In last hard winter—who forgets
> The frost of ninety-five?
> Then all was dismal, scarce and dear
> And no poor men could thrive
> And husbandry long time stood still
> And work was at a stand.

The extent of the suffering in Essex was witnessed first-hand by the Prime Minister, William Pitt when, towards the end of 1795, he went to stay with a friend who lived in the county. According to Lord Rosebery's short biography of Pitt, published in 1891, after a convivial evening spent discussing the good fortune enjoyed by the good and honest labourers of Britain, Pitt was taken by his host to view the homes of some of the poorest people living in the town of Halstead. The Prime Minister was apparently appalled by what he saw, viewing the scene 'in silent wonder', and declaring that 'he had no conception that any part of England could present such a spectacle of misery'.

Wheat, which had averaged fifty two shillings and threepence a quarter in 1794, rose to one pound eight shillings and fourpence in August 1795, an increase of over fifty shillings in eight months. And as prices rose, civil unrest spread throughout the country. JL and B Hammond, in their 1987 book *The Village Labourer 1760-1832* record that in May 1795, for example, 'an unlawful assembly of colliers met on Rodway Hill (near Bristol) on account of the dearness of provisions' and were only dispersed when troops were called out. Similar meetings, some of which led to rioting, took place in other parts of England and Wales with mobs seizing flour or bread and sometimes damaging or destroying mills or bakeries. At Portsea in Hampshire a mob attacked bakers' shops and forced their owners to sell bread at popular prices, and at Seaford in East Sussex the local militia actually joined with the rioters, taking over the town and commandeering all of the flour and other food so that it could be sold at a reduced price. The Seaford rioters moved on to Newhaven and were eventually dispersed by a squadron of the Lancashire Regiment of Fencible Dragoons and a battery of horse artillery that was deployed on the hills overlooking the town.

In *Saffron Walden - Then and Now* (1951) G Brightwen Rowntree writes that the unrest at Saffron Walden was one of the worst disturbances to take place in 1795. Despite an attempt having been made to supply the parish with cheap wheat and flour, on 27th July (a little later than the time that I have placed the event in the novel) a crowd led by Samuel Porter, a

277

cooper, gathered in the Greyhound Inn where a quantity of corn was taken from the loft and monies were raised to pay for drink for the crowd. Porter then moved his headquarters to the White Horse Inn and gangs of men were sent out to gather corn, cheese, meat, and other food at reduced rates. During the whole course of the day the town was in a constant state of riot and confusion with order not being fully restored until two squadrons of the Surrey Light Dragoons were sent over from their barracks in Lexden near Colchester.

Set against this background therefore, the fictitious attack on the Canewdon mill instigated by our very own would be political agitator, John Kettle, does not look that much out of place and, surprisingly, neither do the staunchly loyal attitudes exhibited by our villagers. By this time Britain had been at war with revolutionary France for over two years and, faced with the enemy at the door and the spectre of Jacobin excesses on the continent, an overwhelming majority of the British people of all classes continued to support the established authority. Nine out of ten people cared not a fig for the radical ideals of the French revolution, but stories of churches being desecrated and women and children being murdered rarely failed to outrage public decency. When the situation reached its crisis point in October 1795, with a vast crowd attending a meeting of the London Corresponding Society and listening to speakers openly calling for civil war, and with the King himself being stoned by a mob outside Old Palace Yard, there was seen a massive outpouring of patriotic loyalty. When the King next visited the theatre in Covent Garden the audience sang *God Save the King* six times in succession. And when William Wilberforce travelled to the West Riding district to address a meeting to assist the passage through Parliament of two highly reactionary Bills prohibiting treasonable practices and seditious meetings, he was met by thousands of Yorkshire weavers declaring themselves to be 'Billymen' in support of Pitt, and crying out the slogan 'twenty King's men to one Jacobin'.

That then was the political situation existing in England at the time when Roger was off enjoying his holiday in the countryside, but I think that probably I should also say a quick word concerning the moral attitudes prevalent on the island of Jamaica at the end of the 18th century. At that time white Jamaicans from all levels of society had developed an exaggerated culture of drink and debauchery that elevated white male pleasure above everything else. JB Moreton's *West India Customs and Manners*, written in 1793, evidenced a white Jamaican model of masculinity that emphasised libertinism, drink, dancing, and the sexual exploitation of both enslaved women and free women of colour. Of course, as Roger would have been the first to tell you, libertine culture was a feature of the elite social scene in Britain too. But, as Judith S. Lewis points out in her book *Sacred to female patriotism: gender, class, and politics in late Georgian Britain* (2000) there were two models of masculinity existing in late 18th century Britain, one that revelled in hard drinking, womanising, and sport and another which extolled the virtues of abstinence and the avoidance of sex outside marriage. In contrast, however, there were no such distinctions existing in Jamaica at that time, and there whoring, gluttony, and excessive drinking were as central to the white male identity as they had once been in Restoration England. So, who knows, Roger may be correct when he says that he'll fit right in.

And finally, a bit about the songs I have included in the book. In the 18th century singing was a massive part of the spectacle of punishment, with onlookers as well as the unfortunate victims expected to play their part in what Richard van Dülmen, in his 1990 book *Theatre of Horror: Crime and Punishment in Early Modern Germany*, termed the 'theatre of horror'. Thus, Psalm 51 ('Have mercy upon me, O God, according to thy loving kindness') was at that time known as *The Hanging Song*, and Peter Linebaugh, in his essay *The Tyburn Riot against the Surgeons*, included in *Albion's Fatal Tree: Crime and Society in Eighteenth-Century England* (Hay et al 2011), tells us that the condemned and the crowd alike were expected to belt it out at the foot of the gallows.

The singing would continue even after the condemned had been dispatched to meet their maker with ballad vendors plying their trade amongst the plethora of hawkers selling food, alcohol and other commodities to the crowd. Witness Hogarth's famous engraving *The Idle 'Prentice Executed at Tyburn* which places a scruffy ballad-monger firmly front and centre, singing her wares whilst carrying her child in one arm and waving 'The last dying Speech & Confession of— Tho. Idle' in her hand. *John Kettle's Lament*, though my own invention, is firmly in the tradition of these broadside ballads and is in fact borrowed slightly from a ballad entitled *The Riot - Or Half a Loaf is Better than no Bread*. In its original form this song, published in around 1800, argued that rioting was pointless, and that the Government could not be blamed for either a poor harvest or bad weather. Which is, of course, most probably true. But high taxation and high prices though - well, it may be that even over two hundred years later this might still become the inspiration for an altogether different song.

The third and most important song so far as Roger's story is concerned, however, is the very well-known ballad *The Lark in the Morning*. An English folk song, *The Lark in the Morning* is both a celebration of the life of the ploughboy, and a warning against the dangers of engaging in a little how's-your-father outside of wedlock. Many broadside printers published versions of this song, the earliest known printed text being included in *Four Excellent New Songs*, a garland (a broadside comprising a number of different songs) printed in Edinburgh in 1778. And it is possible, that the song could date back even further. Sometimes the broadside versions, such as *The Plowman's Glory*, for example, focused coyly on the more seemly aspects of pastoral life, but happily most traditional versions of the song tend to concentrate much more on the earthy side.

THE MOON DANCERS

So, that's that, except to say that I hope you will take this book at face value. It is not intended to be an historical or sociological treatise, nor are there any hidden agendas within its pages. Any errors in the text are mine alone and, as the editor of my local newspaper used to say, 'are placed there solely for the entertainment of those who wish to find them'. And moreover, *there is no intention to offend anyone.* The attitudes, speech, and actions of Roger and all the others in this book can sometimes be very much 'of their time' and should not be taken as in any way reflective of my own - that is, unless they reflect on me in a good way, of course…

The Moon Dancers is simply an old school adventure story - with a fair bit of naughtiness and some genuine 18th century jokes thrown in - and, although not a horror novel *per se*, it is in some way a homage to those old fashioned British horror films, like Hammer's *The Devil Rides Out*, British Lion's original version of *The Wicker Man*, or Tigon Films' *Witchfinder General*, that I used to watch with my Dad when the Midnight Movie was on telly way back in the day. Anyway, for what it's worth, I think it's a rattling good yarn, and I hope you like it.

John Pitman
Chipping Ongar, Essex
2021

ABOUT THE AUTHOR

JOHN PITMAN read law at university before working as traditional publisher for almost twenty years and as an online publisher for nearly the same again. When the pandemic struck he decided that enough was enough and retired from the world of work to spend more time with the people he loves and generally 'find himself'. After teaching himself to play the guitar (very badly) and mucking about with shabby chic furniture for a while he decided to go back to his roots and publish a novel. The result is *The Moon Dancers*, an historical fantasy set in the heart of his native Essex.

John lives in Chipping Ongar with his wife, Linda, and his cat, Foxy. He has one grown-up son, Tim, who lives up the road in Brentwood. For the record, none of the family has ever lived in Canewdon.